THE HAUNTING
OF TORRE ABBEY

Also by Carole Buggé

The Star of India

Who Killed Blanche Dubois?

Who Killed Dorian Gray?

THE HAUNTING
OF TORRE ABBEY

CAROLE BUGGÉ

St Martin's Minotaur
New York

Bug

Library of Congress Cataloging-in-Publication Data

Buggé, Carole.
    The haunting of Torre Abbey / by Carole Buggé.
        p.   cm.
    ISBN 0-312-24557-2
    1. Holmes, Sherlock (Fictitious character)—Fiction.   2. Private
investigators—England—Fiction.   I. Title.
PS3552.U389 H38 2000
813'.54—dc21

                                                      99–053751

First Edition: April 2000

10   9   8   7   6   5   4   3   2   1

For Marvin

ACKNOWLEDGMENTS

FIRST I would like to thank my editor, Keith Kahla, for making this book possible, and also for his invaluable and perceptive insight during the rewriting process. Thanks to Chris Buggé for acting as my consultant on the proper procedures of British fox hunting, and to Derrick Seymour for his fascinating book on Torre Abbey. Thanks also to my agent Susan Ginsburg, as well as her assistant, Anne Stowell, at Writers House. My gratitude to Anthony Moore for his Internet research into Torre Abbey and letterboxing. And, of course, to Marvin Kaye, both for introducing me to Torquay as well as offering me assistance during the research phase of this book. Finally, thanks to my father and his bedtime ghost stories featuring the unforgettable Uncle Evil Eye, one of the most memorable characters I have encountered. You will be missed.

AUTHOR'S NOTE

THOUGH TORRE ABBEY is of course a real place, and the Cary family did indeed own it for several centuries, I have fictionalized certain aspects of the abbey—and the members of the Cary family in this book are in no way meant to represent the real Cary family.

THE HAUNTING
OF TORRE ABBEY

CHAPTER ONE

 W ATSON, DO you believe in ghosts?"
        I was used to strange utterances from my friend
Sherlock Holmes, but this one caught me off guard. Sitting in
front of a blazing fire on a misty October evening in our sitting-
room at 221B Baker Street, nothing was farther from my mind
than ghosts.

Before answering, I took a sip of the spirits which did
occupy me at present, in this case a very good glass of Montra-
chet '82. It was a useful tonic against the bitter biting rain which
fell outside our window, pelting the cobblestones and stinging
the cheeks of the poor souls who had the misfortune to be out
on such a dreadful night.

I myself had just come in; after an unusually busy couple of
weeks at my practice, I was worn out. An early flu epidemic had
forced me to keep long hours for days on end, and now that the
outbreak showed signs of being over, I had left the surgery in
the hands of my capable assistant, Dr. McKinney, for a few days.
A cab had been hard to come by, and I arrived at our rooms in
Baker Street soaked to the skin. Now, however, the combination
of the fireplace and red wine was reviving me in both body and
spirit.

"Why do you ask?" I replied to my friend's strange question.

Holmes let one hand drop from the sofa, where he lay outstretched in his mouse-coloured dressing gown. He was in one of those languorous moods which often descended upon him between cases. The sitting-room was in a state of disarray: his makeshift laboratory table sat gathering dust at the far end of the room, and the remains of breakfast or lunch sat uncollected upon the dining table at the other end. Holmes was surrounded by discarded newspapers, strewn about everywhere like fallen leaves. When not at work upon a case, he devoured the papers eagerly in search of "crimes of interest"—anything out of the ordinary which might engage his restless attention.

"Because Lord Charles Cary seems to think that he is being haunted," he answered. With that he produced a letter from his dressing gown and flung it in my direction.

I leaned over and picked it up. The stationery was a rich, creamy ivory colour, the paper of the highest quality; the watermark clearly showed the imprint of the best stationer in London.

"What do you make of it, Watson?"

The writing was in a clear, firm masculine hand. "A man," I opined, "of some strength of character—"

"Would you be so kind as to read it aloud?" Holmes interrupted, fishing some tobacco out of the Persian slipper where he kept it. "It will give me a chance to hear anything I may have missed the first time."

I knew that was hardly likely, but I complied and read the letter aloud to him.

Torre Abbey
Torquay, Devon

Dear Mr. Holmes,

First of all, lest you think I am mad, let me state right away that I am in full possession of my faculties. But that I experienced the events which I now relate to you, there can be no doubt. On the seventh of October of this year occurred the following series of events at Torre Abbey, which has been in my family now for two centuries.

Upon being summoned by an urgent telegram, I hurried from my graduate studies at Oxford to join my mother and younger sister at the abbey. My father having passed away recently, I am now the sole male member of the family and naturally feel a duty to protect the members of the weaker sex.

Holmes raised an eyebrow in his half-cynical way.

"Gallantry, Watson—always an attractive quality in a man, though it has been my observation that women are far from being the weaker sex. In fact, did you know that the lion himself is not the king of beasts everyone takes him for? It is the lioness who hunts and kills the prey, while the lion is content to sit idly by, preening his mane or sunning himself," he remarked, stuffing his pipe.

"Very well, Holmes," I replied somewhat irritably. "Have it your way: women are the very devil incarnate. Now, may I continue?"

Holmes knit his brows in mock contrition. "Oh, dear, Watson, have I offended the gallant in you? I do apologize. I am sure women are the meek, fragile creatures you suppose them to be."

I ignored him and continued reading as a tremendous thunder clap sounded outside the window, rattling the window panes.

Upon arriving at Torre Abbey, I found my mother in an excitable state and my sister bordering on nervous collapse.

Holmes stuck the pipe in his mouth, crossed his hands behind his head and kicked a newspaper from under his feet. "Here comes the good part, Watson."

Let me say that if I were you I would hardly have credited what I am about to tell you. And yet I saw it as clearly as you now see the paper you hold in your hands.

There are many legends associated with Torre Abbey, some going back centuries. The townsfolk like to talk, of course, but superstitions run rampant as rabbits in the West Country, and I never paid much attention to any of them.

Briefly, the story is this: In the late fourteenth century a certain William Norton, who was then the Abbot of Torre, was suspected of committing a foul and cowardly murder. The alleged victim was a monk by the name of Symon Hastynges—

"Note the Welsh spelling of the name, Watson," Holmes said, lazily waving a hand in my direction.

"Yes, quite. May I continue?"

Holmes smiled. "By all means."

I turned my eye back to the page before me.

To quell the rumours, Abbot Norton produced a man who resembled Symon Hastynges, but even then people claimed the man was an impostor and that the real Symon Hastynges lay buried in the churchyard—minus his head, which the abbot had done the courtesy of removing. The case against the abbot was never proved, but ever since then there have been reports of a headless monk who wanders the halls of Torre Abbey—and some claim they have seen him galloping along the avenue leading to the abbey, riding a blind ghost horse.

Holmes chuckled. "It's all deliciously chilling, is it not, Watson? Ancient abbeys, ghost horses, beheaded monks . . . the stuff of children's bedtime tales." He yawned and stretched and flicked another newspaper onto the pile which lay on the floor.

"That well may be," I replied, "but Lord Cary seems to be rather upset by it."

"Ah, yes, you're getting to that part," he said, putting down the unlit pipe and closing his eyes.

I leaned forward closer to the fire and turned to the second page of Lord Cary's letter. If his handwriting was any evidence, he was indeed a man of strong character. He crossed his *t*'s with decisiveness, and the ink was pressed firmly onto the paper with the conviction of a man who knows who he is. He went on to say that, having arrived at Torre Abbey on a Friday night, he listened with a sympathetic but skeptical ear to the tale his sister and mother told. It seems that two nights earlier, his sister, whose name was Elizabeth, heard what she thought to be rats scurrying in the hallway outside her room. Upon rising from her bed, she proceeded into the hall with a lit taper—except that instead of rats, she saw the ghostly form of a headless man dressed in a monk's habit!

She could not say where he had come from or indeed where he went, because she fainted immediately upon seeing him. The ghostly visitor had vanished by the time she awoke, but she could swear she heard the sound of horses' hooves on the lane outside. It was a dark night, and by the time she got to the window, there was no sign of either horse or rider. She went straight away to her mother's room, awakened her and told her what she had seen. Together they agreed to send for her brother Charles—Lord Cary—and had done so by urgent telegram the next day.

I glanced over at Holmes. His lean form was still; one arm was thrown carelessly over his head, his eyes were closed, and he gave every sign of being asleep. However, I knew him well enough to realize that he was listening intently, in spite of all evidence to the contrary.

Upon arriving late Friday night, I comforted my mother and sister and assured them they had nothing to fear. I did not attempt to explain what my sister had seen, for I was not yet convinced she had seen anything. My sister has a vivid imagination, and is of a high-strung and nervous disposition, unlike myself. For all I knew, it could have been an arrangement of shadows that frightened her. The abbey is old and damp, and there are nooks and crannies in the stones that, under the right lighting conditions, can even seem to move.

After a light dinner, I prepared to retire; it had been a long day and I was tired. My bedroom is on the third floor, in the stone tower overlooking a courtyard which was once the back garden of the abbey. As I lay in my bed with a chemistry book—I am reading medicine at Oxford—I thought I heard a sound out in the courtyard below.

Another deafening clap of thunder sounded outside, and I practically leaped from my chair, dropping the letter onto the carpet at my feet. A shiver coursed through my body as I bent to pick up the missive, and I glanced over at Holmes to see if he had witnessed my alarm. He lay there peacefully as ever—though I thought I saw one eyelid twitch. I took a sip of my wine, which I had quite forgotten about, then turned back to the letter, eager to read what happened next.

I went to the window and pulled back the curtains. Even now as I write this it seems so preposterous and unlikely that I would laugh at it myself had I not seen it with my own two eyes. There in the courtyard stood a man—or rather, the figure of a man—for he had no head. The night was dark but there was a faint moon, and I could make out that his clothing was that of a medieval monk. He was turned towards me, and stood there as if waiting for something. My first thought—or rather, my second, for I admit that my first was pure terror—was that someone was playing a trick on us. I seized my robe, threw it on and dashed down the stairs and out into the courtyard, but by the time I got there the figure had vanished.

As I say, the night was dark, but I went back inside for a torch and poked around the grounds for upwards of half an hour before I gave up and went back to bed. I did not sleep much that night—for, trick or not—it was, as you can imagine, a most unsettling experience.

I know you are a busy man, Mr. Holmes, and hope you will forgive me not coming to you in person with my story, but I am certain that, under the circumstances, you can appreciate my desire to stay near my sister and mother. I have cabled Oxford that I may not return to classes for some time, for I am determined to find who is behind this scheme. I do not know what they want or even who they might be, but if a trip to Devon is at all possible, given your busy schedule, I would welcome your help in this matter. Money is no barrier; please feel at liberty to name your price, and please also consider yourself my guest at Torre Abbey for as long as you like.

Yours truly,

Charles Cary

P.S. Doctor Watson is also most welcome, should his schedule permit him to accompany you. I am an avid reader of his adventures and would be honoured to have him stay with us.

I put the letter down thoughtfully. Though naturally gratified by the compliment in his last lines, I was most struck by the sincere tone of the letter. I did not think it was a hoax, and believed entirely that the man had indeed seen what he said he had seen. I stared into the fireplace at the orange and blue flames which crackled and leaped before me, and thought about the West Country. Not since our adventure at Baskerville Hall had Holmes and I visited the moors and bogs of Devon, and the mournful cry of the ghostly Hound still rang in my ears.

"Well, Watson, what do you think?"

Startled from my reverie, I turned to look at Holmes, who was sitting up now. He had been silent so long that I had practically forgotten about him. He lit a cigarette, awaiting my answer, his thin brows drawn together in an attitude of concentration.

"Well," I said, choosing my words carefully, "it is possible that the entire family suffers from hallucinations, but I don't think so."

"Oh? Why not?" He sat Indian-fashion on the sofa, his long legs tucked underneath him, a curl of blue smoke twisting from his lips as he exhaled.

I held up the letter. "This, mostly. Lord Cary strikes me as a man of sense and reason, not given to flights of fancy. He was skeptical about what his sister saw, but then was man enough to admit it when he saw a similar apparition."

"Quite," said Holmes, with a glance at Nature's fury raging just outside our window. The slanting rain pelted the panes and the wind howled like a living thing.

"What do you make of it, Holmes?"

"Oh, I quite agree with your conclusions. Lord Cary took special care to mention his sister's excessive imagination before relating his own encounter."

"What do you think it could be?"

"I can't possibly answer that without an examination of the abbey—and the Cary family."

"What do you propose to do?"

Holmes leaned back on the sofa.

"Do you have any pressing business in the next few days, Watson?"

I explained that as I had left my surgery in Dr. McKinney's hands for a while, I was quite unencumbered.

"Well, what do you say to a trip to Devon? Could you leave, say, tomorrow?"

"Yes, indeed," I replied, picking up my empty wine glass and placing it on the sideboard. "But now, how about some dinner? I'm famished." I was in fact feeling faint from hunger, having had very little time to eat all day long.

Holmes regarded the nest of newspapers scattered about the room. "I suppose I have to eat sooner or later," he sighed. "I'll ring Mrs. Hudson and see what she's up to."

Our ruminations were interrupted by a knock on the door.

"Come in," Holmes called from the couch, and the door swung open to admit the short, stalwart figure of our estimable, long-suffering landlady.

"Ah, Mrs. Hudson, right on cue," Holmes remarked amiably.

"I don't know about that," she replied, "but a telegram's just arrived for you and I thought I'd better bring it up quickly." Her red face and laboured breathing were a testament to how quickly she had rushed up the stairs.

"Indeed," said Holmes, flicking an ash from his sleeve. "What urgent business, I wonder, would bring someone out on a night like this?"

"That's what I said to the poor fellow who delivered it," she answered, fanning herself with the paper as she waded through the pile of discarded newspapers to where Holmes sat on the sofa. "You should have seen him—soaked to the skin he was—I thought he must be crazy and said as much, but he told me there was half a crown in it for him if he delivered it to you straight away."

She stood, hands on her ample hips, her broad face still flushed from her efforts.

But Holmes was not listening to her. He sat studying the telegram, his whole body motionless, in an attitude of deep concentration. Then he stood up abruptly and thrust the telegram at me.

"There is no time to waste, Watson," he said, his voice suddenly clear and sharp. "We must leave immediately."

"Leave? Where to?" Mrs. Hudson said, a bewildered expression upon her kindly face.

"To the West Country—Devon, to be exact," Holmes replied, striding off in the direction of his bedroom.

"Good Lord, why would you need to be going there on a godforsaken night like this?" she said, taking a few steps after him.

"Because someone's life may very well depend upon it," Holmes replied, and disappeared into the bedroom.

Mrs. Hudson turned to me. "What's he on about, Dr. Watson?"

I stared at the paper in my hand. The message was clear and yet cryptic:

FEAR WE ARE ALL IN DANGER STOP
PLEASE COME AT ONCE STOP

It was signed "Charles Cary, Torre Abbey, Torquay, Devon."

"Good Lord," I said as Holmes came back into the room. "It's the Cary family again."

"Who are the Cary family?" Mrs. Hudson said.

"A family that has the misfortune of owning a haunted house," Holmes replied. "And now, Mrs. Hudson, might I impose upon you to pack us some sandwiches for our trip?"

Our good landlady stood still for a moment, then she threw her hands straight up into the air.

"I don't know," she muttered. "Sometimes I just don't know how I stand it."

"Has the boy left yet?" said Holmes.

"Well, no—he was soaking wet, and I brought him inside to give him a cup of—"

Holmes interrupted her. "Send him back with a telegram to Lord Cary that we will arrive tonight if at all possible."

"We may just catch the last train out of Paddington tonight, Watson," Holmes called after me as I hurried upstairs to pack.

TORQUAY WAS just coming into its own as a resort town, and as it turned out, there was a six forty-five train leaving from Paddington, scooping up the last of the London businessmen hurrying out to join their families at the country houses dotting the coastline of Tor Bay.

And so, less than half an hour later, I found myself seated beside Holmes in a railway carriage speeding through the darkened English countryside.

"How long do you think this will take to sort out?" I said as I hungrily devoured the cold roast beef sandwiches Mrs. Hudson had provided us.

Holmes stared out the window at the darkened landscape rushing by. "It's difficult to say, Watson," he replied, stroking his chin thoughtfully. "Lord Cary provided so little information in his telegram."

He turned back to the window, his profile sharp in the flickering gaslight. We sat without speaking, surrounded by the sounds of the train: the low, rhythmic pulse of the engine, the chunk-a-chunk beating of pistons in their chambers, the clatter of metal wheels on the rails, and the squeaking and groaning of the wooden carriage as it swayed to and fro. Holmes sat looking out the window, his dark eyes narrowed, his brows furrowed, his long fingers fidgeting with an unlit pipe. Finally he spoke.

"A curious thing, the human imagination, Watson. As far as I know, it is one of the things separating us from the rest of the animal kingdom."

"I suppose so," I replied, staring out the window at the dim landscape. "I've never heard of a wildebeest imagining the presence of a lion when none was there. On the other hand, perhaps we just don't know enough about animals."

"Perhaps," Holmes answered, shrugging. "Speaking of animals, Watson, you could always give the cat to one of your patients."

I stared at him. "How did you know about the cat?"

He dismissed my astonishment with a wave of his hand. "Oh, come, Watson. When you arrived at Baker Street tonight you were sneezing; rubbing your eyes and wheezing—and you are still wheezing slightly, I can hear it. What am I to deduce but that you have an animal singularly noted for producing allergic reactions even among fanciers of the breed?"

I shook my head. "Really, Holmes, you might have come to the conclusion that I have a cold."

He shook his head. "You rarely get colds, Watson—you seem to be blessed with an iron constitution—and besides, the symptoms you display are of an allergic reaction, not a viral infection."

"Very well, Doctor," I said somewhat brusquely. "Then I suppose you can give me a full description of the animal in question."

Holmes smiled. "Really, that would be asking too much. I'm afraid I shall have to disappoint you on that score. I can only say that it is of a suspicious, violent disposition, is a rather small calico, oh—and that it is of course a female."

I threw up my hands. "Very well; I should have known better than to challenge you. Of course you are right, and now do me the kindness of describing how you arrived at your conclusions."

"Well, the scratches on your left hand, which you have dressed with iodine, were the first clue as to the animal's disposition. As to the coat, I can just make out three colours of hairs clinging to your overcoat—hence my conclusion the cat is a calico. And, as you may know, calicoes—and the closely related tortoiseshells—are always female. Females tend to be smaller than the males of the species, and since this was most probably a stray cat and therefore undernourished, I gambled that it was not a large cat."

"Very well, Holmes, once again you are correct."

"I only hope I am so fortunate with the Cary family," he replied, turning again to look out the window.

"Holmes, you don't think . . ." I began. He turned to look at me, his eyes keen in the dim light. "Before, when you asked me if I believed in ghosts," I continued, "you didn't seriously think . . ."

He smiled grimly. "What I think," he said slowly, "is that the Cary family is in danger—and that I take very seriously indeed."

I nodded and turned away; I had nothing else to say. We sat for some time in silence as the train hurtled through the night toward its dark destination.

CHAPTER TWO

T HE CITY of Torquay lies tucked away in a wide pocket
of the English Channel where the coastline is curved
inward—the convex shape on a map is rather like the outer rim
of a scallop shell. Protected from the treacherous currents for
which the channel is famous, this part of Devon's coast is distinguished by a series of bays—Start Bay, Babbacombe Bay, and of
course Tor Bay, on the southern end of which stands the city of
Torquay. Blessed with a deep natural harbour, Torquay is shel-
tered from the harsher climate of its neighbouring Cornish
coast, and in the last few years has been gaining a reputation as a
fashionable resort town.

The streets of the town rise sharply from the harbour up
into the bluffs surrounding the shoreline, offering many oppor-
tunities for grand views of the harbour. Taking advantage of
these natural geological features, builders of recent years have
begun to exploit the financial possibilities of a location deemed
more fashionable than a middle-class resort such as Brighton.
Situated more or less midway between Dartmouth and Exeter,
Torquay has a history which dates back to Roman times and
beyond—and by far the oldest and most distinguished building
in this historic city was Torre Abbey.

The abbey was a short drive from the train station, past an
apple orchard and down a wide sweeping boulevard lined with

majestic elm trees. The rain had stopped by now, and I inhaled the salt sea air as Holmes and I alighted from the cab in front of the main gatehouse of Torre Abbey. It was an imposing medieval tower of thick Normanesque architecture, and in the moonlight its massive limestone façade loomed three stories above us. As Holmes paid the driver, the heavy wooden door swung open and a tall man emerged whom I took to be Charles Cary. He held a gas lantern, and approached us with a vigorous stride, his right hand outstretched.

"Oh, Mr. Holmes, Dr. Watson, thank you for coming!" he cried, shaking first Holmes's hand and then my own. His grip was as forceful as his handwriting, bespeaking a man of firm and decisive character. Over our protests, he insisted on helping us with our luggage, and, handing the lantern to me, seized both bags and led us into the interior of the gatehouse.

"Our butler Grayson would normally have been here to greet you, but it's late and he's not as young as he once was," our host said, closing the heavy door behind him. The sound echoed through the vaulted chamber of the gatehouse with a dull thud. He led us through the gatehouse and into an enclosed courtyard. Passing through the courtyard, we entered what appeared to be the main living quarters of the abbey, a vine-encrusted three-story structure. It was a long building, lower than the gatehouse, with second-floor balconies opening up onto the courtyard.

"He wanted to stay up, but I insisted he retire at his normal time. Grayson's been with us since I was a child," Cary continued as we entered the dimly lit foyer. He turned up the gaslights, and I was able to get a better look at our host. To my surprise, he was very fair, with blue eyes and delicate facial features; for some reason, I had expected a shorter, darker man. He spoke quickly, gesturing rapidly with his hands, the fingers of which were long and white—the hands of a surgeon or an artist, I thought. His skin was the kind that burns and freckles in the sun, and his eyelashes were so blond they looked almost powdery in the gaslight. His hair was darker, a coppery-red colour, thick and curly, and he wore it rather longer than the fashion of the day, so that it curled over his collar in the back.

"It's so good of you to come," he said as Holmes and I stood in the foyer looking around. He rubbed his hands together briskly, and I noticed that the room was cold and damp. It occurred to me that the climate was ideal for bronchial infections, the humid seaside air combining with the natural moisture of the stone and brick buildings.

"You must be hungry after your journey," said our host. "If you like, we can leave your luggage here and get you something to eat."

Holmes deferred to me, and I nodded quickly. It had been some hours since our roast beef sandwiches, and I was quite famished.

"I let the staff retire for the night, but I believe my sister is still up and about," he said as we entered a long hallway lit by a few scattered wall sconces. Our steps reverberated hollowly down the chamber as we followed our host.

"You did not explain in your telegram the urgent matter that caused you to summon us tonight, Lord Cary," Holmes remarked as we followed our host.

"It's Elizabeth, Mr. Holmes," he replied. "She's seen it again."

"The ghost, you mean?" I inquired.

"Yes, and she's in quite a state about it. I am seriously concerned about her. When I told you she was excitable, Mr. Holmes, I was not exaggerating. Elizabeth is easily agitated, and this has all been terribly difficult for her."

"I see," Holmes replied as we turned a corner.

I held the lamp aloft, casting rather sinister shadows as we walked single file down the hallway. The abbey was elegantly appointed, with all the comforts of a grand country house—carpets upon burnished wooden floors, curtains of the finest lace, beautifully carved furniture and stuffed leather armchairs, but I could just imagine ancient monks in procession down the dusky passageways, chanting in low voices, their brown robes swinging from side to side.

"You know," remarked Lord Cary as he led us from room to room, "the locals will tell you that Torquay is as full of ghost stories as London is of hansom cabs."

"You are familiar with London?" Holmes inquired as we stood in an elegantly furnished room, which I took to be a study of some kind. On the wall was an impressive medieval tapestry, a hunting scene of a deer being chased by a pack of hounds.

"Well, I've been there but I'm not sure I'd say that I know it," Cary replied. "Oh, that's one of my ancestral legacies," he said when he saw me studying the tapestry.

"I believe you said your family has owned the abbey for some two hundred years?" said Holmes.

"Yes, since the seventeenth century."

"And the estate passed on to you following the death of your father?"

Lord Cary nodded. "Yes. In addition to the abbey itself, the Cary family has amassed a rather extensive art collection over the years."

"So I see," Holmes replied, examining an elaborate gilt framed portrait of a Cavalier on horseback. The man was very elegantly dressed all in black, in the style of the seventeenth century, with long leather boots and a tall feathered hat. He sat astride a huge black stallion frothing at the bit, showing its gleaming white teeth.

"Oh, that's one of my ancestors, so they say—Hugo Cary," Lord Cary said. "There are all sorts of stories about him."

"Hmmm," Holmes murmured, "very impressive. I can't say there's much family resemblance, however," he added, studying Charles Cary's face.

Our host shrugged. "He looks more like my father. I take after my mother."

"I see. Was your father—"

Cary fixed Holmes with his striking blue eyes. "Pardon me, but I must ask you this. You do believe that I saw something, don't you, Mr. Holmes?"

Holmes smiled. "It is of no importance what I do or do not believe, Lord Cary. 'Belief' is better relegated to matters of religion than science—and I use methods which I believe to be as scientific as possible, as my friend Dr. Watson here can confirm."

But our host would not be deterred. "It is important to me, Mr. Holmes, that you not think I am mad or delusional," he said earnestly, but Holmes dismissed this with a wave of his hand.

"Oh, I think nothing of the kind, Lord Cary. The question is not one of your sanity; please rest assured of that."

Cary appeared somewhat placated, and turned to me.

"I am a man of science myself; in fact, I am studying medicine at Oxford, with the aim of becoming a doctor. As a physician yourself, Dr. Watson, do you think it possible my sister and I are suffering some form of—hallucination?" He pronounced the word with the greatest disgust, as though he were speaking of leprosy or the bubonic plague.

"Well, the fact that you both saw something makes it more unlikely," I replied slowly, weighing my words carefully. "However, matters of the brain are not my area of specialty."

"I see," he replied, leading us from the tapestry room into a large, drafty dining hall. Sitting at one end of a long oaken table was a young woman of about eighteen years of age.

"May I present my sister, Elizabeth," Lord Cary said as she rose to greet us. "This is Sherlock Holmes and Dr. Watson, who have come to help us," he said gently, taking her hand, which, even in the dim light, I could see was shaking.

"Oh, thank you for coming," she said, with a nervous glance at her brother. Her voice was low and smooth, with a pleasing, bell-like cadence to it, even distraught as she obviously was.

Holmes took her hand and held it for a moment, an

uncharacteristic gesture for him, but it was clear the girl needed comforting.

"Don't worry, Miss Cary, I shall do everything I can to solve this troublesome situation."

She nodded and turned again to her brother. It was evident that she relied upon him greatly for moral strength.

Elizabeth Cary was swarthier than her brother, with a broad, sensuous face and lustrous, dark curly hair, which she wore pulled back from her face; it hung in a shiny cascade down her back. She wore a simple white dress with a high neck; it was old-fashioned-looking, and suited her admirably, I thought. I am no connoisseur of women's accoutrements, but there was something old-fashioned about Elizabeth Cary which the dress brought out, a sense of centuries gone by . . . or perhaps it was the setting and I was just imagining it to be the girl herself. Standing in the dusky dining hall of Torre Abbey, it was hard to imagine we were in the middle of this modern age of gaslighting and telegraphs; the walls themselves seemed to contain within them the spirits of ancient times.

I shivered and drew my ulster closer around me.

"Well, let's get you something to eat—something hot, I think, Dr. Watson?" said our host.

We followed Lord Cary and his sister into the kitchen, which was situated just in the other side of the dining room. It was a large, tidy room festooned with every type of cooking implement, all hanging on hooks from the whitewashed plaster walls. Brightly polished copper saucepans hung next to wire whisks and silver colanders; sets of blue china serving plates sat neatly stacked in a grand armoire in one corner of the room. At the far side of the main room was a door leading to what appeared to be a butler's pantry, and next to it was a line of bells, one for each room of the house.

As we entered the kitchen I heard footsteps in back of us

and turned to see a stout woman standing behind us. She was dressed in a white robe and nightcap and stood with her arms folded, as if waiting for an explanation for our presence.

"Ah—may I present my cook, Sally Gubbins," Lord Cary said. "Sally, this is Mr. Sherlock Holmes and Dr. Watson."

"Pleased to meet you," I said politely, but my greeting was met with only a grunt by way of reply.

"Humph. I suppose you'll be wanting something to eat," the cook muttered, brushing past us with hardly a glance. It was clear she regarded us as intruders in her terrain.

"Don't trouble yourself, Sally—Elizabeth and I can manage," Cary protested, but his comment was met with another, louder grunt.

"Humph! And make a mess of my kitchen? No, thank you, sir," the cook grumbled as she set pots and pans to clattering upon the stove, jangling my already thin nerves. As she bustled about, I studied her.

Sally Gubbins was a large, round woman with the kind of sturdy, comfortable body I had seen so often in English women of her class. She had a brisk, preoccupied manner, as though she had a million things to attend to; she did not so much enter the kitchen as storm through it, rather like a weather pattern. She expressed her irritation with the rest of humanity in the heavy shrug of her shoulders and the constant shaking of her head, all the while muttering under her breath. The occasional word or phrase was audible in her low mumblings; as she stood at the stove warming up the soup, I made out the phrase "outrageous behaviour," and "too much to bear."

Evidently the arrival of Holmes and myself, though welcomed by our host, was not by his cook. Lord Cary seemed aware of her attitude, because he went out of his way to placate her, thanking her profusely for her efforts.

"It really is good of you to do this, Sally," he commented as she plunked plates of bread and cheese down on the kitchen table. "Really, you didn't have to bother."

"Yes, I did," she replied, a great sigh escaping her generous bosom. "They would have made an utter mess of my kitchen," she added with a roll of her eyes, addressing me for some reason.

She trundled back to the stove on her heavy legs, thick and solid as mooring posts.

"It's no good saying you can look after yourself, because you can't," she muttered, turning the gas down under the soup kettle before expertly ladling it into blue china bowls. "Now go along with you," she said, handing each of us a bowl of steaming soup. "Go eat your soup so I can clean up my kitchen. Just pile the dishes in the sink when you're done. Don't leave them lying about in the house or you'll attract vermin," she added darkly. "I'm going back to bed—that is, unless there's anything else I can do for you, sir?"

"No, thank you, Sally, you've been most helpful," Cary replied.

With a final sigh and rolling of her eyes, Sally withdrew into the butler's pantry, where I could hear her clanging pans about as we carried our soup from the kitchen.

"You see who runs the household, Mr. Holmes," Lord Cary remarked as we made our way through dim hallways to the parlour.

Holmes allowed himself one of his dry little laughs.

"I do indeed, Lord Cary, I do indeed."

Cary shook his head. "It's hard to believe sometimes a woman like that has a son."

"Oh?" said Holmes. "Does he live with you, too?"

"Yes."

"And the father?" I said. "Where is he?"

"Apparently she became pregnant by some local roué, now long gone, moved on to greener pastures, no doubt."

"So the boy never knew his father?"

Lord Cary shook his head. "No, none of us did. Taking her on in her—condition—was one of my father's rare forays into charitable works. It's just as well, perhaps, that we never met her . . . paramour. I gather that Sally never had much good to say about him. I say, we men can be appalling creatures, can't we?" he sighed as he led us into a small, cozy parlour. The sight of the room made me feel better. It was cheery and comfortable; the floor was lined with rich Oriental rugs, and hunting prints hung upon the walls. A fire was blazing in the grate, evidently prepared in advance for our arrival.

Holmes opened his mouth to reply but I cut him off before he could launch into one of his invectives against women. I was not in the mood; I was tired and jumpy and altogether worn out.

"What's the boy's name?" I said.

"William," Lord Cary answered as we settled in front of the fire. "He cleans the stables and does the odd job or errand for us, poor boy. He's not quite right in the head," Cary added gently, stroking his sister's hair. She sat on a cushion at his feet, her soup on her lap, and it was evident to me that an unusually close bond existed between brother and sister.

"Poor little bird," she murmured, almost to herself.

"Elizabeth is very fond of William," said Cary. I looked over at Miss Cary and saw that her hand was shaking as she ate her soup.

"I have some valerian drops I could give your sister as a sedative, if you like," I said to Lord Cary.

"Elizabeth, would you like some medicine to make you feel calmer?" he asked gently. She turned to him and burst into tears.

"Oh, Charles," she said, burying her head in his lap.

"Yes, I believe we will take you up on that offer, Dr. Watson," Cary replied, with a glance at Holmes.

"A wise move, bringing your medical kit, Watson," said Holmes.

Warmed by his words, I left the parlour and retraced our steps back to the front hall, where our luggage still sat. I walked through the dining room, back into the long hallway, my footsteps reverberating hollowly, the sound fading away as it was soaked up by the thick walls of the abbey. As I entered the wide front hall, I thought I detected a movement out of the corner of my eye. I spun around, heart pounding, but I saw nothing. The darkened corners of the room were still and quiet, and all I could hear was the slow drip of water from the eaves.

Although the rain had stopped, a steady drip of rain water fell from the eaves onto the ground below. Not wanting to remain in that room any longer, I quickly retrieved my medical bag and headed back to the parlour. This time I walked briskly, without looking behind me, my eyes fixed straight ahead, concentrating on reaching my destination.

But as I entered the long hallway, I felt a chill sweep over my body unlike any other I had ever experienced. It was not the kind of a breeze such as is found in a drafty old building; no, it was an icy, bone-deadening cold, as though all the air in the room had been sucked out and what remained was the kind of vacuum which I imagined existed only in the cold dark vastness of outer space. It quite took my breath away, and I stopped, frozen in my tracks; I had an impulse to run, and yet I felt unable to summon the will to move. I looked around me—at the wall hangings, with their hunting scenes and elaborate Eastern designs, shadowy in the dim light, at the moonlight streaming in through the long vaulted windows. All was motionless and silent around me, and yet I had the distinct impression I was not alone in the room. It was as though there were another presence—a consciousness which did not harbour good will toward me.

Finally I summoned my will and took a deep breath, and suddenly the spell was broken. I was able to move my limbs, and I walked quickly from that dark place toward the light coming from the parlour.

"I was just complimenting Lord Cary on his cook's soup," Holmes remarked as I entered the room.

"Leek and potato, one of Sally's specialties," Lord Cary said. I noticed that his soup sat untouched on the table in front of him. The day had evidently taken a toll on him, because in the firelight his face looked pale and tired. Holmes, however, seemed to be eating his soup; though a natural ascetic, he was capable of eating his food with gusto.

I took the little brown bottle of valerian drops from my bag. "It's not a very pleasant taste, I'm afraid," I said to Miss Cary, "and it's a rather strong tincture, so if you would hand me your glass of water, I'll add the medicine. That should be more palatable."

She complied, and I measured out a dose and added it to the water, watching the brown liquid swirl slowly in the clear water. "There, drink up," I said, handing the glass to Miss Cary. She raised it to her lips and as she did I saw a thick white scar on the underside of her left wrist. She must have seen that I noticed it, because she turned away immediately after drinking the medicine.

"That's very bitter," she said, setting the glass upon the table behind her.

"Yes, it is unpleasant," I replied. "Still, it usually does the trick." I liked to reassure my patients in this way, because I had noticed over the years that a physician's confidence in his cures often seemed to increase their effectiveness. At first, I found this difficult to believe, and it took me a while to accept the role subjectivity seemed to play in medicine. I could only explain this effect as being a result of the power of suggestion—and, in my experience, some people are very suggestible indeed.

In any event, I could sense Miss Cary's body begin to relax as I spoke—and I knew in this case it was the power of my words alone, because it was too early for the medicine to have any effect.

"Now please, Dr. Watson, why don't you relax?" said our host, indicating a comfortable-looking leather armchair to one side of the fireplace.

"Thank you," I said, settling into the chair gratefully. My feet hurt, my joints were stiff from the cold, and my head was beginning to ache from hunger. I broke off a piece of bread and smeared it thickly with sweet yellow butter.

Just then I saw a movement at the other end of the room, by the entrance to the dining room. A shaggy dark head appeared at the doorway and then quickly withdrew.

Elizabeth sat up in her chair. "William, is that you?"

There was a pause and then a little sound came from the other side of the doorway. It was like the whimpering of a small animal, faint and high-pitched. Elizabeth rose and followed, withdrawing into the other room. I could hear her voice, soft and low, as she spoke with the person I presumed was William, but I could not make out the words.

A few minutes later she entered the room again, holding the hand of a boy whom I took to be about twelve years of age. He was possessed of an unusually delicate, pretty face for a boy, with pink cheeks and long dark eyelashes. His hair, though unkempt, was as thick and curly as Elizabeth's, and so black it shone almost blue in the dim light. His mouth was a perfect Cupid's bow, and it occurred to me that some day many girls would long to kiss that mouth, except for one thing: the light of intelligence did not shine from the boy's eyes. Beautiful though they were, with their thick long lashes, there was a dull and haunted expression in them which bespoke the tragedy of a disturbed mind.

Elizabeth pulled the boy gently forward; he resisted, but was reluctant to let go of her hand, clutching at it with all his might.

"This is William," she said, and, turning to him, spoke gently. "William, these are the men who have come to help us."

"Hello, William," I said. "I'm Dr. Watson and this is my friend, Mr. Sherlock Holmes."

William looked at me and then at Holmes, his lower lip trembling all the while. He opened his mouth but all that came out was a little gurgling sound. He looked back at Elizabeth, terror in his eyes. He shrank back against her side like a frightened animal.

"I'm afraid William is rather shy," Cary said. "It's difficult for him to meet people. He trusts Elizabeth and me because he knows us—isn't that right, William?"

In reply William seized a strand of his rather long hair and twisted it between his fingers, rocking gently back and forth.

Holmes crossed his arms and cocked his head to one side. "Hello, William."

William's eyes followed the faces of each person as they spoke, but I couldn't tell whether or not he understood what they were saying. I had seen cases like his in mental institutions when I was in medical school, and it always affected me deeply to see a soul so locked up within a body that communication with fellow human beings was difficult or impossible.

"Can he speak?" I said to Lord Cary.

Cary shook his head. "Well, Elizabeth says he talks to her."

Elizabeth nodded vigorously. "He does—don't you, poor little bird?" In response, William touched her cheek.

Lord Cary sighed. "He understands what we say, because he can follow simple orders. But I've never heard him use language in any sense that I understand it."

"He's just frightened, aren't you?" she said, stroking his hair. William looked up at her and made the same little whimpering sound I had heard earlier.

"Poor little bird," Elizabeth said again, stroking his shaggy head.

He looked up at her. "Po lel bur," he said, forming the

sounds with some considerable effort. He appeared to be trying to repeat her words.

Holmes nodded slowly. "I see."

Lord Cary rose and stretched himself, and I noticed that his build was very slim—unlike his sister's, who, I thought, was given to plumpness. Though quite slender now, I expected she would in a few years grow into the stockier frame Nature had provided her with.

"You mentioned Elizabeth takes after your father?" I remarked, but Lord Cary didn't seem to hear me. He went over to the armchair near the fireplace where his sister was sitting with William and leaned one arm upon the mantel.

"Well, Elizabeth," he said, "now that our guests have come all this way to help us, why don't you tell them what you saw?"

The girl's lower lip trembled a bit, but her brother put a reassuring hand on her shoulder. "It's all right, don't be afraid. Mr. Holmes and Dr. Watson are here to help us."

"Yes," Holmes repeated. "Don't be afraid—you can tell us what happened."

"Well," she said, stroking the boy's hair as he lay in her lap, "I was asleep and then I felt a gust of wind or something against my cheek." She shuddered and wrung her hands. "I woke up feeling cold, as if there was a draft in the room. And then . . . he was there."

"Where?" said Holmes, his grey eyes keen as razors. "Where was he?"

"At the foot of my bed," she replied, trembling. "I felt cold all over, so cold."

As she spoke, I felt a corresponding chill run through my own body. My mind was hurtling back to the deadly cold I had experienced in the hallway, and the accompanying sense of dread. It was enough to shake my nerve—and in my experience as a soldier and a doctor I had seen some pretty disturbing things. I had no doubt that such an experience as this could shatter the delicate sensibilities of a young girl such as Elizabeth.

"What did you do?" I said.

She looked at me blankly. "I'm not sure. I think I screamed . . . and then I must have fainted, because when I came to again, he was gone."

"She screamed, all right," Cary remarked, lighting a cigarette. "Everyone in that part of the house heard her."

"What exactly did you see, Miss Cary?" said Holmes, leaning forward. His eyes were keen as a crow's, and shone out of his aquiline face with an intensity I have yet to see in another man.

She rubbed her eyes as if to rid them of the awful spectre. As she did, young William reached up a hand to stroke her cheek. He had been lying quietly in her lap, curled up almost as if he were an infant and she his mother. The touch of his hand appeared to comfort her, for she took a deep breath and answered my friend's question.

"It was the Cavalier," she said firmly, though her chin trembled as she spoke.

"The Cavalier?" said Holmes, with a look at her brother.

Instead of replying, Charles turned away and flicked his cigarette into the fire. He watched it flare up briefly and disappear into the flames, then he turned back to us.

"Do you remember the picture you saw when you came in, of my ancestor, Hugo Cary?" he said.

"Ah, yes—the seventeenth-century Cavalier," I replied.

"Is that whom you saw, Elizabeth?" said Holmes. "Hugo Cary?"

She nodded, one hand to her lips while the other stroked William's hair.

Charles Cary sighed, a deep heavy sound which seemed to resonate through his whole body. He sat down again and regarded Holmes and myself with a serious face.

"There is an old legend that whenever a member of the

Cary family sees the Cavalier, it means that someone in the family is about to die."

There was a silence, and then Holmes spoke.

"Do you believe that?"

Charles Cary snorted. "Of course not—it's typical West Country superstition. But that's not what concerns me. My sister seems to believe it, and given her fragile state of mind, that is worrisome."

"I saw him, I tell you!" Elizabeth said quietly but with such fervour that we all looked at her. "I saw the Cavalier," she repeated slowly. "One of us is going to die."

"Don't be foolish, Elizabeth—no one is going to die!" her brother snapped.

"Miss Cary, I assure you I will do everything within my power to make certain no harm comes to you or your family," Holmes said quietly. "You have my word upon that."

"You're exhausted, Elizabeth—why don't you go up to bed now?" said her brother, his voice softer now.

I looked at her—her eyelids were indeed beginning to droop, and she sat slumped in her chair, one hand on William's shoulder. He appeared to have fallen asleep; his eyes were closed and his breathing was steady and regular.

"Perhaps we should all retire," our host continued, addressing Holmes and myself. "You have had a long journey, and must be tired yourselves."

I glanced at Holmes, who rarely showed signs of fatigue except when he was bored, which he certainly was not now. However, at Cary's words he rose immediately from his chair.

"I think that would be a good idea," he replied. "We can get a fresh start on things tomorrow. Everything always looks less frightening in the light of day," he added with a look at Elizabeth, who sat staring into the fire.

"Elizabeth, would you take William back to bed while I show our guests to their rooms?" said Lord Cary, rising from his chair. She raised her head and nodded in reply, but did not move. "Come along, then," he said, offering her a hand. "Time for bed. You'll feel better in the morning."

She obeyed meekly, and, taking a sleepy young William by the hand, shuffled off to bed.

"Right," said our host, with a final poke at the fire. "Allow me to show you to your rooms, gentlemen."

We followed him back to the front hall to fetch our bags, and then up the long dark staircase to the second floor.

"That is the Abbot's Tower," he said pointing to a set of narrow stone steps. I caught a glimpse of high, narrow vaulted windows with a cross-hatch design upon the upper third of the glass. Everything at Torre Abbey was reminiscent of the religious history of the place; even the windows in the second-floor hallways resembled miniature church windows, the top panes pointed like tiny chapel roofs.

"Some say this is where Abbot Norton had Symon Hastynges beheaded," Cary remarked as we turned onto the second-floor landing. I couldn't suppress a shudder as I thought of the blunt sound of an axe echoing through these dusky chambers.

Holmes's room was at the southern end of the long hallway, overlooking the gatehouse, and I was to have the room closest to the staircase. We wasted little time saying good night, assuring Lord Cary that anything else we might require could wait until morning.

My room was elegantly but simply furnished, with an old-fashioned poster-bed with thick velvet drapes to keep out the night air, crimson to match the window curtains, which were a heavy brocade material. I lay awake for some time that night listening to the wind as it whistled and moaned in the eaves, restless as an unquiet spirit. On a night like this, it was hard not to think of ancient monks roaming these cold chambers, and try as I might, I could not erase the image of a headless Symon Hastynges from my mind.

I turned over in the bed and pulled the coverlet up to my chin, but it was no use: I fancied I could hear in the pining of the wind the sound of the axe as it whistled through the air on its way to strike the fatal blow. This was followed by the picture of the newly beheaded monk wandering through the drafty recesses of Torre Abbey, perhaps in search of his executioner, looking to even the score, the hood of his brown robe falling loose about his headless shoulders. This image was replaced by one of a smiling Hugo Cary, his grin sinister in the dim light.

I knew these imaginings were silly and useless, and that in the light of day I would have a good laugh at myself. However, in this dark and gloomy fortress, lying upon the Cary family's canopied bed, surrounded by the groaning wind and rain, only a man who was made of stone would have been able to vanquish these thoughts from his mind by sheer power of will. Finally I rose from my bed and administered to myself the same liberal dose of valerian I had given Elizabeth Cary earlier. Slipping back into bed, I pulled the covers up and waited for the drug to take effect. I thought of Holmes in his room down the hall, and wondered whether he was asleep. I had half a mind to go knock on his door, but, foolish as I knew it was, I had no great desire to enter that bleak and deserted hallway.

I had said nothing to my friend of my experience in the deserted hallway, fearing that I might injure the good opinion he had of me. Now, however, given Miss Cary's experience of the night before, I couldn't help but wonder if what I felt had some meaning after all. Holmes always accused me of giving in too much to my imagination, and while on occasion I might agree with him, tonight I was not so sure. I resolved to speak to him about it the following day, and, drawing the covers up to my chin, I closed my eyes and waited for the drug to take effect. At length a heavy drowsiness settled upon my weary limbs, and I slid gratefully into sleep.

CHAPTER THREE

⟨~⟩

Well, Holmes, what do you make of Charles Cary?"
We were in the dining room, lingering over a late
breakfast. Lord Cary had risen early and gone into town on
business, or so we were informed by his ancient manservant,
Grayson, who attended to our needs with the efficient, prac-
ticed air of someone who has spent his life in service. Elizabeth
Cary evidently had accompanied her brother into town, as
there was no sign of her—nor of her mother, who, we were
told, often rose late.

"I will not argue with your conclusions regarding his personality," my friend replied, "except to add that he is more
attached to his mother and sister than he was to his father."

"Oh? How do you arrive at that conclusion?" I said, spear-
ing another kipper with my fork.

"Oh, just little signs that he gives off, really; his tone of
voice, the way he looks at his sister as opposed to the way he
speaks of his father."

"Yes, I know what you mean. I get the distinct impression
that he avoids saying much at all about his father, perhaps to
avoid saying anything bad?"

Holmes poured himself another cup of coffee and settled
back in his chair. "Yes, I was thinking the same thing. Loyalty is

important to our young host . . . unless, of course, he is playing a deeper game than we could ever guess."

"Oh?" I said, surprised. "Such as what?"

Holmes shook his head. "I don't know as yet. But I am beginning to believe that everything is not as it seems at Torre Abbey."

"By the way, I saw something which I thought might be of some significance."

"Oh?" Holmes said, and I proceeded to tell him about the scar I had seen on young Elizabeth's wrist.

Holmes's lean face grew even more grim as he contemplated this new information.

"Self-inflicted, do you think?" he said.

I shook my head. "It's impossible to say for sure, but it is suspicious, to say the least."

"Yes, isn't it?" Holmes replied, his deep-set eyes narrow in the silky morning light which fell upon our table, shining on the brightly polished silver tea service on the sideboard. Old as he was, their manservant Grayson kept Torre Abbey in ship-shape; there was not a spot of tarnish on the silverware or a fleck of dust upon the windowsills.

Just then Grayson entered the room again, and we fell silent. I took the opportunity to observe him more closely than I had earlier: he was thin and wizened, with papery skin, shrunken as a mummy. A few greying wisps of hair clung to a head which looked larger than normal, seated as it was on such a bony frame. His skin was a faded brown colour, like old parchment, darkened and brittle with age. His eyes were large and watery, so dark they were almost black. His eyebrows were bushy and thick, though dead-white, and sat over his eyes like overhanging snow drifts on a cliff. His shoulders were bent over from arthritis, but his knotty hands were steady as he poured fresh coffee into our pot.

Holmes got up from his chair, wandered over to the window and stretched himself. "This is excellent coffee, Grayson—is it Kenyan?"

"Is everything satisfactory, sir?" the butler said, turning around to look at Holmes.

"Yes, thank you, Grayson," Holmes replied, eyeing the man through half-closed eyes. I knew, of course, that he was keenly observing the butler and that his sleepy look was deceiving.

"If you need for anything, Master Cary says you are to ring for me and you shall have it at once," Grayson said, brushing a few crumbs from the table into his hand.

"We are much obliged, I'm sure," Holmes replied.

Grayson bowed stiffly and withdrew from the room.

"Well, Watson," Holmes said, looking after him, "there goes a rather unusual individual."

"Oh? How do you mean?" I never ceased to be impressed by the inferences my friend made based upon the same observations of people as myself—his eye was always keener, and went beyond the obvious. Try as I might, I could not match his acuity and ability to transform an encounter into a series of astonishing conclusions.

"Well, I cannot tell you that much about him," Holmes said, stirring milk into his coffee, "but it is certain that English is not his native language, that he has spent time in the East—probably India—and that in spite of a considerable hearing loss he continues to play the tin whistle—or some such instrument."

I shook my head and laughed. "I give up, Holmes. I won't even attempt to follow you this time, so you might as well tell me how you arrived at these conclusions."

Holmes shrugged. "You perhaps remarked the musical cadence of his speech, and the way he pronounces his *r*'s—not at the back of his throat, like an Englishman, but more to the front, with a very slight rolling sound?"

"Well, now that you mention it, yes, I did notice there was

an unusual lilt to his speech . . . and there is something different about the way he pronounces his words."

"Yes. Even though he has evidently lived here the better part of his life, he has not quite eradicated the music of his original language from his speech. Hence my conclusion that English is not his first language. And you probably failed to notice his ears?"

"His ears?"

"Yes," Holmes replied. "There is an identical indentation in each of them. I would be willing to bet good money that he has had his ears pierced."

"Really?" I said. "So you concluded that he is most likely of Indian origin?"

"Just so, Watson."

"And the hearing loss?"

Holmes took a sip of coffee. "Did you notice that when he was not looking at me he was unable to understand what I was saying?"

"I did notice that he didn't seem to hear your question about the coffee."

Holmes nodded. "I noticed that when speaking to us he looked keenly at our faces, and guessed that he might be lip-reading, so when he came in just now I turned away from him and complimented him on the coffee, which you noticed he did not respond to. He immediately afterwards asked if everything was satisfactory."

"I see," I said, nodding slowly. "So you came to the natural conclusion that he was in fact reading lips to compensate for a hearing loss."

"Precisely."

"And the tin-whistle playing?"

"Well, you may have remarked the slight round indentations on the first three fingers of both his left and right hand . . . and when you realize that there are six holes on a tin whistle, and that it is played with the first three fingers of both hands, the conclusion becomes rather obvious."

"Obvious to you, perhaps," I said. "However, to the rest of us—"

I was interrupted at that moment by the appearance of Lady Cary. My mind was immediately drawn from what I was saying by the sight of her, and I am afraid I looked rather foolish, my mouth half open in mid-sentence, as she made her entrance. Indeed, I quite forgot what I was saying; I quite forgot everything except the presence of that extraordinary woman. Since the death of my wife, my feelings towards women had been blunted, but the appearance of Marion Cary seemed to awaken dormant emotions within me.

The resemblance between her and her son was evident at first glance: she had the same slim build, the same fair skin, the same striking blue eyes. But on her the effect was one of astonishing beauty: the subtle colouration of her skin, the delicacy of her facial features, the calm dignity with which she carried herself, all combined to produce a startling effect. Her hair was that shade between red and blonde which is described as "strawberry blonde" but does not convey its true beauty, the highlights which seem to shine from every strand, whether in the gaslight or in the mid-morning sun that shone now through the gauzy lace curtains, falling upon her white neck, long and curved as a swan's. In the sunlight her hair looked exactly like what I had imagined spun gold would look like when I was a child and read about it in fairy-tales. I knew she must be at least forty-five, but to me at that moment she looked a good fifteen years younger, so lithe was her figure and so luminous her skin.

I could not help staring at her, and turned to Holmes to see what impression she was making on him. (He was not so much impervious to feminine charms as wary of them; I had gathered that much from his reaction to Irene Adler, whom he still referred to as "*the* woman.") But Holmes was unreadable, and I could not gather from his expression what he thought of the lady.

"Good morning, madam," he said cordially, rising from his chair. "I am Sherlock Holmes, and this is—"

"Dr. Watson," she replied, smiling, and all the world was not large enough to contain the radiance of that smile. "My son said he had summoned you; I cannot thank you enough for coming on such short notice. Poor Elizabeth," she said softly, the smile fading from her face, and it was like the sudden appearance of a cloud cover on a sunny day. "Your reputation has reached as far as Torquay, Mr. Holmes," she said. "Even out here people have heard of you."

Holmes brushed a crumb from his sleeve. "I thank you for the compliment, Lady Cary, but notoriety can be a hindrance in my line of work."

"I see," Lady Cary replied, seating herself at the end of the table. She reached for the silver coffeepot, and I sprang from my chair to pour her a cup.

"Shall I ring for some hot coffee?" said Holmes, but she shook her head.

"No, thank you; this will do nicely," she said, stirring in some sugar with a delicate white hand. "Grayson is old," she sighed, "and I sometimes think I should relieve him of his duties and just let him live here at his ease, but then I think that would send him to an early grave. He is so used to looking after us . . ." She lifted a laced handkerchief to her face and dabbed at her forehead. As she did so, I noticed that the nails on her hands were bitten to the quick, the cuticles red and irritated. I glanced over at Holmes to see if he was taking this in, but once again it was hard to tell from his expression what he was thinking. He saw everything, however, so I had no doubt that he had observed the condition of her hands.

"These past few days have been very hard on all of us," Lady Cary sighed as she poured cream into her coffee.

"Yes, I've no doubt," Holmes replied sympathetically. He could, when he wanted to, project the utmost compassion—a stark contrast from the cold reasoning machine which he had on many occasions described himself as being.

Just then Grayson entered the room with a plate of bacon and eggs, which he set down on the table.

"Thank you, Grayson," she said warmly. "How did you know I was here?"

"I heard your voice, mum. I hope everything is to your liking."

"I'm sure it will be fine," she answered with a warm smile, and again I felt as though the sunlight which already suffused the room had suddenly become brighter. "You're a wonder, Grayson," she said with a little sigh, plucking a kipper from the plate and putting it onto her own. Peering at it closely, she made a face, and Grayson stepped forward.

"Is everything to your liking, madam?"

"Yes, fine, thank you."

Giving a little bow, the butler withdrew back to the kitchen.

"He really is a wonder, you know," she said to Holmes, who sat drumming his fingers on the table, a sure sign that his brain was working even more rapidly than usual.

"Has he been with you since he came over from the East— India, is it?" Holmes inquired with a little smile.

"Oh, my son has been telling you the family history, then, Mr. Holmes?" she said. It seemed to me that his question had taken her a little off guard, for the spoon slid out of her hand as she helped herself to some eggs.

"As a matter of fact," I began, "he didn't tell us—"

"Watson is quite correct," Holmes said. "Several factors suggested to me that Mr. Grayson was not only not a native of this country, but that his origins were somewhere in the East."

"Well, you are correct," the lady replied. "He has been with my late husband ever since Victor was stationed in India. In fact, it seems my husband saved his life, and to show his gratitude he insisted on staying on as Victor's manservant—it was a point of honour for him, apparently, to repay such a debt. But you interest me, Mr. Holmes—how did you know Grayson was not an Englishman? Certainly he looks like the perfect English butler, or so I have always thought."

Holmes smiled and leaned back in his chair. "The first thing that alerted me was the slight cadence of his native language which still informs his speech, as I explained to my friend Watson—but there were one or two other little points as well."

"Oh?" she said, leaning closer to him, and I could smell a faint breath of perfume coming from her creamy neck—something floral, like lilies in the spring.

My friend settled back in his chair, his long fingers around his coffee cup. "Well, for one thing, it is very unlikely that an Englishman would have his ears pierced."

"Oh?" said Lady Cary with some surprise. "I was not aware that—" She stopped and looked at Holmes. "Grayson, Mr. Holmes? Are you certain?"

Holmes smiled. He enjoyed the suspense in which he kept his listeners. "They have healed over, of course, but if you look closely you will observe on either ear the small but unmistakable holes in the lower lobes."

Lady Cary sat back in her chair. "Good heavens, Mr. Holmes, I never noticed! Well, I don't know what to make of this information."

Holmes shrugged. "Only perhaps that there is more to most people than one would at first suspect."

At that moment a young servant girl appeared at the door holding a broom and dustpan. When she saw us, a blush bloomed in her already red cheeks; she evidently had not realized the room was occupied. She was short and plump, with a little button nose set in a round rosy face. It was a face so like the ones I had seen on the streets of London's East End, where grime and poverty turned even those rosy cheeks sallow, but here in the country, I thought, a young girl was allowed to bloom, round and rosy, fresh as a spray of daffodils in April.

I was interrupted in my poetic musings by the entrance of Grayson, who saw the girl and frowned.

"Annie, what are you standing there for? Go on about your duties."

"Begging pardon, sir, I only come in to sweep the dining room," she said meekly, a hint of Dublin in her speech.

"Well, you can see it's occupied at present. There's no shortage of rooms to clean, now, is there?" he said sternly.

"No, sir," she replied, and scurried from the room as though a cannon had been fired behind her. Grayson made a little bow to us and withdrew from the room.

Lady Cary smiled. "Poor Annie. She's the chambermaid, and is quite terrified of Grayson, though I can't imagine why. He's gentle as a kitten, really."

Holmes regarded her languidly, one thin arm draped over the arm of his chair. "You employ a fairly small staff, then, Lady Cary?" he said.

"Yes," she replied. "With only Elizabeth and myself here these past few months, I see no need to have scads of servants marching about all day. In addition to Grayson and Sally, our cook, there's only Annie the chambermaid—oh, and there's a gardener who comes once a week to trim the hedges and look after the flower beds—but we won't be needing him much until spring. How long do you expect to be with us, Mr. Holmes?"

Holmes rose from his chair and went over to the window. "Well, Lady Cary, that all depends."

"Upon what?"

"Several things, actually—some of which I am only beginning to understand myself."

"Yes, I have heard that you have an uncanny ability to deduce facts about people upon first meeting them."

"Well, it's hardly uncanny," Holmes said modestly. "My 'ability' is merely based upon observation."

"Very well, Mr. Holmes; tell me everything you have observed about me," she said, leaning towards him.

Holmes considered this proposition for a moment. "Everything, Lady Cary?" he said carefully.

"Yes, indeed! It's hardly any good if you keep something to yourself. I want to hear it all," she laughed, but as she spoke a flush crept up her beautiful neck.

I had an impulse to tell Holmes not to go on, but I must admit I was curious to hear what he had surmised about our hostess.

"Very well," Holmes replied smoothly. "Beyond the obvious facts that you are a practicing Catholic, left-handed, disciplined, and that you enjoy the company of a small brown terrier, I also observed that you are nearsighted, averse to fish, and have recently decided to give up smoking. Also, if you will pardon me for saying so, you are a bit on the vain side."

"I say, Holmes!" I protested, thinking this last statement was a bit much, but Lady Cary laid a cool white hand upon my arm.

"It's all right, Dr. Watson—I asked Mr. Holmes to tell me everything. He is quite correct in observing that I am vain," she said with a smile. "I am not ashamed to admit it."

"Well, I am certain you have a perfectly good reason to be," I said huffily, still put out at Holmes for his remark.

"Well, Mr. Holmes," said the lady. "You are of course correct in every particular—except for the fish. It is only that I don't like the smell of it first thing in the morning."

Holmes smiled. "I see. When you reached for the platter of

bacon, which Grayson placed near the kippers, and got the plate of herring instead, the look on your face was one of extreme distaste. In order to make such a mistake one would have to be quite nearsighted. When a woman does not wear her eyeglasses—even though they help her distinguish a plate of bacon from kippers—I am apt to conclude that she does so out of vanity rather than absentmindedness."

Lady Cary laughed again, a deep chortling sound I found quite musical. "You are really too frightening, Mr. Holmes. Do you also have the ability to read minds?"

Holmes smiled drily. "Hardly. I think you will find all of my conclusions based upon fact rather than conjecture and intuition. For instance, when I saw the nicotine stains upon the fingers of your left hand, together with the greyish colour of your teeth, I concluded that you are a smoker, accustomed to holding a cigarette in your left hand. However, the way you fidget with your fork, together with the fact that the nails on both hands are bitten to the quick, lead me to the logical deduction that you are recently attempting to quit this unhealthy habit."

Lady Cary sighed. "Yes, and it is one of the harder things I have ever attempted to do."

Holmes nodded. "Very commendable, I'm sure. I for one do not have your discipline, for it takes discipline and willpower to quit the evil weed—as my colleague here, Dr. Watson, can tell you."

I nodded. "It is indeed a most addictive substance, I'm afraid."

Lady Cary absently ran a hand over a few scattered curls which had escaped her chignon. "And the Catholicism—and the terrier?"

Holmes waved his hand dismissively. "Mere child's play. That cross you wear around your neck—surely it is an unusual ornament for a Protestant, and more likely to be worn by a Catholic, do you not agree?"

Lady Cary nodded. "Perhaps."

"An interesting religion, Catholicism," Holmes remarked. "They are especially given to secrecy, which is not surprising, considering the history of the religion in this country."

Lady Cary smiled. "The Cary family have always been Catholics, even when they were persecuted for it—but you could have found that out from anybody in town."

Holmes smiled. "Ah, but I didn't."

"Very well. And the terrier?"

Holmes shrugged. "Again, child's play. The short brown hairs which I observe are only on the lower part of your dress indicate a small dog. I'll admit the actual breed was a guess, but an educated one. Terriers are not only a popular breed but also have short, stiff hairs such as those."

Lady Cary laughed her musical laugh again. "Well done, Mr. Holmes!"

"One thing puzzles me," I interjected. "Terriers are notoriously territorial. Why didn't he bark when we came in last night, I wonder?"

Lady Cary smiled. "He's not a young dog, and his hearing is not what it used to be, I'm afraid—though his sense of smell is as good as ever. He's a Skye terrier, actually, and goes by the name of Callie—short for Caliban. My daughter named him after reading *The Tempest* at school."

"Yes, and a terrible little monster he is!"

I turned just in time to see Charles Cary enter the room, his face flushed and healthy-looking—a marked contrast to the drawn and haggard visage we had seen on the previous night. He kissed his mother on the cheek and then settled himself at the table with the air of a man who has just concluded some satisfying business.

"It seems your errand in town was a successful one, Lord Cary," Holmes remarked, as if reading my thoughts.

"What? Oh, yes, it was; nothing much, just a small matter," he replied. He appeared to be distracted by something, but turning his attention to Holmes and myself, he smiled. "Please call me Charles," he said. "I don't like all this 'Lord Cary' business—it makes me feel terribly old and responsible."

"Oh, but you are," his mother replied warmly. "Charles has not gotten used to being the man of the house—have you, Charles?"

Charles looked at her from under his blond lashes and bit the nail of his right index finger. "Well, it was a damn bloody nuisance of Father to go off and drown like that—it upset poor Elizabeth terribly."

"Elizabeth is a high-strung child," his mother replied dismissively.

"Where is your sister, by the way?" Holmes inquired.

"She went up to her room when we returned . . . she wasn't feeling well," Cary replied, stretching out a hand towards the coffeepot. In the morning light I could see that several of his nails were also bitten to the quick. I glanced at Holmes to see if he too noticed this, but his attention was focused upon Lady Cary.

"I'll ring for some hot coffee," she said as her son lifted the empty coffeepot.

No sooner had she spoken, however, than the door to the kitchen swung open and Grayson emerged, a steaming pot of fresh coffee in one hand and a tray of cinnamon buns in the other.

"Good man, Grayson," said Charles Cary, plucking a bun from the tray as the butler set it down upon the table. "Always one step ahead of us, aren't you?"

"I do my best, sir," the old man replied as he poured his young master a cup of coffee. "Will Miss Elizabeth be taking her coffee upstairs today?" he inquired in a voice that I thought contained the slightest hint of disdain.

"She's resting just now, so I think perhaps not," Cary

responded, biting into the cinnamon bun. "She's still rather upset today," he said after Grayson had retired from the room.

"Understandable, I'm sure," Holmes replied, leaning back in his chair. I wondered what he thought of the Cary family. There seemed to me to be undercurrents of unresolved tensions between everyone in the household. I couldn't put my finger on it, but I had the feeling that they were all watching each other—and watching us as well, waiting to see what we might do.

Lady Cary turned to her son. "Mr. Holmes has just been telling me the most ingenious things about myself. He really is wonderfully observant, Charles—it's rather like being under a microscope."

Charles Cary turned to look at my friend. "Oh? What have you gleaned in your short time here, Mr. Holmes?"

"Well, he knew that Grayson was not an Englishman, for example," said Lady Cary.

"Actually, he's half English—his mother was a high-caste Indian woman, and his father was a British cavalry officer," Cary replied.

"I see," said Holmes.

Lady Cary rose gracefully from her chair. "If you gentlemen will excuse me, I will leave you to your coffee—I know you have many things to talk about."

"By all means," said Holmes, rising as Lord Cary and I did the same.

She turned to her son. "If you need me, I will be in my rooms."

Charles Cary took his mother's hand and pressed it to his lips—not an unusual gesture in some circumstances, perhaps, but it seemed a little out of keeping with his natural air of reticence and dignity. Holmes showed no expression. Either he did not think it odd, or, more likely, he was keeping his thoughts to himself.

After his mother had gone, Lord Cary ran a hand through his hair and sighed.

"I do not expect much help from the local police in this matter, you know, Mr. Holmes. However," he said, looking at Holmes intently, his blue eyes blazing with emotion, "I hope that you will stand by us and get to the bottom of this affair."

Holmes nodded, his face serious. "Have no fear of that, Lord Cary—there are several points of interest about this case. More importantly, I am convinced that, whatever forces are behind these events, you and the other members of your family are in some peril."

Cary looked at Holmes. "Really, Mr. Holmes? What makes you say that?"

Holmes waved off the question with a flick of his hand. "I make it a habit not to reveal all that I observe, Lord Cary—a trait that you may well imagine is taxing to the patience of my ever tolerant colleague, Dr. Watson. However, I have my reasons. There are some things that my clients have no need to know— facts and observations that would not only be useless but upsetting to them and to my investigation. And, of course, I do not like to proceed upon any information unless I am very certain of it. Being a man of science, I'm sure you can appreciate that."

As Holmes spoke, Cary's face grew redder, until it nearly matched the rich hue of his copper-coloured hair.

"I can well appreciate your need for some secrecy, Mr. Holmes, but I hope you will share with me anything which will help me to protect my family," he replied, his voice tight. "After all, I feel it is my duty to see that no harm comes to them."

Holmes nodded. "I understand, Lord Cary, and rest assured that I will do everything in my power to ensure the safety of everyone at Torre Abbey . . . By the way, may I ask how your father died?"

Cary looked down at his coffee cup, his jaw clenched. "He

was drowned in the bay. He went swimming one day and never returned . . . his clothes were found upon the beach later that day."

"I see. So the death was ruled an accident?"

"Yes."

"But no body was ever found?"

Cary shifted restlessly in his chair. "No, Mr. Holmes—and now, if you will both excuse me, I have some business to attend to."

"Before you do, Lord Cary, I would like to ask you one or two things," said Holmes.

"By all means," Cary replied, but I could see that he was anxious to leave. "What do you want to know?" he said, drumming his fingers on the table.

"Have you considered asking for protection from the local police?"

"I have spoken with the local authorities, but they are not anxious to become involved. They claim this is because nothing has been stolen, and no one has been injured—"

"As yet," Holmes interjected.

"As yet . . ." Lord Cary shook his head. "I may as well tell you, Mr. Holmes, that I'm afraid my family's relationship with the local constabulary is somewhat compromised. My father . . . how to put it delicately? He could be a harsh man, and once or twice he had occasion to clash with the forces of the law. In the process, I'm afraid, he made no friends."

"I see. Very well . . . and now, I don't wish to detain you any further from your business."

"Thank you," our host replied, and practically bounded from his chair. "I will see you at dinner, then, which is served at eight."

When he had gone, Holmes turned to me and smiled. "Well, Watson, have you ever seen a man more anxious to avoid a conversation?"

"He was rather intent on leaving, wasn't he?" I answered. "He clearly didn't want to talk about his father's death."

"No, indeed he didn't," Holmes said, shaking his head slowly. "I'll tell you something else: that chambermaid knew perfectly well we were in the dining room but she came in anyway."

"So when Annie came barging into our breakfast carrying a broom—"

"I suspect the broom was just a pretense. She came in to talk to someone, but whoever it was, she clearly couldn't do it in front of Grayson."

"Yes that much is clear."

"I'm not a betting man, as you know, Watson, but I would be willing to wager a substantial amount that Lord Cary is not the only one at Torre Abbey hiding something."

I was thinking exactly the same thing.

CHAPTER FOUR

Holmes spent the morning going from room to room of the abbey, examining each one. He began with the upstairs bedrooms, beginning with the one I was occupying. He explained that this was because it was closest to the stairs, and had been empty until our arrival. It was therefore a perfect hiding-place for an intruder, he claimed, and should therefore be thoroughly examined. Though he drew his magnifying glass from his pocket several times, peering through it closely, I gathered from his attitude that his search was not particularly fruitful.

Next we went into Elizabeth Cary's room. She had gone out for a walk with young William, and Holmes was especially interested in the foot of the bed and the area of the windowsill, which he looked at very carefully through his lens, plucking from the window seat what looked like a few threads of fabric and placing them carefully in a small pouch.

"Did you find anything of value?" I asked as we left the room.

"Possibly," he replied enigmatically. "Time alone will tell."

Holmes and I found ourselves alone at luncheon that day. We were told that Elizabeth Cary was indisposed, and it seemed that Marion Cary rarely ate lunch. As Lord Cary was away attending to business for the remainder of the day, and Grayson was in town running errands for the family, Holmes and I had the dining room to ourselves.

Our meal was being served by a somewhat trepidant Annie, with much loud verbal assistance from Sally in the kitchen. The chambermaid's hand shook as she placed the platter of salmon in cream sauce on the sideboard, and she scurried back into the kitchen immediately when Sally summoned her.

I could hear Sally in the kitchen muttering to herself. Though I couldn't make out the words, the aroma of discontent was heavy in the air, and there was much banging of pans and rattling of cutlery.

"I can't for the life of me understand why Cary keeps on that cook," I said as I sat down across from Holmes. "She's a good enough cook, but—"

My ruminations were interrupted by the sound of breaking china in the kitchen, followed by a loud curse. This time there was no mistaking the words: the oath was both colourful and specific.

"I dare say Lord Cary has his reasons for keeping her on," Holmes remarked drily, unfolding his napkin.

A moment later Sally lumbered into the room, carrying a platter of beef medallions.

"Stupid girl," she muttered as she half-hurled the platter in the general direction of the table, much as one might throw a discus. Luckily for us, the meat and platter arrived more or less intact, and once the cook was safely out of the room, stomping loudly back to the kitchen, I helped myself to some beef medallions. I was almost afraid that Sally might reconsider her beneficence and take them away from us, just out of general spitefulness, so I took two just in case.

They were delicious, as was the salmon—in fact, everything that emerged from Sally's kitchen was superb. I had to agree with Holmes—Lord Cary *did* have his reasons, and miraculously, Sally's disposition did not seem to affect the quality of her cooking. Fortunately for us, her sour moods did not seem to seep into her sauces. I had imagined radishes withering under her touch, turnips turning brown at her fingertips, but such was not the case. She was not a warm person—even her attitude towards her son was solicitous without being warm—but she was an inspired cook. I took another bite of salmon and sighed. Mrs. Hudson's cuisine at Baker Street, while plentiful and hearty enough, lacked the subtlety of flavor that characterized Sally's cooking.

All day I had been wondering whether I should relate to Holmes my experience of the night before. Now seemed like a perfect opportunity, so I decided to take advantage of it.

"Holmes," I said slowly, "I have struggled with myself whether or not to mention this to you, and I'll admit that in the light of day I'm even more reluctant, and yet . . ."

Holmes set down his wine glass. Torre Abbey had a formidable wine cellar, it turned out, and before he left for town, Grayson had chosen a lovely light Chardonnay to accompany the salmon, and a Bordeaux to go with the medallions of beef.

"What is it, Watson?" Holmes said. "If it has any bearing on this case, I suggest you tell me."

"Well, Holmes," I replied, fingering my napkin, "as to whether it has any bearing on this case, I rather think that's for you to say. However, I would be remiss not to tell you, even though you may think me somewhat—addled."

Holmes put down his fork and looked at me.

"My dear fellow, I assure you I would never think anything of the kind. I should hardly need to remind you that I consider you to be one of the most sensible and level-headed of men."

Warmed by his words, I nevertheless shook my head. "I might in all immodesty have agreed with you—until last night, that is."

I proceeded to tell him of my strange encounter (if that's what it was) in the hallway upon the previous night. Though he listened attentively, I was nonetheless somewhat embarrassed by what I had experienced. I related the whole thing carefully, however, taking care to omit no detail—and being certain to mention my exhausted, perhaps overwrought state of mind at the time.

When I had finished, Holmes sat back in his chair and lit a cigarette.

"Well, Watson, it seems that it is not only the Cary family who is being plagued by visitations from the other world."

"But I saw nothing," I protested. "And surely you don't believe—"

"Ah," Holmes interrupted. "I will let you in on a little secret."

"Very well," I replied, curiosity getting the better of me.

Holmes leaned back in his chair and blew a smoke ring, which hovered above his head before dissipating into a grey mist. Everything about Torre Abbey seemed to suggest the presence of spirits, and even the cigarette smoke reminded me of a miniature will-o'-the-wisp as it rose and curled before disappearing into the air.

"What is it?" I said impatiently. "What is your secret?"

"Oh, it is merely this: though I do believe in the primacy of logic and deduction above all other qualities in an investigative detective—as I have on many occasions stated—I am by no means solely the cold reasoning machine you have described so often to your readers."

I smiled in spite of myself. "You need hardly tell me that, Holmes. After all, there was the affair of the—

Holmes interrupted me sharply. "This has nothing to do with Miss Adler, Watson; let me finish, if you would. What I mean to say is that there are occasions upon which so-called intuition has played a larger role in my conclusions than I admitted at the time, even to you. For example, in the case of 'The Giant Rat of Sumatra,' you may remember I set my sights early on upon Colonel Throckmorton?"

"Yes, but you always claimed—"

"Yes, yes; there was the evidence of the rare cigar ash, most assuredly. But it was by no means conclusive."

"But the stain on his jacket—"

"I was about to say that even the curious stain upon his jacket could have been explained away a number of ways. What really led me to close in on him, finally, was a feeling all along that he was responsible for the smuggling operation, and the series of murders that followed it."

"I see," I replied slowly. "So you are saying—"

"What I am saying, Watson, is that there are aspects of the human brain we have not as yet fully explored. As much respect as I have for the primacy of observation, fact, and deduction— science, in other words—what I am suggesting is that even science has its limits—or rather, there are occurrences science has not yet been able to fully explain."

I nodded slowly. "I see. There are more things in heaven and earth, Horatio?"

"Something like that," he answered with an enigmatic smile. "Mind you, I am fully confident that science will no doubt someday provide the answer to these puzzling questions."

"No doubt," I replied, still a little taken aback by Holmes's unaccustomed frankness. My friend was, if nothing else, unpredictable. Just when I thought I had the measure of him, he would surprise me. It made being around him stimulating, if occasionally trying.

"So what do you think I experienced last night, Holmes?" I said. "Are you saying that you believe—"

"Believe what, Watson?" Holmes smiled. "That what you

experienced was the presence of an evil spirit?" He shrugged. "Who can say, Watson, who can say?"

Our conversation was interrupted by another entrance into the room by Sally. Her already sour disposition was evidently not improved by the absence of Grayson and the clumsiness of the chambermaid, forcing her (as she evidently saw it) not only to prepare lunch but serve it as well. She clumped even more loudly into the room, heaving a great sigh as she tossed a dish of watercress salad on the table.

"Can't trust that stupid cow to do anything," she muttered as she rearranged the platters to make room for the salad.

"The salmon is quite delicious, Sally," I commented, "and so is the beef."

She regarded me dolefully, then her face softened.

"Thank you, sir," she replied. "It's nice to know as how one is appreciated by someone around here."

With that she turned and stomped back into the kitchen.

"I believe she rather likes you, Watson," Holmes remarked after she had gone, helping himself to salad.

"Don't be absurd," I replied, feeling my face redden.

"Oh, no, she definitely favours you, no question about it." Holmes smiled and plucked a sprig of watercress from his plate.

That afternoon I accompanied Holmes on a tour of the abbey ruins. The remnants of once proud medieval buildings lay all around the grounds of the abbey, their sturdy stones crumbling under the weight of centuries and the damp Devon air. We stood for a moment by the tomb of William Brewer the Younger, son of the founder of Torre Abbey, and then headed out across the orchard, where we came upon a small graveyard nestled just the other side of the apple trees.

I looked across the cemetery, where a thin white mist hung over the gravestones like a shroud. The rain had lifted, leaving the white fog behind it. As dusk descended over the cemetery, not a breath of breeze stirred the air around us, and we stood among ancient crumbling tombstones, mist swirling around our feet, pale and damp as death, a worldly reminder of what lay deep in the ground underneath our feet. The musty smell of earth and dried leaves invaded my nostrils as I watched our breath come in little white puffs of air.

A movement at the far side of the cemetery caught my eye. As I turned to look, Holmes clamped a hand upon my shoulder.

"Look, Watson," he whispered, "just there. We're not alone."

I could make out through the descending darkness the figure of a woman, dressed all in white, moving among the graves.

"Who is it, do you think?" I whispered back.

He shook his head in reply and stepped behind the weathered oak tree, its branches spread out over the ancient gravestones like the wings of a mother hen guarding her chicks.

"Perhaps we can watch unobserved," he said as I joined him behind the thick trunk of the old tree. We watched as the lady knelt before one of the more recent graves, the headstone still relatively untouched by the harsh effects of the Devon seaside air. She sank down to her knees upon the soft ground, her head bent as if in prayer, and remained thus for some time. I could not make out her face, but I thought there was something familiar in the attitude of her shoulders.

After spending some time in this position, she rose and moved off through the graves. With the mist covering her feet, she appeared to be floating over the ground, smooth and effortless as a spirit, gliding with an unearthly grace.

"Well, Watson," Holmes said when she had gone, "shall we see who is the fortunate recipient of this visit?"

I followed him across the damp ground, picking my way carefully so as not to do dishonour to the bones of those who lay buried here. At length we came to the grave; it was on the far side of the cemetery and the fresh shoe prints in the ground around it left no doubt that it was indeed the same grave visited by our mysterious lady in white. I looked at the headstone, which contained only a name and the dates of birth and death:

CHRISTOPHER LEGANGER
1832–1867

"Hmm," said Holmes, kneeling to examine the imprints in the ground left by the lady.

I ran my hand over the top of the tombstone, which was grey and rough to the touch. "Who was he, I wonder?"

Holmes stood up and brushed the dirt from his trousers. "Whoever he was, he evidently inspired great devotion."

I nodded, and thought of the lady in white gliding through the misty air, in search of the lost love who lay buried beneath the damp Devon ground.

AT PRECISELY eight o'clock we were called to dinner by the resonant rumbling tones of the large brass gong hanging in the small antechamber off the main dining room. Dinner at Torre Abbey was a formal affair, complete with cut-crystal goblets and gold-rimmed china. I was glad Holmes had suggested packing formal wear as we left Baker Street, and though my evening clothes felt stiff and uncomfortable as I took my place at the table, I was glad I had brought them.

Lady Cary was already at the table, and Charles arrived moments later, his rust-coloured hair wetted and neatly combed back from his forehead, his face shiny from a recent scrubbing.

"How was your meeting, dear?" his mother asked as he kissed her cheek.

"Fine, thank you," he replied as he took his place at the other end of the table.

"Where's Miss Cary?" said Holmes.

Mother and son exchanged a look, and although they tried to hide it, I could tell they were keeping something from us.

Just then Elizabeth Cary appeared at the doorway. Wearing a white dress, her dark hair loose about her shoulders, she reminded me of Ophelia. There was something ethereal and otherworldly about her, an untouchable quality perfectly suited to this drafty old building. In the pale, warm candlelight, she seemed to have stepped into the room from the deep, dark past of this place, after wandering the stone hallways with softly chanting brown-robed monks.

"Hello, Elizabeth," Charles Cary said, rising from his chair.

She looked at her brother with a vacant gaze, and at that moment the truth was so blindingly evident to me that I wondered I had not seen it before: Elizabeth Cary was a dope addict.

CHAPTER FIVE

I T WAS not until the next day that I was able to share my observation with Holmes. When we were finally alone upstairs following breakfast, I ventured upon the topic. We had breakfasted early, before either Lady Cary or her daughter were up, though we were told Charles Cary was already up and out on his morning ride.

"Yes, I was thinking something along the same lines," Holmes replied after I voiced my suspicions. He shook his head as he lit his cherrywood pipe. We were settled comfortably in his sitting room enjoying a smoke after breakfast. "What gave her away to you?"

"Well, I sensed there was something odd about her the first night—an overwrought quality, perhaps," I replied as a thin swirl of smoke enveloped his head. "But it was only last night that I realized she . . . I'm not sure what it is, but she is undoubtedly under the influence of some drug or other. I'd say an opium derivative, if I had to guess."

Holmes blew a smoke ring, a white circle which spun and curled briefly in the air, then dissipated slowly into a grey wisp. "I agree," he replied. "I'd put my money on laudanum. Her behaviour has all the earmarks of the opium addicts I have observed."

I frowned in spite of myself. I knew Holmes occasionally

visited opium dens in London in his pursuit of the criminal element, but I didn't like it all the same. I couldn't help worrying that the seductive poppy derivative might some day wrap its claws around him. My concern was probably for naught, however; cocaine was much more to his liking, with its sharp corners and drug-induced energy spurts.

"Oh, don't look so disapproving, Watson," Holmes said. "It's not as if I was ever seriously tempted by the substance myself."

I raised an eyebrow. " 'Seriously' tempted, you say? Do you mean to imply—"

"My dear fellow," he said, "really, you should try to worry less. I've lasted this long, and I expect I'll muddle on for a good while yet."

I couldn't help smiling. "Very well, Holmes. I take your word for it that opium has never presented you with serious temptation."

He nodded and leaned back in his chair. "I fear the same is not the case with our young friend, however—did you remark the blankness of her gaze last night? It was as if she were looking right through us without even seeing us."

"Yes, it was rather disconcerting. I wonder if her family realizes it."

Holmes flicked an ash from his sleeve. "Oh, I dare say they are quite aware of it—it is hardly the kind of thing one can easily hide. The wonder of it is that they thought they would be able to conceal it from us."

"Perhaps they don't think that."

Holmes looked at me, his grey eyes narrowed. "Her mother certainly doesn't seem to think much of her. She can barely conceal the disdain she feels for her daughter. I wonder . . ."

"If there's a connection between her addiction and the 'apparitions'?"

"That, and . . ."

"What?" I sat barely breathing, thinking Holmes was about

to reveal one of his startling conclusions, but to my disappointment he just shook his head and sighed.

"I don't know, Watson . . . there's something at the centre of this that just doesn't sit right."

He rose and went to the window, his lean form outlined against the glare of daylight from the window frame. "I get the distinct feeling that everyone around here is hiding something." He rubbed his brow wearily. "There are unseen forces at work here, Watson . . . human ones, no doubt, but unseen nonetheless."

Our ruminations were interrupted by the entrance of Annie the chambermaid, who tiptoed shyly up to the open door.

"You sent for me, sir?" she said, her voice trembling, her head bowed.

"Please come in, Annie. I'd like to ask you a few questions, if you don't mind," Holmes answered.

She raised her head and looked at us imploringly. "I does my best, truly," she said, clenching her hands in front of her as she entered the room.

"It's all right," Holmes replied kindly, seeing the state she was in. "You haven't done anything wrong. I just want to ask you a few questions."

Her body relaxed a little, but there was still tension in her voice. "About what?"

"Oh, nothing much important," Holmes replied carelessly. "I just wondered if you had to clean any boots last night."

She cocked her head to one side and wrinkled her pert little Irish nose. "Funny you should ask, sir. My mistress gave me a pair of walking shoes—they was terrible dirty, and it took me quite a while to get all the mud off. I did a good job of it, though," she added hastily, looking at me for support.

Holmes gave one of his rare chuckles. "I'm sure you did, Annie, I'm sure you did. Was there anything else you noticed about her?"

"There was something else, now that you mention it, sir,"

she replied in a low voice. "It struck me as a bit queer at the time."

"Yes?" Holmes was all attention.

"Well, when she come in from her walk, I noticed her dress was all dirty, as though she'd been kneeling in the dirt. 'Now that's odd,' I says to myself; 'what would a grand lady such as her want to be kneeling in the dirt for?' "

"Did you mention it to her?"

Annie stared at Holmes, her eyes wide. "Oh *no,* sir; I would never presume . . . I mean, it isn't my place now, is it?"

Holmes smiled. "No, I suppose not. You're a good girl, then, are you?"

Her face flushed, Annie smiled broadly at Holmes, displaying a missing front tooth. "Well, now, sir, I'll leave you to judge that for yourself. I make no claims to virtue, really I don't. I just try to do my best and leave it at that." She paused, then added, "I don't have no truck with those what think they're better than other folks."

"Yes, quite right you are," Holmes replied languidly. "Do you have anyone in particular in mind?"

Annie looked at us through wide blue eyes and shrugged. "All I'm saying is how those what think they're very grand aren't always so smart, is all, even if they is people of the Church . . . everyone's equal in the sight of God, is all I'm saying."

Holmes allowed himself a slight smile. "I see. Quite right you are, too, if I may say so. That's good sensible reasoning."

Annie beamed at him, showing the gap where her tooth had been. "You really think so, sir?"

"Oh, undoubtedly. I'm sure Watson would agree with me— wouldn't you, Watson?"

"Oh, most certainly," I replied automatically, my mind not fully engaged in what they were saying. I was still brooding about Lady Cary and her dead suitor, trying to imagine what sort of man he must have been to capture the heart of such a woman.

Annie stood for a moment waiting and then spoke. "Will that be all, then, sir?"

"Yes, thank you," Holmes replied, smiling kindly. "You have been very helpful." He could be brusque and even rude at times, but when dealing with those subservient to or weaker than himself he was often kindness itself; he was far more likely to show courtesy to a chambermaid than to a baron.

Annie gave a quick curtsy and withdrew from the room. I listened as her quick light steps echoed down the hall.

"Well, Watson, what do you think of that?" Holmes said when she had gone.

"So Lady Cary was the lady in white?" I said.

Holmes spread his long fingers. "It would seem the inescapable conclusion, don't you agree?"

I sighed. The idea of the beautiful Marion Cary mourning for a long-lost love was sad, but it also served as yet another reminder of her unobtainability—not only was she nobility, but she had given her heart to him who lay buried beneath the cold dank Devon soil.

"I suppose you're right," I replied moodily.

"The plot, as they say, thickens," Holmes said, rubbing his hands together. He was beginning to enjoy himself; his eyes were bright, his step full of spring, and his lean body quivered with purpose—he was like a bird dog on a scent.

I, on the other hand, could not remember feeling so listless. Whether it was the lingering effects of the long days at my surgery, the depressing atmosphere of the abbey, or the damp Devon air, my body felt sluggish, as though I was moving underwater. I observed Holmes's boundless energy as though from a foreign country, watching him move energetically from one action to another, as a sleepwalker might view the conscious. It was almost as though I was being sucked into the atmosphere of the abbey, becoming one of the languid troubled spirits who roamed these ancient hallways at night. I had no sound medical explanation for any of this, but I would be glad to quit Torre Abbey, when the time came, for the more familiar haunts of London.

WHEN CHARLES Cary returned from his ride, Holmes discussed with him the details of his investigation.

"If you don't mind, Lord Cary," he said, "I'd like to look through each room in the abbey—that is, if you and your family have no objections."

Cary shrugged. "I can't imagine why any of them would—after all, you're here to help us."

"Thank you. It won't take long, but it would be good to begin as soon as possible."

Cary nodded. "Certainly. Whatever you want—I assure you, Mr. Holmes, I shall do everything in my power to assist you."

"Good," replied Holmes. "I should like to start with Lady Cary's quarters, if you don't mind."

A look of apprehension passed briefly over our host's face, but he quickly mastered himself. "By all means, Mr. Holmes—as I said, whatever you wish. My mother's apartments are located in the east wing," he said, leading us to the back of the building. "They call this the night staircase—I'm not exactly sure why," he remarked as we followed him up a narrow twisting staircase.

"Perhaps it's the one the monks used to return to their quarters after vespers," I offered.

"I know very little about medieval religious life, I'm afraid," Holmes remarked.

"Nor do I," Cary replied as we climbed the narrow stairs, single-file. "My father was really the historian in the family. My tastes run to other things—horses and medicine, mostly."

He led us down a dimly lit hallway; a long thin carpet ran the length of the hall. It seemed to have been there for quite some time, as I noticed it was rather worn in several places.

"I'll just see if Mother's in," Cary said, knocking on one of the doors lining the hall. Like the others we had passed, the door was highly polished, and appeared to be either maple or elm. As we stood there I thought I detected a faint scent of lilacs.

"Yes?" came the reply from within.

"It's Charles," Cary said. "Mr. Holmes and Dr. Watson are with me."

There was the sound of light footsteps, then the door opened and Lady Cary appeared. She was wearing a light-green silk dressing gown, the colour of early spring grass. It suited her slim figure so well that I had to counter an impulse to stare. Her golden hair was piled somewhat haphazardly on top of her head. Though it was well past noon, she clearly had not yet completed her toilette.

"Yes?" she said, looking from her son to Holmes and myself.

"Mother, Mr. Holmes would like to . . ." Charles Cary began, but he faltered a bit, so Holmes intervened smoothly.

"I would like to have a look around your rooms, if you have no objections."

Lady Cary looked a bit startled by the suggestion, and I hastened to add, "We can come by another time if this is inconvenient."

To my surprise, she shook her head. "No, this is as good a time as any," she replied, opening the door to admit us.

The apartment was large and airy, with a sitting room in the front leading through to a bedroom in the back. The sitting room overlooked the old abbey cloisters. A small brown terrier sat primly perched upon a crimson velvet settee. I assumed this was Lady Cary's dog, Caliban. He didn't bark as we entered, but cocked his head to one side when he saw us. I could hear the chirping of the birds in the ivy outside—such a peaceful sound,

I thought, and I suddenly had trouble imagining anything could go wrong in a place like this. Lord Cary excused himself, saying he had business to attend to, and so we were left alone with the lady of the house.

"Please, make yourselves at home, gentlemen," Lady Cary said, sitting on the end of the settee and running her hand over the silky head of the little terrier, who wagged its tail and licked her hand. Her voice was cordial enough, but I thought I detected an ironic edge to it. Holmes took a glance around the room and disappeared into the bedroom. Left alone with her, I busied myself examining a small, ornate gilt clock on the mantelpiece. The edges were inlaid with fat porcelain cherubs, their plump fingers wrapped around the face of the clock.

"A birthday present from my son," Lady Cary said as I studied the clock.

"Very nice," I murmured, fearing my face would betray my discomfort with the situation. My neck felt hot, and knowing I coloured easily, I turned away, hoping she would not notice. Just then Holmes called out from the other room.

"Lady Cary, would you be so kind as to come in here for a moment?"

"Excuse me, please," she said, and went into the other room. I wandered over to where the little dog sat upon the settee, and sat down beside him to stroke his head. As I did so, my eye was caught by a single piece of paper protruding from behind a pillow. I slipped the paper out, and went to place it upon the writing desk, but my curiosity got the better of me and my eyes perused the page; it appeared to be a poem of some kind. I knew it was wrong, but I read the text.

> *She shares her secret fancies with the moon, her only confidant;*
> *She smiles and hugs her deep dark secrets close to her breast.*
> *She keeps them tightly locked away within her heart*
> *Until under a cold white stone she finds her final rest.*

At night she lies upon the bed and imagines it her grave,
But the moon is cold and dark
So she waits for daybreak and the singing of the lark.

She trembles at the sound of footsteps through the garden gate,
But when he arrives it is already too late.
Now from her lips there comes not a single breath,
Silence her only company,
Her only lover Death.

I heard the sound of approaching footsteps and hurriedly shoved the poem back behind the pillow where I had found it. Holmes and Lady Cary entered the sitting room at that moment. I could feel the blood creeping up my neck, and once again I feared my red face would give me away. Worse, the little dog suddenly found the pillow extremely interesting, and began sniffing around it. Mortified, I glanced at Lady Cary, but she was busy watching Holmes, who was examining an elaborately carved secretary which sat against the far wall.

"A family heirloom, Mr. Holmes," the lady said, as he ran his fingers over the polished wood.

"Have there been any burglaries at Torre Abbey since you came to live here, Lady Cary?" Holmes said abruptly, fixing her with his keen stare.

"No," she replied. "Why do you ask?"

"Then how is it that this lock has been recently forced?" he inquired, pointing to the side drawer of the desk. Sure enough, the lock showed signs of being tampered with—the wood was scratched and scarred, and the lock itself was bent and scoured by some sharp instrument.

"Oh, I lost my key and had to ask Charles to force it open for me," she replied a little too quickly.

She was a very poor liar, and even I could see that she was hiding something. She fingered the belt of her dressing gown as her eyes darted nervously from side to side. To my surprise, however, Holmes merely nodded, as if she had given the most natural explanation in the world.

"Very well," he said. "Thank you for your time, Lady Cary. I apologize if we disrupted your day."

"Not at all," she answered warmly, no doubt relieved not to be called on her lie. She scooped the little terrier up in her arms and went to the door to see us out.

As we walked down the hall toward the stairs, I couldn't resist commenting. "She was lying about the lock, Holmes, I'm certain—"

"Not now, Watson," he said in a low voice. "You never know who might be listening," he added with a glance over his shoulder.

"I know she was lying, my dear fellow," he chuckled as we made our way down the narrow stone steps. "The interesting question is why? What—or whom—is she protecting?"

Again my thoughts turned to the man lying alone in the cemetery beneath the cold Devon soil. I thought of Marion Cary's poem, so sad and wistful, a tragic lament to lost love. I sighed deeply and considered the lucky man who had been the recipient of such devotion from such a woman.

CHAPTER SIX

THAT NIGHT we were visited by a terrific storm. It ripped and tore at the abbey, howling like a mad dog outside the window, hurtling rain so hard against the panes that I was afraid they might break. There was no question of sleeping during the height of the storm's fury, so I crept from my bed and sat at the window gazing out onto the courtyard below. The rain fell relentlessly in steady sheets upon the already soggy ground. Puddles formed, soon becoming rivulets, which then turned into small lakes. A sudden loud clap of thunder rent the air, resonating through the halls of the abbey itself. It was followed by a white flash of lightning so bright that the entire room was illuminated for a few seconds by its pallid glow.

I was entranced by the storm, captivated by its unfettered energy, much as I was captivated by the charms of Lady Cary. I thought of her alone in her room, listening to the storm— I didn't see how anyone could sleep in weather such as this. I wondered if she liked the spectacle of Nature's fury, or if she was frightened by the thunder and lightning. My mind drifted and I imagined myself comforting her, holding her hand when she was startled by a particularly loud clap of thunder . . .

The storm abated and I had dozed off in the chair when suddenly I was awakened by a loud ringing which seemed to fill the building. It reverberated through the hallways, resounding against the stone walls with a deafening volume. I jumped out of bed, threw on my robe, and dashed into the hallway, where I saw Holmes coming from the other end of the hall.

"What on earth is it?" I cried over the din.

"It would seem to be coming from the Abbot's Tower," he replied, pointing to the clock tower which rose just above us. Then, just as suddenly as it had begun, the sound stopped.

"Come, Watson!" Holmes cried, and took off in the direction of the stairs leading to the tower. I followed, my robe flapping behind me. We dashed up the two flights of stairs to the top of the tower, where the great bell hung from its pulley. The ringing had not yet completely died out; the air still vibrated with the hollow remnants of sound. But there was no one in sight—impossible as it seemed, it was as though the giant bell had somehow rung itself!

Holmes examined the heavy rope which hung down from the great bell, peering at it in the dim moonlight. Suddenly the air was rent by another sound—a woman's scream. It was no ordinary scream, however; it was a blood-curdling yell of pure terror.

Holmes let go of the rope and sprang towards the stairs.

"Quickly, Watson!" he cried as he dashed down the narrow steps. I followed close behind, stumbling as my feet searched for footing upon the ancient crumbling stones.

The screams died out as we reached the first floor of the abbey, but it was clear the sound had come from the direction of the kitchen. Holmes and I reached the kitchen at the same moment as Charles Cary—he evidently had been as hurriedly roused from his bed as we had, because his dressing gown was unbelted and there were no slippers upon his bare feet. He carried a torch, though, and his face appeared even paler than usual in the dim light.

"What on earth was that?" he exclaimed as Holmes and I arrived. He appeared to be as breathless as I was, though whether from exertion or apprehension I could not tell.

"This way," Holmes said, brushing past him and heading into the kitchen. Cary and I followed close behind, Cary holding the torch aloft so that we could see. It was strangely quiet now, and the only sound I could hear was a muffled rapping—like a door that had been left open banging against its frame, blown by the wind.

We crossed the kitchen to where Holmes was standing. The sound I heard was indeed the outside door to the kitchen, which was open. But I quite forgot about the door when I saw what Holmes was looking at.

There, in the narrow alcove leading to the outside door, was the outline of a prostrate form lying upon the ground. I took a few steps closer, and as Cary held his torch aloft, we saw that it was the cook, Sally Gubbins.

"Good Lord!" Cary said as Holmes knelt over her and turned her over gently.

One look at her face and it was clear to me that the poor woman was dead. Her eyes were wide open and staring straight up at the ceiling, and her mouth was open as if she had died in mid-scream. Her face, in fact, was a perfect mask of terror—as though whatever she saw in her last moments of life had frightened her so much that it was imprinted on her features.

I felt for a pulse even though I knew there would be none, then I closed the lifeless eyes out of respect for the dead. I examined the body for signs of injury but found none. Cary had lighted one of the wall sconces, and I looked around the room. There was no sign of struggle—no overturned chairs or scuff marks on the floor—no outward indication of violence of any kind. Holmes, meanwhile, was occupied with his own investigation. He disappeared through the back door out into the night, only to return a few minutes later shaking his head.

"We are too late," he said in response to Cary's inquiring look. "Whoever or whatever was here is gone now."

He closed and latched the door behind him. "Do you keep this door locked at night, Lord Cary?"

"Well, yes—I mean, it's Grayson's job to lock up at night, and though we have sometimes been lax, ever since the events of the past few days I have asked him particularly to be certain to lock the house at night."

Holmes nodded. "I see. And does anyone other than members of your household have keys?"

"No, not that I am aware."

Holmes turned to me. "Well, Watson, what do you make of it? Is there any sign of injury?"

"None that I can find." There were indeed no bruises or cuts or other obvious signs of trauma, only the horrified expression on the cook's face.

It wasn't long before the other members of the household showed up. The first to arrive was Grayson, whose calm manner was only slightly ruffled by the gruesome sight in the kitchen. Marion Cary, though greatly affected by the news, insisted on seeing the body, even though her son tried to persuade her not to look. Charles would not allow his sister anywhere near the body; she dissolved into tears upon hearing the news. Annie, the chambermaid, took it upon herself to comfort her mistress, patting her hand and murmuring, "There, there, miss. Don't worry now. It'll be all right."

"Where's William?" Elizabeth said suddenly, looking around, and I realized at that moment we had not seen him. As if in response to her query, a shaggy dark head appeared around the corner of the butler's pantry.

"William! Have you been in there all this time?" Elizabeth cried, catching the boy up in her arms and holding him to her breast. He laid his head on her shoulder, shoved his thumb in his mouth, and made a little gurgling sound. She took him quickly from the room, so that he could not see his mother's body around the corner.

Everyone except Holmes retired to the west parlour, where Grayson, with his usual efficiency, had laid a fire in the grate. He even bustled about the kitchen and fixed tea for us, apparently not bothered by the presence of poor Sally, who, after covering her, we left where she was so the police could see her lying where we found her.

Holmes continued to prowl about the grounds of the abbey, and dawn was peering through the lace curtains by the time Grayson set out for town to fetch the police. I offered to accompany him, but he declined my assistance, preferring to go himself.

We all sat around the fire, hunched over within the circle of its welcome heat, teacups clutched in our stiffened fingers, as a weak October sun struggled up through the dissipating clouds.

The stout, sleepy-eyed police sergeant who turned up to supervise the removal of the body seemed unimpressed by Lord Cary's recounting of the various apparitions, and I thought his examination of the area around the body was cursory at best. As Lord Cary had warned us earlier, the police were not particularly interested in the goings-on at Torre Abbey, and the fat sergeant's attitude seemed to confirm this.

"Well, Sergeant?" said Cary as the body was loaded into the back of the police wagon.

"We'll have the coroner's report for you as soon as we can, sir," the sergeant replied, then he shrugged. "Looks like natural causes to me, sir, if you don't mind my saying so."

With that he climbed into the front of the wagon, signalled the driver, and the horse was off at a trot. And so poor Sally made her exit wrapped in a blue blanket with the letters *Coroner* emblazoned on it in yellow.

"They couldn't even be bothered to send a proper detective inspector," Cary muttered as the police van drove off. "Well, Dr. Watson?" he said as we watched the police wagon disappear around the corner of the long drive through the orchard. "What could have killed her, do you think?"

"Well, only an autopsy could reveal that with any degree of certainty," I replied. The words sounded strange as I said them, but nonetheless I found myself uttering the phrase almost before I could stop myself.

"It sounds odd, I know, Lord Cary, but it looks to me very much as if she died of fright."

CHAPTER SEVEN

FATHER JOHN Norton had a face like a fallen soufflé. With its creases and swirls around the jaw, it was like the sagging remnants of a once proud egg dish left too long on the counter to cool. His heavy-lidded eyes with their downturned corners reminded me of a bloodhound. His face was all skin folds and flaps; even his ears were large, with heavy hanging lobes, fleshy as fresh fungi. For all that, it was a handsome face; his olive skin, though creased, was ruddy and healthy-looking, and with his jet black eyes and hair he made a striking impression. A faintly ironic smile played habitually about his lips, which were surprisingly full and red.

He sat in the west parlour at Torre Abbey, a cup of tea balanced on one knee, awaiting the attentions of the Cary family so he could discuss with them the matter of Sally's funeral services. Sally had attended his church in the nearby village of Cockington, where Father Norton presided, if not regularly, then at least often enough that he considered her one of his flock.

Holmes was out prowling the grounds of Torre Abbey, Elizabeth Cary had not been seen all day, and Charles Cary had gone riding, so I had been selected to keep the priest company whilst he awaited the appearance of Lady Cary, who was upstairs dressing for dinner.

"I do apologize for keeping you waiting, Father," she said as she swept breathlessly into the room, pinning up one last strand of her golden hair as she crossed the carpet to where we were seated in front of the fire, her little terrier trotting faithfully after her. The day, which had started out promisingly enough, had turned grey and blustery by mid-afternoon, with a chill in the air that cut through to the bone. I was cold no matter where I was in the drafty and dank rooms, and only a chair near the fire felt warm enough.

Father Norton rose from his chair immediately, and, grasping her hand, kissed it—perhaps a little too long for a man of the cloth, I thought, but if Lady Cary noticed she gave no indication of it.

"I see Grayson has seen to your tea," she remarked, seating herself gracefully in a low-backed French provincial-style armchair, gold with vermilion trim. The furniture in Torre Abbey was a mix of so many styles and designs that it was difficult to sense an overlaying plan; Charles had told us that the Cary family was a very old one, and the collections of various generations over the centuries had ended up in Torre Abbey. Caliban the terrier, showing no respect for the venerable status of the furniture, jumped up alongside Lady Cary and put his silky head in her lap.

"It is a sad duty I am to perform for you now, Lady Cary," Father Norton said with a sigh, laying his teacup aside. There was something of the actor about him, as I suppose there is with all good clergymen, but in his case it was difficult to tell if the sentiments he expressed were entirely genuine. Lady Cary did not seem to feel this way, however, as he pressed her hand between his own. "Please rest assured that I will do everything in my power to make poor Sally's final farewell a memorable one. She was a good girl, and I know you were fond of her."

Lady Cary nodded sadly, absentmindedly stroking Caliban. "Yes, she has—had—been with us a long time."

"Thirteen years, I believe your son said," said Holmes from the doorway where he stood. Droplets of rain clung to his hair, and his face was flushed.

Lady Cary turned her haunting blue eyes upon him, and a shiver of excitement shot through my spine. Holmes, however, gazed back at her impassively as he removed his coat and walked over to stand in front of the fireplace.

"She was with us since before William was born, so that would be—let me see—thirteen years now," she replied softly. "Allow me to introduce Mr. Sherlock Holmes," she continued as Holmes moved to the fireplace. "Mr. Holmes, this is Father Norton."

The priest rose from his chair. "A pleasure to meet you, Mr. Holmes."

"The pleasure is mine," Holmes replied as they shook hands. "Your name sounds familiar, though I can't quite place it."

"I believe I can help," I offered. "Wasn't there an Abbot Norton mentioned in Lord Cary's letter to us?"

"Ah—that's it! Yes, according to Lord Cary, he was accused of murdering one of his monks. An ancestor of yours, perhaps?"

The priest frowned. "No, my family came here this century from Scotland."

"Well, it's just as well," Holmes smiled. "By all accounts, this Abbot Norton was quite a villainous fellow—"

But the priest interrupted him. "I was going to say before, Mr. Holmes, that your fame has spread far and wide throughout England, even reaching sleepy backwaters like Torquay."

"You flatter me, Father," Holmes replied. "Torquay is hardly a sleepy backwater—it has become a thriving resort town."

"Yes, it hardly seems possible . . . I can't understand where time goes sometimes," Lady Cary mused.

Father Norton nodded sympathetically. "Yes, that's true for all of us, I'm afraid. Still, we must make the most of what's given to us, you know." He handed Lady Cary a couple of sheets of paper. "I've written down here the basic funeral service. Sometimes my parishioners like to add a few words of their own . . . please let me know if you would like to amend the proceedings in any way."

Lady Cary took the papers and smiled sadly. "Thank you, Father—you've been such a comfort to me in these hard times, and I do appreciate it."

"Think nothing of it," he replied, rising from his chair. "Please let me know if there's anything else I can do."

"Well, there is one small thing," she said with a glance at Holmes and myself. "You may think me rather silly for asking this, but . . . do you know any mediums?"

Father Norton's handsome face registered surprise, then amusement. "A medium? Do you mean as in . . . ?"

Lady Cary nodded. "You see, my daughter has gotten it into her head that we are being visited by spirits, and she is absolutely convinced that what we need is . . . well, a séance."

"A séance, Lady Cary?" I said, unable to contain my astonishment. "Do you seriously mean to hold a séance at Torre Abbey?"

Lady Cary folded her hands in her lap and looked down at the glowing fire which danced in the grate. "You must understand that Elizabeth has been through some very difficult times lately. Her father's death was very hard on her, you know—they were quite close." Her tone of voice as well as her words suggested that this was not the case with Charles Cary and his father.

"You see, Charles and I thought that if we held a séance, as she wishes, then she would come to accept her father's death in time. I know it sounds fanciful," she added, "but Elizabeth is a fanciful child."

Father Norton raised his thick dark eyebrows. His expressive face registered skepticism, but before he could speak, Holmes broke in.

"It sounds like a very good idea to me, Lady Cary." More than a little surprised, I turned to look at him, but his face revealed nothing, leaving me to conclude that he was sincere.

Even Lady Cary looked surprised. "You think so, Mr. Holmes?" she said dubiously.

"I do indeed," he replied, settling his long body in the depths of an overstuffed armchair across from me. "It seems to me that whoever—or whatever—is at the bottom of the strange events these past few days is likely to tip their hand at such a gathering. I believe your daughter has the right idea—though perhaps for the wrong reasons."

Lady Cary glanced at me, her fingers absently pulling at a loose lock of hair at the back of her neck.

"You will attend, then, Mr. Holmes?" she said.

"By all means—Dr. Watson and I will be pleased to attend."

"Now see here, Holmes," I protested, but Holmes waved me into silence.

"Come, come, Watson—it will be of great interest to you in particular, as a man of science—think of what you can learn from a communication between our world and the next!"

Now I was certain he was putting us all on, and I was more than a little irritated.

"Look, Holmes," I began, but he rose and laid a hand on my shoulder.

"Let's talk about it later, shall we, Watson?" he said, with a firm squeeze. I realized then that it was my job to go along with the scheme, and that he would explain his reasoning later.

"Very well," I replied. "I will be happy to attend the séance."

"Well, that's all very well and good," Father Norton said as he took his hat and coat from Grayson, who had appeared, noiselessly as usual, with our visitor's things. "But I'm a pastor, not a witch doctor. If I agree to participate, it would be strictly as a friend to the family, and not in my official capacity as a man of the cloth." He shook his head. "I have no doubt the Church would not look kindly upon such matters."

"I don't see why the Church need know anything about it," Lady Cary replied. "I'm a good Catholic, as you know, Father," she said, placing her white hands upon his arm. A sigh escaped me as I watched her escort him out into the hall.

"I do hope you and your sister will be able to attend," she continued. "I would feel much better if you were here."

"I cannot speak for Lydia," the vicar replied. "However, I will certainly attend if you think it would help Elizabeth."

"Thank you," Lady Cary said warmly as she walked with him toward the front door, her little terrier trotting faithfully behind.

When they had gone, Holmes leaned back in his chair. "Well, Watson, what do you think about that? A séance, of all things!"

"I can't understand why you would go along with such a plan, Holmes," I whispered, afraid of being overheard by a member of the family.

"I'll explain later," Holmes answered as Lady Cary came back into the room.

"Father Norton is such a comfort," she said, perching on the armrest of a mahogany sofa upholstered in a rich crimson velvet.

"So your cook was also a Catholic?" Holmes said, pouring himself a cup of tea.

"Yes. She was Irish Catholic. The Cary family have been Catholics for centuries, of course. It's only fitting they ended up at Torre Abbey." She paused. "Did you know that during the persecution of Catholics under Henry the Eighth, a secret chapel was built underneath Torre Abbey?"

"How interesting," I said. "Is it still there?"

Lady Cary nodded. "No one goes there anymore. It's fallen

into ruins." She reached for a piece of cake, the skin of her delicate white hands almost translucent in the pale afternoon light. "Until the middle of this century, the abbey served as the Torquay parish church for local Catholics."

"I see," Holmes replied. "And you? You're not a Cary by birth; were you always a Catholic?"

A cloud passed over her lovely face. "I am a Lawrence, and we are Scottish Presbyterian. My husband insisted I convert when we were married. Both of our children were raised Catholic, though Charles has never been exactly . . . fervent."

"I see," Holmes answered. "Where is your daughter, by the way? I don't believe I've seen her all day long."

Marion Cary flicked an imaginary strand of hair from her neck. "She's not feeling very well today. I believe she's upstairs lying down. Will you excuse me for a moment, gentlemen? I need to see to dinner. With poor Sally gone, Grayson is handling the kitchen duties with only the help of Annie, our chambermaid."

Later, as we followed Lady Cary through the long front hallway, her little dog began sniffing at the floor along one wall. He looked up at his mistress, wagged his tail, and barked.

"What is it, Caliban?" she said. In reply he only wagged his tail harder. "That's odd," she mused. "I wonder what he's on about?"

"Is there any significance to that particular spot?" Holmes inquired.

"Do you remember the secret chapel I told you about?"

"Certainly."

"Well, that used to be the entrance. Behind the wood panelling was a secret door leading to an underground tunnel which comes out in the chapel. But the door was boarded over years ago—no one ever uses it."

I realized at that moment this was the same spot where I had felt the awful chill three nights ago. After Lady Cary had gone up to her room, trailing a faint odour of lilies after her, Holmes turned to me.

"Would you like to take a look at the grounds of the abbey with me?" I shook off my mood and said that I would.

"There is something of the rogue about Father Norton, unless I miss my guess," I said to Holmes as we walked across the broad expanse of lawn toward the old tithe barn, which the Carys referred to as the Spanish barn. The name dated back to 1588 and the unsuccessful invasion of the Spanish Armada, Charles told us, when a Spanish galleon was captured off the coast of Devon. The four hundred members of the crew were brought to the abbey and kept as prisoners in the tithe barn until they could be transferred. In the meantime, many had died of privation and disease.

As I contemplated this tragic chapter in English history, an offshore wind brought the smell of the sea, sharp and clear, rolling across the sloping hills surrounding the abbey. We could see the tithe barn, a low, long flagstone building a few hundred yards south of the abbey's main buildings. Holmes had not yet explored the barn, and was intent on gleaning any clues he could from it.

"I don't know what you think you'll find there; we always keep it locked," Charles Cary had said the night before as he handed over the key, a heavy, old-fashioned iron affair that looked to be straight out of the Middle Ages.

"So you think the rector is a rogue?" Holmes said as we walked over the soft lawn, still damp from the rain of the previous two days. "What makes you say that?" he said, his keen eyes fixed upon the ground.

"Well, the fervour with which he kissed Lady Cary's hand seemed a little out of keeping with my image of a man of the cloth."

"Ah, I see," Holmes replied, the corners of his mouth

twitching. "His presence evokes in you a need to protect Lady Cary's honour."

I felt my face redden. "No, that's not what I said. It's more than the way he treats her. There's a—well, a sort of twinkle in his eye, a sardonic attitude that puts me in mind of rogues I have known."

"Well, you will have your chance to observe him again at the funeral," Holmes remarked as he paused to study some little bit of ground beneath our feet. He sank down onto his heels and leaned over, his long back bent in a convex curve, and peered at the grass.

"Hmmm," said he, "interesting."

Then, just as abruptly, he stood and began walking away again rapidly. I was going to ask him what he had found, but I was caught flat-footed and had to hurry to catch up to him.

"So you think the good Father has things on his mind other than the ways of the Lord?" Holmes said.

"Well, if I am any judge of character," I replied. "He is clearly smitten with Lady Cary, and makes no attempt to hide it."

"Oh, come, Watson—after all, you are rather taken with the lady yourself," Holmes remarked, a wicked twinkle in his eye.

"Well, I—I mean, that may be," I stuttered, taken off guard.

My discomfort caused him to burst out laughing, and he clapped a friendly hand upon my shoulder. "Oh, I am sorry, Watson; it is indelicate of me to refer to it. Do forgive me, please—it's just that it really is so obvious."

"As obvious as all that?" I replied sulkily.

"I'm afraid so. It is to me, at any rate, but perhaps not to others who do not know you quite so well."

I took some comfort in this idea, for I had no wish to make a fool of myself mooning over a woman who was quite beyond me.

"I cannot say I share your sentiment, but neither do I blame you," Holmes said as we approached the tithe barn. About a hundred feet from the barn was the stable where the Carys kept their horses; Charles Cary had promised to show us the stables himself later that day. I could hear the horses pawing the ground in their stalls and whinnying softly; evidently they could smell us as we approached.

As we neared the barn, I thought I saw a flash of movement just the other side of the stables. I turned to Holmes to see if he had noticed, but he was busy studying the ground under our feet.

"Hmmm," said he, "it's a pity there's been so much rain. These tracks are difficult to make out."

"Holmes, did you see that just then?"

"See what?" he said, looking up.

"I thought I saw something move over by the stables."

He peered in the direction I was pointing. "Could it have been one of the horses?"

"Maybe—but I don't think so."

From where we stood we couldn't really see the horses; their stalls were facing the other direction, and we could only see the back of the stables. Whatever it was I saw, it was gone now, and we proceeded to the barn. We stepped up the couple of stone steps leading to the front door, which was locked with a large rust-encrusted padlock attached to a thick metal loop on the barn door. Holmes inserted the key, and with a turn and a creak of metal, the padlock fell away. He pushed open the door, which squeaked on its rusted hinges. We stepped inside the cool dark interior of the old barn, and were greeted with the close smell of dirt and ancient stones.

I looked around at the interior of the barn and tried to imagine four hundred people crammed inside its mouldering walls. The building consisted of a single cavernous room with a high, wood-beamed ceiling, and was lit only by the pale light coming from half a dozen narrow slit windows. I noticed that it was eerily quiet, as though no sound from the outside could penetrate the thick stone walls. The atmosphere was suffused with a dampness that seemed to seep into my bones, a cutting chill that felt as though it were not so much a result of the temperature as the sheer weight of the air itself.

Standing there, I experienced a feeling of oppression such as I had never felt before—as if the stones themselves had absorbed the suffering of the poor souls who perished here three hundred years ago. It was a horrifying thought. I had seen misery as a doctor in London, certainly, but the idea of man's cruelty to his fellow man depressed me more than the worst disease epidemic ever could.

I glanced at Holmes, who stood silently gazing out one of the tiny windows, the pallid light falling upon his ascetic face. I wondered if he was feeling the same thing I was, but didn't want to interrupt his contemplations. He looked at me and shook his head.

"It's a bad business, Watson, and I don't envy those caught up in it."

Caught up as I was in my contemplation of the past, I thought at first he was referring to the unfortunate Spanish prisoners, but then I realized he was talking about the Cary family. I nodded, too disturbed by the barn's grim past to be much concerned about the Cary family. I wandered to the far end of the cavernous room, where a few pieces of old furniture sat gathering dust in the corner. The floor was stone, with occasional patches of packed dirt where the stones had sunk into the damp ground.

I stopped in front of a window from which there was a full view of Torre Abbey. As I stood gazing at the Normanesque columns of the gatehouse, the call of a whippoorwill perched on the branch of an old gnarled oak tree outside floated in through the narrow window. The bright and cheerful sound, full of gay disregard for life's suffering, took hold of my imagination. Suddenly I imagined myself as one of the unfortunate prisoners, standing inside this dark and comfortless place, listening to the chipper songbird sitting on its tree branch—cut by the cruel irony of this insouciant creature, utterly free, while he remained a prisoner. I wondered if he had stood there listening day after day, and if so, whether he had come to hate the bird for having the precious freedom he himself lacked—or if he welcomed the bird's appearance, maybe even looked forward to it, representing as it did a connection, however tenuous, to the world outside.

I walked to the other side of the barn, my boots scraping against the damp stones at my feet. I fancied I could hear the moans of the stricken prisoners as they lay on the damp floor, their faces swollen with fever. Finally I went over to where Holmes knelt underneath one of the windows, examining the ground. He carefully swept something up from the floor, putting it in a small leather pouch he often carried on such occasions.

I could stand it no longer; the feeling of loss and sorrow inside this place was almost unbearable.

"Holmes," I said as casually as I could manage, "I'm going outside for a breath of air."

"Very well," he said without looking up, and began examining the windowsill. Pushing open the heavy wooden door, I stumbled from the building and stood outside, breathing heavily, much relieved. Even though it was a foggy day, the air outside seemed sweeter than the close and stifling atmosphere inside the barn.

I gazed up at the gnarled oak tree and wondered if this same tree had stood in this spot three hundred years ago. I looked for the whippoorwill, but the bird was gone, flown away to more pleasant environs. After a few moments Holmes emerged from the barn. His trousers had patches of dirt from where he had knelt upon the ground, and his forehead glistened with sweat, but he looked relaxed and cheerful. I was glad Holmes had not noticed my condition—or so I thought.

As we approached the abbey, I thought I caught a movement out of the corner of my eye up in the Abbot's Tower. However, when I turned to look, shielding my eyes from the glare of the shrouded sun, there was nothing there. The tower stood empty and dark, the heavy hands of the clock pointing to three o'clock.

I am not one given to swooning, but as I stood looking up at the tower, everything went black for a moment. I staggered and caught my balance. I passed a hand over my forehead; the momentary dizziness passed as quickly as it had come. I felt Holmes's firm hand upon my elbow.

"Steady on, Watson. Are you quite all right?"

"Yes, quite," I replied, touched by the concern in his voice.

"Perhaps we should go inside," he said, frowning. "You've likely had enough for one day."

"I'm all right," I answered, but followed him back inside all the same.

THAT NIGHT, as we went up to bed, he surprised me by laying a hand upon my shoulder.

"Had a rough time of it, Watson?" he said gently, and I nodded.

No further word was spoken, for which I was grateful, but once again Holmes continued to surprise me by revealing the heart hidden beneath his aloof exterior. Once again, I could only shake my head and wonder if I yet knew the full measure of my friend.

CHAPTER EIGHT

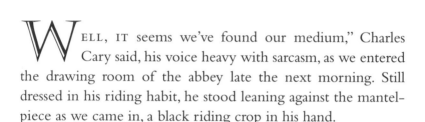

"WELL, IT seems we've found our medium," Charles Cary said, his voice heavy with sarcasm, as we entered the drawing room of the abbey late the next morning. Still dressed in his riding habit, he stood leaning against the mantelpiece as we came in, a black riding crop in his hand.

"Oh?" I said, taking a chair by the fire. I still felt chilled to the centre of my being, a chill which even the leaping flames of the fire did little to dispel.

"Yes—it seems there's a thriving business for mediums in town," Cary replied, "what with all the well-heeled Londoners who come down here to 'take the waters,' you know." He shook his head and tapped his leg impatiently with the leather crop. "There's several of them about who prey upon credulous wealthy dowagers. It wasn't hard to locate them—they leave calling cards at all the tea-houses."

Holmes leaned an arm upon the mantelpiece. "You don't seem to have much faith in the practitioners of this particular profession, Lord Cary."

Our host rolled his eyes. "Good Lord, Mr. Holmes, you don't mean to tell me that you do?"

Holmes smiled enigmatically. "I neither believe nor disbelieve. Belief based upon faith is always suspect in my eyes—and anything which I cannot confirm for myself by observation is in that category as far as I am concerned." He bent down and put another piece of wood on the fire. "However, one can be equally at the mercy of prejudice by rejecting an idea out of hand, so I attempt to maintain an open mind as much as possible when it comes to things of which I have no firsthand knowledge."

"Commendable, I'm sure, Mr. Holmes," Lord Cary remarked, but without an attempt to conceal the disdain which had crept into his voice. "I wish I shared your open-mindedness. And you, Dr. Watson," he said, turning to me. "Have you ever attended a séance?"

"No, indeed I have not," I replied, "but I must admit I am rather looking forward to it."

Cary sighed and threw himself into one of the armchairs closest to the fire. "Well, I think it's stuff and nonsense, and if it weren't for my poor sister Elizabeth's delicate condition, I would have none of it. I'm only going along with it to humour her."

Holmes looked as if he were about to say something, then changed his mind and was silent.

"So if you don't think the manifestations at Torre Abbey are of supernatural origin, Lord Cary, what do you think they are?" I said.

Cary looked at me as if the question surprised him. "That's what I brought you down here for," he replied, a hint of irritation in his voice.

"And we shall do our best to ferret out the answer," Holmes said genially, "but in the meantime, I don't believe you should reject the supernatural explanation out of hand."

Lord Cary looked at Holmes as if he'd just taken leave of his senses. "Good Lord," he said, "you don't really think—"

Our conversation was interrupted by the arrival of Grayson, who announced solemnly that luncheon was being served in the dining room. As he turned to leave, Holmes spoke to him. "Grayson, who in this house smokes cigars?"

The butler's creased face expressed surprise.

"No one that I am aware, sir."

Holmes nodded. "I see."

After Grayson had gone, Cary turned to Holmes. "Why did you ask him that, Mr. Holmes, if I may ask? After all, you could have just as easily asked me."

But Holmes sidestepped the question with one of his own.

"There was someone out around the stables yesterday," he said. "I don't suppose you have any idea who that might be? Whoever it was, they were careful to make sure we didn't get a good look at them."

"Oh, that must have been young William," Cary replied. "He loves the horses, and he does a few odd jobs around the stables. He's very shy, though, as you've seen."

"Yes," Holmes murmured almost to himself, "so I have observed."

"He's very good with the horses, though," Cary continued as we seated ourselves around the long table in the dining hall. "You should see how they respond to him—he has a real way with them. And they seem to have a calming effect upon him as well."

"Do you let him ride them?" I inquired.

"Oh, no—I shouldn't think that was wise," Cary replied, unfolding his napkin and laying it neatly upon his lap. "I wouldn't want to be responsible for something happening to him in case the horse panicked or bolted or something."

"Yes, quite," Holmes said as Grayson appeared with a steaming tureen of soup.

"By the way," said our host, "there's a hunt coming up next weekend, and if you're still here by then, I'd love to have you join up, if you care to. We can put you on a couple of good mounts from our stable, if that suits you."

"What do you say, Watson?" said Holmes. "Have you ever ridden to hounds?"

"I can't say that I have," I replied. "My background is a bit less aristocratic, I'm afraid. But I can ride, and I'm game to try."

"Splendid!" Cary exclaimed. "The countryside around here is perfectly suited to a hunt—a few fences, some shallow streams, and plenty of meadows for a good gallop."

As Grayson was serving the last of the soup, Lady Cary entered the room, flushed and out of breath. Caliban the terrier followed after her, his sharp little nails clicking on the hardwood floor.

"Have you seen Elizabeth?" she said to her son.

"Perhaps she's with William," Cary replied.

Marion Cary shook her lovely head. "William's in the kitchen with Annie, having his lunch."

"Why don't you—" Charles Cary began, but was interrupted by the appearance of his sister.

Elizabeth Cary looked even more wraithlike than she had the previous evening. Her hair was loose and dishevelled, and her eyes stared straight ahead, the pupils fixed and dilated. Charles Cary was evidently alarmed by her appearance, for he rose from his chair upon seeing her.

"Elizabeth," he said. "What is it? What's wrong?"

She gazed vacantly at her brother. When she spoke, her voice was muffled and flat.

"He came to me again last night."

"Who? Who came to you?" Charles replied, but I had a strange sense that he knew the answer to the question.

"The Cavalier . . . Hugo Cary."

Upon hearing this, Marion Cary stiffened. "That's nonsense," she said tersely. "Don't be a foolish girl."

Her daughter turned to her. "You've seen him, too," she said in a flat, expressionless voice which was all the more eerie for its lack of emotion.

Lady Cary looked at her son for help, but Charles Cary was already at his sister's side. "Come on," he said, taking her by the shoulders. "Let's get you upstairs. You're not well and you need some rest."

She went along willingly enough, but I sensed in her docility a kind of awful hopelessness, as if she believed she was beyond help.

Lady Cary turned to me with a strained laugh. "I believe my daughter has more imagination than is entirely healthy. This . . . Cavalier she spoke of . . ."

"An ancestor of yours, I believe," Holmes replied smoothly. "There's a picture of him in the room your husband used as his study."

Lady Cary fidgeted with her hair. "An ancestor of my husband's, to be exact," she corrected. "Remember, I am not a Cary by blood."

"Just so," Holmes answered. "This Hugo Cary—what was he like?"

"Oh, I don't suppose any stories one hears can hold much evidence—you know how the people around here talk," she said, twirling a golden strand of hair between her fingers.

"Tell them, Mother."

We turned to see Charles Cary standing in the doorway, his face grim.

"Oh, Charles, don't be absurd," she replied, but without conviction.

"Very well; I'll tell them," he said firmly, seating himself once more at the table. "They say he was a murderer, a cruel man who was responsible for the Cary family curse."

"Oh?" said Holmes. "What's that?"

"That in every generation of Carys a family member will die a violent death."

There was a silence, and then Holmes spoke.

"Do you believe that?"

Charles Cary snorted. "Of course not—it's typical West Country superstition. But that's not what concerns me. My sister seems to believe it, and given her fragile state of mind, that is worrisome. Who knows what she may do?" He ran a hand through his hair, his expressive face glum.

Marion Cary leaned forward in her chair. "Perhaps we should—" she began, but broke off when her son looked up at her. I wasn't sure, but I think I sensed an admonition in that gaze.

"What were you going to say?" Holmes said when she did not complete her thought.

In response she shook her head, her eyes downcast. "Nothing," she replied. "I really don't know what to do. Perhaps the séance will calm her down, convince her that there are no spirits wandering around Torre Abbey."

"Or perhaps it will convince her of just the opposite," Charles Cary said tersely.

LUNCHEON WAS a strained affair that day. Marion Cary made an attempt at polite conversation, but it was clear that her daughter's condition was deeply disturbing to her. Caliban sat at her feet throughout the meal, very well behaved, and she occasionally slipped him a tidbit, but her manner was distracted. Charles Cary went back upstairs to see to his sister, then reappeared after a while, but he was no more relaxed than his mother, and barely touched his food. To my surprise, Holmes made no reference to Elizabeth Cary's condition or to the mysterious Cavalier throughout the meal, but made small talk about events in and around Torquay. This was so unlike him that I wondered what he was up to.

Later, as we sat alone in the parlour watching the pale October sun slip behind the trees outside, I asked him why he had avoided the obvious questions about Miss Cary.

He smiled in reply. "Sometimes a loose rein is necessary, Watson—you have to give a horse its head occasionally to learn more about it."

"What exactly do you hope to learn in this case?" I said, moving my chair closer to the fire. Ever since our visit to the barn I could not seem to get warm, and wondered if I was perhaps coming down with a chill or something.

Holmes gazed into the glowing flames of the fire.

"Well, one curious thing strikes me. Torre Abbey has an impressive array of apparitions, doesn't it?" he said thoughtfully.

"I was just thinking that myself," I replied.

He rose from his chair and stood before the fire, one sinewy arm resting upon the mantelpiece. His eyes were dark in the yellow firelight.

"Yes—curious, isn't it? It's as though the hauntings were tailor-made, as one might make a suit to fit a customer."

"What does it mean, do you think?"

Holmes shook his head and stared into the grate. "Whoever is behind this knows the family—and knows them well."

I too looked into the flames, which leaped and danced before my eyes. Mesmerized by the golden glow of firelight, I couldn't help wondering if I too would find my deepest fears reflected in the spirits—real or otherwise—that walked the dusky chambers of Torre Abbey.

Just then Charles Cary entered the room. "You wished to see me, Mr. Holmes?"

"Yes," Holmes replied as our host took a chair by the fire. "Do you own firearms, Lord Cary?"

"Yes—yes, I do. I have a revolver."

"Do you know how to use it?"

"Oh, yes. My father believed every country gentleman should know how to ride and shoot."

"You'd best sleep with it loaded next to your bed," Holmes

remarked. "And after tonight I would like everyone to move into a bedroom close to the centre of the house, so that I can more easily keep an eye on things."

"I wonder if it would help to move your family somewhere where they might be safer—a hotel in town, perhaps?" I suggested.

Lord Cary looked at my friend, his pale eyebrows knit. "Do you think that would be wise, Mr. Holmes?"

Holmes leaned back in his chair and rubbed his eyes. "Not necessarily. If this were London, I would have the Baker Street Irregulars at my disposal, but here . . . of course, Watson and I will do what we can, but . . ."

"What about the servants? After all, it was Sally who died," Lord Cary pointed out. "It would hardly do to move my family out of danger and not the servants, too."

"True—and I'm not at all certain that moving them into town would remove them from danger—in fact, it might encourage whoever is behind this to engage in even bolder behaviour," said Holmes. "As for Sally, it is true that she was most probably a casualty in this case, but I feel confident that your family is the real target."

Lord Cary's face turned a shade paler and he swallowed hard. "Really? What makes you say that, Mr. Holmes?"

Holmes passed a hand over his face and sighed. "A number of factors. If you don't mind, though, it is late and I think I'd like to retire."

I knew Holmes well enough to know that the lateness of the hour had nothing to do with it. When he was on a case, fatigue was unknown to him—he was capable of feats of endurance beyond other men. For whatever reason, he clearly did not want to reveal all that he knew to Charles Cary—either because he did not entirely trust him, or because he feared it would compromise Cary's safety.

After Cary had gone, I turned to Holmes.

"What exactly did you find in the Spanish barn, Holmes?"

"Cigar ash, Watson. A rather rare blend of tobacco, in fact, found most often in Turkey, though I have heard tell of it being sold on the streets of Kashmir as well. In my monograph on cigar ash I devote a paragraph to this particular blend."

"I see. So that is why you asked if anyone in the house smoked cigars."

"Indeed. Someone stood in that spot rather recently and smoked a cigar, Watson. In fact, judging by the amount of ash, they were there for rather a long time. An expensive cigar like that takes a long while to smoke."

"Do you think . . . ?"

"That is all I can safely conclude, though I have my theories. In any event, I intend to keep a close eye on the Spanish barn, Watson, and I would appreciate it if you did the same."

I shivered. Though I did not say so, I had no desire ever to go near the Spanish barn again.

CHAPTER NINE

I
N THE middle of the night I was catapulted out of sleep by a blood-curdling scream. It was the most hideous, utterly terrifying sound I had ever heard. It slashed through the night like a sword, cutting the air and piercing my ears with its horrible, shrill cry. My heart beating rapidly my chest, I tore off the covers and launched myself from the bed. But the second my feet hit the ground, the sound stopped, leaving in its wake only a faint dying reverberation in the air. I threw on my robe, and, flinging the door open, plunged out into the hallway.

To my relief, I was not alone. In the moonlight filtering in from the windows, I could see the tall spare form of Holmes coming towards me from the other end of the hall. The sound of footsteps from around the corner moments later announced the arrival of a very out-of-breath Charles Cary. He wore a dressing gown and carried a gas lantern in his left hand.

"Good God!" he exclaimed. "What on earth was that?"

"It sounded like a woman screaming," I replied.

Cary's handsome face clouded over. "Have you seen my sister?" he said to Holmes as he joined Cary and myself.

Holmes shook his head. The same thought had crossed my mind: it seemed only logical that the scream came from a member of the household. At that moment, however, Elizabeth Cary appeared, her dark hair in disarray, clutching her robe to her breast.

"What is it, Charles?" she cried, falling into her brother's arms.

"Have you seen Mother?" he said by way of answer.

"No," she replied, but just then Marion Cary came rushing down the hall.

"What can it be, Mr. Holmes?" she said, shivering. "It was horrible—it sounded almost inhuman."

"I don't know," Holmes responded, "but I intend to find out. The servants' quarters are in the north wing, I believe?"

"Yes, yes," she replied breathlessly.

"Lord Cary, if you would be so good as to accompany me, I shall ask Watson to remain here to make sure the women come to no harm," Holmes said.

"Yes, of course," Cary replied, following my friend down the hall towards the servants' quarters.

As I watched them disappear down the darkened hallway, I thought of my service revolver sitting in the drawer next to my bed. I looked at Marion Cary, whose face was flushed and glowing from exertion and emotion. In spite of my concerns for the safety of the household, I confess that the sight of her golden hair, loose about her shoulders, caused my heart to beat even more rapidly.

Embarrassed, I averted my eyes. "Did either of you get a sense of where the scream was coming from?"

Marion Cary shook her head. "It woke me from a sound sleep. It seemed to be everywhere at once."

"It—it seemed to me that it was coming from the cloisters," Elizabeth Cary said haltingly.

I was itching to join the search in finding the source of the scream, but Holmes had told me to watch over the women, and I resigned myself to fulfilling my duty.

"We would probably all be more comfortable in the library," said Marion Cary. "We could at least light a fire there."

The hallway was indeed draughty, and a sneeze caught in my throat as I replied. "I think we should wait here until Holmes returns. Then we can all go down to the library together."

Elizabeth Cary pulled her cloak around her shoulders. "I want to go find William. I'm worried about him."

"I think we'd best leave that to Mr. Holmes," said her mother. "Dr. Watson is right—we need to stay here and wait for him."

It wasn't long before I heard the quick, firm tread of my friend coming down the hall. He was followed by a very bewildered-looking Annie: nightcap askew, she stood shivering in her bare feet, with only a thin robe over her long white nightgown.

"Are you all right, dear?" Lady Cary said, and the little chambermaid nodded in reply, as if she didn't trust herself to say anything. "You look cold. Why don't you wear this?" Lady Cary said, taking off her own dressing gown and putting it on the girl's shoulders.

"Oh, no, mum, that's quite all right, really," the poor girl replied, but Lady Cary wrapped the robe snugly around the maid.

"Nonsense. You're shivering, and likely to catch cold."

"Where's William?" Elizabeth asked.

"Right here," said Charles Cary, rounding the corner. Young William trailed after him, clutching a stuffed bear.

"Come here, little bird," Elizabeth said, folding the boy in her arms and stroking his shiny black curls.

He made a sound which was indeed very much like the cooing of a pigeon or some other such bird as she caressed his hair.

"The only person unaccounted for, then, is Grayson," said Holmes, but as he spoke the butler appeared at the other end of the hall.

"Where have you been, Grayson?" said Cary.

"I was looking for the source of that scream, sir," Grayson replied smoothly. In contrast to the rest of us, he gave the impression of being entirely calm and collected. His appearance lacked any sense of disarray: his dressing gown showed no sign of having been donned quickly. "It seemed to me the scream came from the east wing, sir."

"Hmmm," I said. "Miss Cary seemed to think it came from the area of the old cloisters."

"Did she?" said Holmes, peering at Elizabeth intently.

"Well, I—I can't be sure, of course," she replied. "It's just the impression I had."

"I see," said Holmes.

"Well, now that we're all present and accounted for, I believe I shall have a look round the abbey," Holmes declared.

"We were just about to go down to the library and build a fire to warm ourselves," said Lady Cary.

"That sounds like a fine idea," Holmes replied. "Lord Cary, if you will assist your mother, Watson and I will try to find the source of that mysterious scream."

"Very well, Mr. Holmes," Cary replied.

Though I said nothing, I was much relieved that my guard duty was ended; I much preferred to remain at my friend's side while he ferreted out the cause of the nocturnal disturbance.

"If you would be so good as to take that lantern from Lord Cary, Watson," Holmes said, "and follow me, I would be grateful."

"If none of us screamed, it means there must be someone else in the building," said Lady Cary as we all filed down the stone staircase to the first floor.

"Not necessarily," Holmes replied mysteriously.

"But there are no other houses within a mile of here," Charles Cary protested. "The scream must have come from within the abbey."

"I do not argue with you there," said Holmes as we parted from the little group. As they made their way to the library, Holmes turned and headed down the hallway in the direction of the gatehouse.

I followed, much puzzled. "I don't understand, Holmes. If the sound did not come from within the abbey, then why was it so loud?"

"Oh, I am convinced that it came from within the abbey," he replied, leading me into the back courtyard, which was formerly the abbey's cloisters. An oval flower bed at the centre of the courtyard was enclosed by the thick vine-covered walls of the abbey. A series of stone paths crisscrossed the grassy interior of the cloisters. "I think the erroneous conclusion is that it was of human origin," Holmes continued as we picked our way over an ancient stone walkway toward the flower bed, which now contained only a few browning chrysanthemums.

"What, then?" I said as a thin cold chill made its way up my spine. The memory of the terrible howl of the Hound of the Baskervilles was still fresh in my mind. Standing upon the dark ground in what was once an ancient medieval cloister did nothing to improve my mood. "What do you think it was, then, Holmes?" I whispered.

"Well, suffice it to say for now that I have my theory," he replied mysteriously.

"Good Lord, Holmes, you're not saying that . . . ?" I said, hardly believing my friend would credit the existence of supernatural forces.

"No, no, Watson; have no fear. I merely suspect that it is not human. Would you be so good as to hold that gas lamp closer to the ground?"

I complied, lowering the lantern so that it cast a halo of light upon the ground around our feet. A thin mist rose from the spot Holmes indicated, and I noticed there was a puddle of water upon the stones, seeping slowly into the already waterlogged soil. The glow of the lantern caught the flash of a shiny metal object on the ground, and Holmes bent down to pick it up.

"Well, well, well," he chuckled, holding it up so that I could see. "Look what we have here, Watson."

It was a half-crown piece, dripping wet from where it lay in the middle of the slowly spreading puddle.

"What does it mean?" I said, completely at sea.

"Perhaps nothing," he replied, "but if I am right, it confirms what I already suspected."

I was used to my friend's cryptic ways, but I confess I was burning with curiosity as I followed him back into the abbey. I could not imagine what a half-crown piece could have to do with the horrible scream which had awakened us all so abruptly.

We found the Cary family in the library. Charles had lit the fire, and everyone sat huddled around the flames. Charles and Lady Cary sat in the stuffed armchairs at either side of the fireplace, and Elizabeth had settled herself upon one end of the settee, William curled up in her lap.

As I watched them, I was struck by how the two of them resembled a medieval painting of the Madonna and Child. The orange glow of the firelight fell upon the boy's face, which was nestled in the young girl's arms, his round cheeks as smooth and white as the plump arms which held him. It was a pretty sight, his black curls against hers, so that one could hardly tell which was which. I looked at Holmes, wondering if the beauty of the scene was lost on him. He too appeared to be studying the pair, but the expression on his face was one of scientific curiosity rather than aesthetic appreciation.

Annie the chambermaid sat at the other end of the sofa, wrapped in a blanket, looking ill at ease; no doubt she was unused to relaxing in the presence of her employers. Grayson, efficient as usual, was passing round cups of tea. He alone looked utterly unmoved by the strange events.

Charles Cary rose from his chair the moment we entered the room.

"Well, did you find anything?" he said, coming towards us.

"I believe we can account for the source of that terrifying sound," Holmes replied calmly.

"Oh? Who was it?" Marion Cary said anxiously.

"Not *who*—but rather *what*," Holmes answered, holding up the half-crown piece.

Charles Cary's face darkened. "Mr. Holmes, this is not a laughing matter. No doubt you find it very amusing, but I can assure you that we—"

"You are mistaken, Lord Cary; I don't find it amusing at all," Holmes replied calmly.

"Then why do you taunt us with such an outrageous suggestion?" Cary sputtered, his face red as a beet.

"Oh, there is nothing outrageous about it, Lord Cary, and if I had some dry ice I could show you right now why it is a perfectly reasonable conclusion."

Marion Cary rose from her chair. "Dry ice? I don't understand."

All eyes were on Holmes as he held up the half-crown piece. The little group on the couch—Annie, Elizabeth, and William, were silent, their eyes round as saucers as they watched him.

"I have made some small study of magic, which is proving very useful in this case, involving as it does the use of certain illusions. One rather unusual but very simple trick involves dropping a coin into dry ice to produce a very effective and chilling sound that sounds very much like a human scream."

Cary turned pale. "Do you mean to say that—that *noise* wasn't a person at all, but was made by—by a *coin*?"

Holmes nodded. "Precisely."

Marion Cary shook her head in disbelief. "But how—I mean, how did you know it wasn't a person?"

Holmes shrugged in reply. "I didn't—not at first, at any rate. But then, when all the members of the household were accounted for, and none confessed to being the source of the scream, I decided to look at other options. The first possibility was that one of you was lying, but for several reasons I didn't think it particularly likely. Also, there was something odd about the sound—as you pointed out, Lady Cary, it was not quite human. That's when it occurred to me that it might indeed be not human at all, and that was when the magician's ploy occurred to me."

Charles Cary sat back down in his chair, amazement on his face. "By God, Mr. Holmes, you don't miss a trick, do you?"

Holmes smiled. "In this case, I was literally looking for a trick, you might say. Dry ice can be stored for short periods of time in an ordinary icebox, so the most logical spot for the commission of such a trick would be near the kitchen, where transport would be simple. The cloister courtyard was a perfect choice; because of its central location, the sound would travel equally throughout the abbey, and even be magnified somewhat because of the acoustics. There is, I observed, a pronounced echo effect when one stands in certain areas of the old cloisters."

He settled his lean form upon a low chair next to the settee, where William and Elizabeth sat curled up around one another like two squirrels in a nest. Annie sat at the other end of the sofa, not moving a muscle as Holmes continued.

"Since I knew what I was looking for, it remained only then to locate the coin, which I accomplished with the help of Watson and a gas lantern."

Marion Cary shook her head. "You astonish me, Mr. Holmes, really you do. Everything Charles said about you is true—and more."

Charles Cary nodded in agreement. "I suppose there is no

chance it was just a half crown someone accidentally dropped there?"

"Unlikely," said Holmes. "The coin was extremely cold to the touch—and though the ice had melted by the time I arrived, the ground all around the coin was conspicuously wet."

"I see," said Carey. "But the real question is, who is responsible for this?"

Holmes shook his head. "I'm afraid I don't yet have that answer. All I can say is that I am getting closer—and this is another piece of the puzzle. In the meantime, you are safe for tonight. You and the rest of your family should get back to your beds. I have some thinking to do."

"Very well, Mr. Holmes—whatever you say," Cary replied meekly. "Come along, Elizabeth. It's time to get you and William back to bed."

The boy had fallen asleep on her lap. His face in repose looked angelic, his dark eyes with their long lashes fluttering slightly in response to whatever he was dreaming about. Charles gathered William up gently and carried him from the room, Elizabeth following behind them. Marion Cary stopped briefly to press Holmes's hand between hers.

"Thank you, Mr. Holmes," she said warmly. "I am glad you are here."

Holmes looked uncomfortable, but he managed a smile. "I only hope that I am able to be of some service, Lady Cary."

"You already have been," she replied, giving his hand a squeeze, and I could not help wishing it were my hand she held instead of his.

When they had all gone, Holmes sat staring moodily into the dying flames of the fire.

"I did not want to reveal so much just now, Watson, but I could tell Cary was getting impatient, and I needed to gain his confidence." He sighed. "And so I performed that little parlour trick involving the coin and dry ice."

I looked at him, astonished. "Do you mean that *you*—?"

He laughed. "Good heavens, no, Watson; I don't mean that *I* dropped the coin into the dry ice. No, no—someone else did that. I merely meant that, having discovered its source, I revealed it to everyone. I would rather not have tipped my hand so early, frankly—until I know whom I can trust. In the event that there is an accomplice within Torre Abbey, they now know to what extent we are on to their little game." He sighed and rubbed his forehead wearily. "That is not good—I prefer to operate as secretly as possible."

I knew that to be true, but had often suspected that it was his innate theatricality and love of showmanship that led Holmes so often to keep his conclusions to himself, only to reveal them at the last possible—and most dramatic—moment.

"You think there may be a member of the Cary family involved, then?" I said.

"Let me just say that I think it would be difficult to pull off these tricks without the help of someone within the house. I'm not ruling out the servants, either," he added, "dead or alive."

"You mean poor Sally?" I said. "How could she have been involved?"

"I don't know that she was. But there was a secret involving her no one is telling me—I am certain of it. It may have something to do with this case, and it may not. Only time will tell," Holmes replied, slumping lower in his chair.

His face in the firelight was drawn and haggard, and it suddenly occurred to me that he was the only one who had appeared in the hallway fully dressed. That could only mean one thing: while the rest of us were awakened from deep sleep by the scream, Holmes had not been to bed at all that night.

"You look tired, Holmes," I said gently. "Why don't you try and get some rest?"

He dismissed the idea with a wave of his hand. "I must think upon this while it is fresh in my mind, Watson." He fumbled about in his vest pocket and produced his pipe. "This is a two-pipe problem, I think." He shook his head and sank lower into the chair. "There is something here that escapes me . . . something deep—and dark."

I said nothing, but stared into the dancing flames of the fire. The terrible scream—inhuman though it was—still echoed in my ears.

CHAPTER TEN

THE NEXT day the incident of the nocturnal scream was the subject at breakfast, but by afternoon all talk was of the upcoming séance. It had been arranged for the day after Sally's funeral, which was to be held tomorrow afternoon in Cockington. Besides Holmes and myself and the Cary family, the only other guests in attendance at the séance were to be Father Norton and his sister Lydia, who was a teacher in the parish school run by her brother.

After spending the morning tramping about the grounds of the abbey, Holmes and I sat over a late tea in the library that afternoon. Holmes wanted to research some of the Devon legends which floated about the abbey, and we sat pouring over any books we could find with information about Torquay. In addition to their extensive art treasures, the Cary family had an impressive collection of books, which they kept in the spacious library in the east wing of the abbey.

"Watson, what do you know about letterboxing?" Holmes said, pouring himself a cup of tea.

"Nothing," I replied. "What is it?"

Holmes flicked an ash from where it had fallen on his sleeve. "It is a curious sport," he observed, smiling. "No doubt it serves as an excuse for some otherwise sedentary gentlemen to tramp about the moors of a Saturday."

"Oh?" I said, intrigued. "What sort of sport might that be?"

"I know little other than what I have read," he answered with a shrug. "I believe it involves placing one's card in a sort of container, or letterbox, that is to be found upon the moors—under rocks, trees, even buried in the ground—to show that one has been there."

I reached for my pipe and began filling it with tobacco.

"Really? It sounds an odd sort of activity—why do they refer to it as a sport, I wonder?"

"Well, the sport comes into it in following a rather complicated series of clues which lead you to the next letterbox."

"I see. Sort of like treasure-hunting—only without any real treasure."

Holmes nodded. "Just so. It exists mostly in the West Country, though I believe it is spreading slowly to other parts of the Great Britain."

"Hmm," I said, lighting my pipe. "What significance does it have to us?"

"Well, unless I miss my guess, Father Norton is a participant in this rather odd sport."

"Really?" I replied. "How do you surmise that?"

Holmes smiled mysteriously. "Oh, come, Watson. Do I have to reveal my methods every time to you?"

I laughed. "No, of course not—it's just that I'm curious."

"Well, restrain your curiosity a little while if you can," he said with a sideways glance towards the door. "It seems we have a visitor."

We were indeed about to be joined by another person, though his entrance into the room was a strange one. I looked in the direction Holmes indicated and saw young William lurking just the other side of the door. He may have thought he was out of sight, but his shaggy dark hair was clearly visible, and I could see his pale face poking around the corner. He saw me watching him, though, and the face disappeared, only to reappear again moments later.

"There's nothing to be frightened of, William," Holmes said in a soothing voice. "Come have a cup of tea with us."

The boy took a couple of halting steps into the room and then stopped, and I took the opportunity to study him. His appearance was one of rumpled disorder. His clothes, though clean and in good condition, looked ill-fitting and unkempt on him; it was not so much the clothes themselves as the way he wore them. His shirt-tail hung out on one side, his untied shoelaces trailed uselessly after him, one shirt-sleeve was buttoned, while the other flapped loosely about his wrist. His hair was a frightful tangle of dark curls, and looked as though it had not been combed for some days.

"Would you like some cake, William?" Holmes said softly, watching the boy greedily eye the plate of lemon cake.

William nodded silently in reply, and took a couple of steps towards the tea tray. Holmes reached slowly out for the cake plate, and with a steady, smooth gesture, handed it to the boy. I recalled seeing the same sort of careful movements back when I was serving in India—an Indian comrade had used the same fluid gestures, slow and hypnotic, as he approached a poisonous snake asleep in our path.

William's eyes widened as he watched the plate of cake—then, with a speed so sudden it startled me, he grabbed the plate and began shoving a piece of cake into his mouth rapidly, as though he hadn't eaten for a week. I looked at Holmes, who was observing the boy intently.

"Good, isn't it?" he said softly.

William didn't reply, but nodded vigorously as he ate, crumbs flying everywhere, floating down upon the carpet like tiny yellow snowflakes.

"You like cake, don't you?" said Holmes.

By way of reply, William made a gurgling sound, neither quite human nor animal. It was as though he was trying to speak but couldn't get the words out. Holmes leaned his head back, the fingers of one thin hand drumming restlessly on the arm of his chair. He looked at William through half-closed eyes. A casual observer might think he was napping, but I knew my friend well enough to realize that he was in fact observing the minutest detail of the boy's behaviour.

William's eyes darted around the room as he devoured the cake. He sat on the floor right where he was, stuffing cake into his mouth as fast as he could.

"Is that good, William?" Holmes said gently. "Did your mother used to give you cake like that?"

Suddenly there was a change in the boy. His eyes widened, and he sprang to his feet, gesturing wildly. He seemed to want to show us something, for he looked earnestly at us while making the tortured, half-human sounds which seemed to be his version of speech. Placing his cake on the sideboard, he pointed to himself, then, to my surprise, began stirring an imaginary pot with an imaginary spoon. I looked at Holmes—William was doing a very credible job of miming someone cooking. I began to speak, but Holmes laid a hand upon my arm.

"No, Watson—he's trying to show us something," he whispered.

William continued to stir the pot, adding ingredients from various invisible containers, and then suddenly he stopped, seeming to hear something. He put down his "spoon" and crept in the direction of what would be the outside door if he were indeed in the abbey kitchen. He hesitated, then opened the door. His face expressing utter horror at what he saw, he gave a terrified screech, which sent a chill through me, and fell abruptly to the floor, writhing in agony. So good was his performance that I was half out of my chair to come to his aid when he rose from the floor, evidently uninjured. He stared earnestly at us for a moment, then his face crumpled and he sat down at my feet rocking himself to and fro, moaning and whimpering. His distress was heartbreaking to see, and I reached out to lay a comforting hand upon his shoulder, but he pulled away and continued rocking himself. He then scooted across the floor to where the plate of cake sat upon the sideboard and resumed eating, all the while whimpering softly to himself.

I looked at Holmes. "Do you realize what we've just seen, Watson?" he said.

I nodded. The implication was clear: *William had been present at his mother's death!*

What was not clear, however, was whether he was capable of identifying her "attacker"—it seemed from his re-enactment that poor Sally may have died of a heart attack, after all.

"I wonder if anyone in the household has seen this 'performance,' " Holmes murmured as the boy continued to eat cake. The activity seemed to calm him, and before long his frenetic state evaporated and he sat contentedly upon the sofa, rocking gently back and forth and humming softly to himself, the kind of little wordless melodies a small child might invent.

"Are you going to tell any members of the Cary family about this?" I said.

"I think not," Holmes replied. "I have not decided who can be trusted, and I wouldn't want to do anything that would put William in danger."

The boy looked up at the mention of his name and smiled. He really was a pretty child, with his head of curly dark hair, full red lips and smooth olive skin.

"Do you really think harm could come to him, Holmes?" I said, alarmed at the idea that anyone might think to hurt the poor lad.

Holmes shook his head. "I don't know, Watson; I have many pieces to the puzzle, but so far they are not adding up to a coherent picture."

★ ★ ★

I WAS feeling unusually tired that night, and, excusing myself from supper with the family, went to bed early. I awoke in the middle of the night seized by a chill, shivering so violently that my teeth rattled. I piled every spare blanket on top of me that I could find, but to no avail; I continued to shake. My forehead burned and my eyes ached. Wrapping a blanket around my shoulders, I went over to where my medical bag sat on the window-seat and extracted a thermometer from it. The stone floor was like ice under my feet. Upon taking my temperature, which was a hundred and two, I realized that I had not escaped the flu epidemic after all. Cursing my rotten luck, I wrapped a wool scarf around my neck and returned to my bed, slipping in under the pile of blankets.

I lay there tossing and turning, alternately freezing and burning up with fever. My head felt swollen and fuzzy, and my muscles ached. Fevered images of the poor unfortunate Spanish prisoners invaded my thoughts. I imagined myself one of them, lying in the cold and cheerless barn, the dampness seeping into my bones as the fever ravaged my body . . .

I dozed off, awakening to the sound of voices in the hallway. It was still pitch-black outside, and I strained to catch the words, my head throbbing from the effort. It was a man and a woman; I wasn't certain, but I thought the voices belonged to Lord Cary and his mother.

"Where is she?" the man whispered fiercely.

"I don't know!" came the answer, equally tense.

Then there was the sound of footsteps departing in both directions. I listened for a few minutes more, until, hearing nothing but silence, I finally drifted off into a restless slumber, the blankets pulled up to my chin. I fell into a fever-induced dream state in which I imagined I was a Spanish sailor caught in a storm with the coast of Devon in sight. But the ship drifted farther and farther away from the coastline, until it faded away into the wind and fog. I stood upon the bow surrounded by a thick white mist, cut off from land, from rescue, from any hope of deliverance from the fierceness of the gale.

CHAPTER ELEVEN

I AWOKE to a thin grey dawn outside my window. A pale slice of sun was trying to break through the low cloud cover blanketing the rolling hills of Devon. I sat up in bed; once again I could smell the sea, which lay only about half a mile to the east. I had a sudden urge to go down to the water, through the orchard and down the hill leading to the sandy beach which was the western boundary of the abbey property. But a sudden fit of dizziness reminded me that I was sick, and I sank back upon the pillows and closed my eyes.

Just then I thought I heard the sound of a flute, faint and thin, drifting through the drafty halls of Torre Abbey. I wondered where it could possibly be coming from, and then I remembered what Holmes had said about Grayson. The melody was modal, some kind of Celtic tune, the song sliding smoothly onward like water rolling over stones, moving ahead even as it twisted and turned around itself. The flute had a ghostly sound, echoing through the ancient stone chambers of the abbey as though it were being played by a long-dead hand, a ghost sonata played by the dead for the benefit of the living. My mind turned to all the many rituals the living performed to honour the dead.

I mused upon the deep need we have to maintain contact with the dead. Once someone has passed from this world into the next, we think of ways to keep them with us: hoarding letters, pictures, mementoes, keepsakes, even clothing. Is it to smooth our own entry into this other world, I wondered, or because we cannot bear to say goodbye to dear friends? I had often thought religion was primarily man's response to the catastrophe of death—his attempt to come to terms with Nature's great final insult, to understand and control it, in a way. The upcoming séance, the funeral service—all were attempts to communicate in some way or other with the land of the dead.

And all of this done without the knowledge of whether our communiqués would ever hit their mark, as pure an act of faith as could be imagined, I supposed—love letters sent into the void without hope of acknowledgement. There was something touching about this, I thought; something touching but also disturbing. What a race of necrophiliacs we were, with our endless obsession over the dead. It seemed impossible for us to stick to the business of living; we simply could not leave the dead to lie in peace, quietly mouldering in ancient cemeteries. No, we had to visit their crumbling bones, festoon their rotting tombstones with flowers, and kneel upon the damp ground to show our obeisance to the past and to the certainty of our universal future.

Whether it was the strange Celtic tune that made me think these morbid thoughts, or the effect of the virus upon my weary brain, I could not say. But as I lay there listening to the intricate melodic strains of the flute, my mind looped over and through the music, like a counter-melody curling and twisting around the ancient-sounding Celtic air.

I MUST have dozed off, because I awoke some time later to the sound of rain outside. I didn't know how long I had slept; it was impossible to tell from the dull grey sky what time of day it was. My body still ached, but the fever had broken; my forehead, though clammy, was no longer burning. Lying under the goose-down quilt, I was in fact rather comfortable.

Listening to the steady drumming of rain upon the window panes, my mind wandered to all the thousands of feet which had trod these halls in centuries past, coming and going with the same regularity as the raindrops falling so steadily upon my windowsill. I thought of all the monks and abbots searching for truth through the way of the Church, seeking in God what they had been unable to find in their fellow man. I had never quite understood the compulsion to live the cloistered life—London was such a hodgepodge of people, a veritable symphony of sensations, as stimulating an environment as one could imagine. I had lived there so long that it was strange now to be in the midst of such solitude, sequestered within the thick walls of this ancient monastery.

Now, lying in my weakened state in the seclusion of my room with only the rain to keep me company, I half-imagined myself as one of those ancient monks, wandering the halls in my long coarse robe, carrying a single candle, the wax dripping slowly onto the stone floors of endless passageways smelling of incense and tallow.

There was a knock at the door.

"Yes?" I called out.

"It's Grayson, sir."

"Come in."

The door opened and the butler entered the room carrying a tray. "I though you might like a cup of tea, sir," he said, placing the tray upon the nightstand next to the bed.

"Thank you, Grayson," I replied, pulling myself up under the covers.

"Lord Cary always used to say there was nothing wrong in the world that a cup of tea couldn't make better," he said, arranging the things on the table to make more room for the tray. Large, knotty blue veins protruded from under the skin of his hands, hands which looked surprisingly strong for a man of his age.

"What was that melody you were playing, Grayson?"

"Oh, that was an old English air the master used to like, sir. It's about lost love, I believe."

"It's very haunting."

"Do you think so, sir?" he replied as he tucked the blankets in around my feet. "I always found it rather sad."

"That too—yes, it is sad."

"He was a lover of the finer things in life, my master," Grayson added with a sigh.

"He certainly married a beautiful woman," I replied.

Grayson looked at me as if he was about to reply, then turned away. I thought I sensed disapproval in the set of his shoulders, and wondered if he was about to disagree with my analysis of Lady Cary's charms—or perhaps he knew something about the family which he thought better of telling me.

"What sort of man was Lord Cary, Grayson?"

The old butler took a deep breath and straightened his spine, which, though somewhat stiff with age, was still upright. He carried himself with an almost military vigour, his movements brisk and precise.

"Well, sir, he was the kind of man you would do well not to cross . . . he inspired loyalty, sir, and there's nothing I wouldn't have done for him. If he asked for my firstborn, I would have given it to him."

"He must have been extraordinary," I said. "What a tragedy to die like that."

"Any way to die is a tragedy, sir," he replied solemnly, pouring my tea. "He was a man of the sea, and in the end it seems fitting that the sea took him at last."

"Still, you must miss him."

He paused to consider it for a moment.

"Miss him, sir? Yes, I suppose I do. Who you keep in your heart you never quite lose, though, sir, he used to tell me."

"He seems unusually reflective for such a man of action."

He handed me the tea. "He was a man of many facets, sir, both philosophical and otherwise. Milk, sir?"

"Yes, thank you."

I poured milk into the cup and watched it billow in the hot tea, rolling up to the surface like approaching storm clouds. The tea was strong and smoky, an Assam blend, I thought. As Grayson busied himself fluffing the pillows on the bed, I sipped my tea and thought about the British Empire; how, in our rapaciousness, we appropriated not only the land but the customs of those we conquered, so that tea—unknown to our Anglo-Saxon ancestors—was now commonly regarded as typically British.

The day continued dull and grey, with a steady drizzle of rain pattering upon the window panes. Grayson told me everyone else had gone to Sally's funeral, so I was left to myself for a few hours. Feeling restless, I roamed the draughty hallways of the abbey, finally wandering into the library. The library smelt of damp wood and dried rose petals. The dim light filtering in through the long narrow windows hung like a shroud over the silence of the room. The chirping of the sparrows I had heard outside my bedroom window did not seem to penetrate the ancient stones or thick lead glass of the library windows; all was stillness as I approached the stacks of books which lined the room from floor to ceiling. The smell of cracked leather bindings reminded me of my years at medical school, of days spent studying the thick textbooks which were my constant companions in those times.

I lit a lamp and browsed through the dusty stacks of ancient books until my eye was caught by a title: *Folk Legends of the West Country*. Perhaps it was the grey day, or maybe the abbey itself, its gloomy rooms made even more so by the weather, but whatever the reason, I was drawn to the book. I had not noticed it the day before when Holmes and I perused the books in the library.

The room was not particularly cold, yet I shivered as I

pulled the book from the ancient stacks. My hand trembled as I turned over the crumbling leaves, the pages brittle and brown with age. Turning up the lamp on the table, I settled down in a soft red leather armchair to read.

I really did not believe that the events which had transpired in Torre Abbey were of supernatural origin. I was quite certain, in fact, that some person or persons were playing a nasty trick on the Cary family, and that eventually Holmes would discover who it was. I wasn't thinking of this as I opened the cracked leather binding of the book, however; I just wanted something to pass the time. I leafed through the pages until a title caught my eye: "The Demon Hunter of Devon." My hands trembled as I held the book and read.

The Demon Hunter

At the hour of the moon the Demon Hunter is abroad
On his black stallion o'er the fields he does ride
As an ardent lover comes galloping across the moors
In search of his beautiful young bride
The lover hears the pounding hooves and urges his steed on
He senses danger but does not dare to look
Still the Demon Hunter gains on him, as the day is gone
They ride across glen and dale and over broiling brook
The lover gallops toward the sea, beyond the round face of the moon
But alas, he is too late and night arrives too soon
As over darkened plains the silver moon begins to rise
From his horse the hapless lover falls, and upon the ground he dies
The Hunter goes to claim the widowed bride but finds it is too late
In despair she hangs herself at the castle gate
The lovers now lie buried in the deep dark glen
But the Hunter on his great black steed will ride, and ride
—and ride again

I sat for some time staring at the page. The poem sent a chill through my spine, and the image of the Demon Hunter was as clear in my mind as if I had seen it myself.

All of a sudden I was aware of someone standing at the door. I turned to see Grayson, a tray in his hands.

"I thought you might like some refreshment, sir," he said, entering the room and placing the tray on the table in front of me. A plate of sandwiches sat next to a steaming bowl of soup.

"A day like this calls for soup, I believe, sir," he said, turning up the gas lamp, which had begun to dim and flicker.

"That's very thoughtful of you, Grayson," I replied, "but I'm not very hungry."

"You must eat to keep your strength up, sir. And be sure to keep warm," he added, taking a blanket from the sofa and wrapping it around my feet.

"I don't know what would become of this place without you, Grayson," I said warmly. "You think of everything."

"I do my best, sir." Noticing the book I was reading, he smiled. "That was one of my master's favourites, sir. I'm glad there's someone else to appreciate it."

"Devon seems to be full of ghostly legends," I replied.

"Oh, indeed it is, sir. There are those who believe they are true, too."

"And you, Grayson? What do you believe?"

"I believe in what I can see, sir," he replied solemnly. "I leave superstition to those who need it."

"That's an interesting notion," I said. "I never thought of anyone as *needing* superstition."

He tucked the blanket in around my feet and unfolded a napkin on my lap. "People seem to need religion, and to my mind it's the same thing."

"So you're not a religious man?"

He shook his head. "As I say, sir, I leave that to those who need it. And now, if there's nothing further you need, I'll get on with my duties."

"No—thank you very much."

"Be sure to eat your soup while it's hot, sir," he said, leaving the room as soundlessly as he had entered it.

I took a few sips of soup, then sat watching as the rain slanted onto the window panes. I dozed off after a while, and dreamt of the Demon Hunter riding, riding over the moors of Devon in the driving rain.

B Y T H E time everyone returned from Sally's funeral that evening, I was feeling better. The fever had broken, and although Holmes expressed concern about me, I insisted that I would be well enough to attend the upcoming séance the next day.

Holmes remarked that everyone in the surrounding villages seemed to know the Cary family, and that the turnout had been good. "Whether they came to gape or to sympathize is unclear—some of both, I expect," he observed, wrestling with a cuff link. I sat in a rattan chair in the corner of his sitting room, wrapped in a blanket, while he dressed for dinner. "But gossip about the family is flying about town fast and furious, from what I can see." He looked at me, concern written upon his aquiline face. "But are you certain you're quite all right, Watson?"

"Yes, yes," I replied.

By nightfall the rain had lifted, revealing a brilliant starry sky and a moon so bright that the grounds of Torre Abbey were bathed in its paleblue light. It shone in through the windows of the east parlour, falling softly upon the corners of the room, combining with the gaslight to lend even everyday objects a ghostly brilliance.

After dinner I was feeling well enough to join the others for coffee and cognac in the parlour. Elizabeth did not drink coffee, and Grayson had made her a cup of cocoa. Lady Cary, it seems, had retired to bed after dinner. Elizabeth rose and went to the window, the moonlight falling upon her shoulders. As she stood by the half-parted curtain, her face turned towards the window, her lustrous black hair seemed to absorb the pale rays of light. It seemed to be lost somewhere among those thick dark curls, held hostage within the raven tresses. She heaved a deep sigh and closed the curtains.

"I don't know why moonlight always makes me feel so melancholy," she said, "but it always does."

Her brother rose from his chair and put his arms around her shoulders. "Never mind," he said in a soothing voice. "Come along and have your cocoa, there's a good girl. It'll help you to sleep."

"There is no sleep for us, not we who lie in the dreary deep—only the eternal sleep of the dead," she murmured in an expressionless monotone, as though she were reciting a long-memorized text.

Charles Cary looked at Holmes and then at me. "She gets like this sometimes," he said apologetically.

Elizabeth Cary turned to us and spoke as though she hadn't heard her brother's words at all. "It was in the moonlight I died, and in the moonlight he stood beside my grave and cried." Holmes and I exchanged a look as Cary gently led his sister from the room.

"Come now," he said. "It's time for bed."

He returned shortly. Pouring himself another cognac, he took a swallow before speaking. "I really must apologize for my sister's behaviour. She's gotten it into her head that she is a Spanish girl who died three hundred years ago."

Holmes raised one eyebrow. "Oh?"

Cary sighed. "Yes. There is a legend that among the prisoners taken from the Armada galleon was a Spanish girl who disguised herself as a sailor in order to be near her lover. But they were separated when the ship was taken and she died of the fever without ever seeing him again—or so the story goes."

I leaned forward. "She died in your 'Spanish barn,' then?"

"So they say."

Holmes unfolded his long body from his chair and walked to the window. He looked out into the moonlit night, the glow of the moon so bright that the trees cast long shadows across the abbey lawn. The moonlight fell upon my friend's lean profile, so sharply etched that it could have been cut from glass.

"Lord Cary," he said slowly, "you must find a way to wean her from her drug addiction."

Cary's face went red. He opened his mouth to speak but Holmes cut him off.

"Whatever the poor girl is going through is undoubtedly aggravated by whatever she is taking. What is it, by the way? Watson and I agreed that laudanum was the most likely choice."

Cary nodded, all the fight gone out of him. "Yes. At first it was just every few days, you know, when things seemed unbearable to her . . . but now she seems unable to do without it for more than a day." He hung his head, and I felt sorry for him.

"I have no particular reason to doubt you," Holmes replied icily. "However, that does not change her predicament. I'm sure Watson can describe to you the long-term effects of drug addiction."

It was my turn to go red in the face. I didn't know if Holmes was referring to his own battle with cocaine, but if he was, I certainly had firsthand knowledge of its effects, living with him as I had off and on all these years.

"Lord Cary," I said carefully, "you really should listen to what Holmes says. The longer one remains addicted to a substance, the more painful the withdrawal symptoms can be."

"Yes, yes," he replied. "I know you're right, and I promise you I'll do something about it when this is all over."

I opened my mouth to protest, but Holmes silenced me with a look.

I AWOKE sometime in the middle of the night shivering, and as I got up to get another blanket I heard a sound in the hall outside my room. I crept to the door, opened it slowly, and looked out. To my surprise, I saw Elizabeth Cary walking down the hall towards me, carrying a lantern. I opened my mouth to address her, but the expression on her face stopped me cold.

She walked, eyes fixed straight ahead, her long white nightgown trailing after her. When she passed by without seeming to notice me, it was clear to me that she was sleepwalking. I had heard of cases of somnambulant wanderings, but had yet to see one myself. Concerned as I was for her safety, I confess I also felt a thrill of anticipation at the chance to observe the curious phenomenon firsthand. I followed her down the hall, resolved to waken her at the first sign of danger to her person. She walked ahead with slow but confident steps, as though she knew exactly where she was going.

I followed her down the central staircase to the first floor, and when she headed for the door leading to the outside, I almost put out a hand to stop her. Something stayed my arm, however, and I continued to follow her. She unbolted and pushed open the heavy front door as though it were nothing, and stepped out onto the front lawn. Without hesitating, she continued walking directly south, and I had a sinking feeling I knew where she was headed—the Spanish barn.

I had little desire to go near that structure again, filled as I was with a sense of its tragic past, and yet I followed after her as though I had no will of my own, curiosity driving me on. What could she possibly have in mind to do, asleep or not, at the old tithe barn? She walked quickly across the expanse of yard, going straight as the crow flies rather than taking the curving dirt path to the barn.

My legs trembled as I followed her. The building loomed in front of us, long and low, silent as a tomb. To my surprise, the door was unlocked. She pushed on it and it swung open with a loud creak. I stood upon the sill as she went inside, the flickering light of her lantern creating ghostly shadows on the interior of the vaulted ceiling. Still apparently unaware of my presence, she walked to the far window and gazed out at the dark branches of the old oak tree. And then she began to sing, not in English, but in a foreign tongue which I recognized as Spanish.

As I stood watching her, my head began to swim, and I felt the same sense of creeping dread which had overcome me the first time I entered this place. I put my hand to my head, and as I did, I thought I caught a movement out of the corner of my left eye. That end of the barn was almost entirely in darkness, however, and as I peered through the shadow I thought I could just make out the outline of a person moving towards me. I stepped back instinctively, but at that moment I lost consciousness, falling into an even more profound blackness than the one surrounding me in the Spanish barn . . .

WATSON! ARE you all right?"

I opened my eyes to see Holmes kneeling over me in the semi-darkness. I felt a damp cool sensation at the back of my neck, realized it was grass and that I was lying on my back upon the lawn. I looked up at Holmes's face, framed by a full moon hanging high in the sky.

"What happened?" I said.

The back of my neck hurt, and I felt stiff and sore, as though I had been lying on the cold wet grass half the night.

"I was hoping you'd be able to tell me," Holmes replied with a sigh. "I only arrived in time to find you lying here."

"Where's Miss Cary?" I said, struggling to sit up.

"Steady on, Watson," Holmes murmured, laying a hand upon my shoulder. "Take it easy and don't try to get up too quickly. You don't know yet the extent of your injuries."

"I'm quite all right," I replied, but my words belied how I felt. There was a ringing in my head, and my neck ached. I felt a lump forming at the back of my head.

I told Holmes everything I could remember—following Elizabeth Cary out to the barn, listening to her sing, and then losing consciousness.

"Did you just faint, or did someone hit you?" Holmes inquired, helping me to stand up slowly.

I felt the rising lump on the back of my skull and shook my head. "I'm not sure. I could have sustained this bump when I fell. I can't really say—all I know is that suddenly everything went black, and the next thing I knew I was lying here."

Holmes frowned. "You're not well, Watson, and shouldn't be out at night wandering around. Someone moved you from the barn. I wonder if a young woman could drag a man weighing—what, thirteen stone . . . ?"

"Twelve and a half."

"Even so, it is a distance of approximately twenty yards or so."

"I suppose she could."

"Perhaps, but it would be a fair accomplishment. And you're quite certain she was sleepwalking when you followed her?"

"Either that, or she wanted me to believe she was."

Holmes paused to consider it. "Well, the plot thickens, as they say. Come on, let's get you back to bed," he said, putting an arm around me and helping me to walk back towards the house.

"By the way, Holmes," I said, "what are you doing up at this hour?"

"Thinking," he replied offhandedly. "And actually, I am concerned about young William, so I thought it wise to keep watch over him tonight."

"That's all very well," I remarked. "But you can't keep watch over him every night. There's an extra bed in my room—why not put him in with me?"

"When you are feeling better, Watson," Holmes replied. "I shall catch a catnap later on. As you know, I require little sleep."

This was true enough; however, even in the moonlight I could see the fatigue in my friend's face, the circles under his eyes. Our stay at Torre Abbey, it seemed, was beginning to take its toll on both of us.

CHAPTER TWELVE

THE NEXT day I slept late, rising only in time for lunch, which I had in my room. I still did not have much appetite, and was only able to finish half of my soup before dozing off again. I awoke to a knock on the door.

"Come in," I said sleepily.

The door opened and Holmes entered quietly. He walked across the room and stood over my bed, shaking his head. "You never should have been wandering around last night. However, I wish I had been with you, to see what happened."

"I'm only sorry I didn't see more," I said with regret. "Are you going to tell the Cary family?"

"I think we should mention that you saw Elizabeth sleep-walking, then watch their reaction. It's best not to offer any details other than that, and see what they do."

But when we mentioned it to Charles and Marion Cary, they appeared utterly nonplussed; both claimed they were unaware of any such behaviour on Elizabeth's part. Charles actually seemed very concerned, and said he would speak to his sister about it, but that he would wait until after the séance.

That night we consumed a light dinner of soup and cheese. It seems our medium, Madame Olenskaya, had told Father Norton that too much food could cloud the mind and make communication between this world and the next more difficult.

By eight-thirty we had retired to the west parlour with our coffee. In spite of his evident concern about his sister, Charles Cary made no secret of his contempt of the proceedings. He stood in front of the fire glaring into the flames, an island of isolation, lost in his own thoughts.

Father Norton arrived at precisely nine o'clock, accompanied by his sister Lydia. Lydia Norton was tall and straight in the way Scottish women are, as slim at fifty as she no doubt was at twenty, with sandy hair and a handsome, taut-skinned face ("Good bone structure," my anatomy professor would have said). Her profile was as sharp and clean as the prow of a boat, her eyes bright as a terrier's. All in all, she gave the impression of extreme alertness—the kind of schoolteacher that children would not even try to outwit.

Lydia Norton shared the same ironic half-smile as her brother, except that on her it was not so much droll as a bit arch. It was as if one of them had borrowed it from the other, in a kind of unconscious imitation. In spite of their natural sardonicism, though, even Lydia and her brother looked apprehensive as we awaited the appearance of the medium.

Everything came to a halt with the entrance of Madame Olenskaya. She entered the room with all the theatricality of an opera diva. She was a large, florid woman, with loose folds of skin at her jowls like the dewlaps of a basset hound, and she lumbered into the west parlour of Torre Abbey with an authoritative air, as if unimpressed by its wealth and grandeur.

A heavy aura of perfume hung about her, filling the air with its musky scent, thick as a London fog. There was a familiar odour of sandalwood to it, and I found myself thinking of my days in India and the smell of incense floating over the marketplace, the staccato cries of vegetable sellers at their stalls mixing with the buzz of flies in the torpid air. The medium's fingers were festooned with colourful rings with gems of green, vermilion, and gold, and shiny silver bracelets hung from her arms. Around her neck she wore a single necklace of green and gold beads with a simple carved wooden hand at the end; the little finger and thumb were the same size and curved outward. I had seen that design somewhere before, but couldn't remember where.

She seated herself in the most comfortable armchair and gazed around the room at the rest of us; we all expectantly awaited her cue. I wondered what Holmes thought of her. He sat at one end of the couch, one elbow on the armrest, his chin resting upon his hand. I was intrigued in spite of myself; there was something about her presence which both reassured and commanded, and I was content to sit passively while she spoke in a deep, husky voice with traces of what sounded like a Russian accent.

"There is a time in the final flat grey hour before dawn when the heart sinks, and the spirit is deadened as it is pulled closer to the other world—and the doorway between the two realms slides briefly open. Physicians will tell you that is the time when most deaths occur, and many births as well—that dark hour of the moon when it is not yet day but no longer quite night. It is during that hour you must be most vigilant, for the spirits that walk abroad will come to you then, seeking to pull you into their world. Resist them—resist their soft playing voices and seductive ways, for if they sense you weaken they will surely pursue you until you sink into their world, and are lost to this one forever."

We all sat listening in silence, with only the ticking of the grandfather clock as punctuation to her words. There was something about the way she spoke which was both lulling and mesmerizing; I felt my limbs relax and my heart beat slower as she spoke. Thick waves of her perfume washed over us as she moved her heavily braceleted hands, the jewelry tinkling like so many silver bells.

Madame Olenskaya rose from her chair and pulled the curtains closed on each of the windows. Then she turned down the gaslights in the room one by one, until the only source of light was a single candelabrum in the center of the round oak table. She then approached the table.

"Come, enter the circle," she said, her voice low and resonant. "We must all join the circle of spirits, inviting them back into our world so we can communicate with them. Come," she said, extending a hand in my direction. I rose from my chair, pulled toward her by the power of her personality. I took a chair on the other side of Lady Cary, who sat directly to the right of Madame Olenskaya. On her left was Charles, and to his left sat Elizabeth. Father Norton took the chair to my right, and his sister Lydia sat on his other side.

"We must all join the circle in order to beckon them back into this world," said Madame Olenskaya. "They need to feel welcomed and safe, and when we create the circle of hands we allow them to step out from the shadows and communicate with us."

I glanced at Holmes, who stood calmly and joined the group at the table. He took the only chair left, between Elizabeth Cary and Lydia Norton.

"Now," said the medium, her cheek jowls quivering, "we must all join hands. Once the séance begins, under no circumstances are you to let go of the person's hand next to you. If you do, you shall break the spell prematurely, and injury could result."

She paused and looked around the table to judge the effect of her words upon the assembled company. Elizabeth Cary looked back at her with burning intensity, while Charles appeared bored and impatient. He shifted in his chair and sighed as if he wished this were all over. Lydia Norton glanced at her brother, who smiled back reassuringly. Next to me, Lady Cary trembled a bit and ran a hand over her hair, a nervous habit I had noticed before.

Finally, I looked at Holmes, but the expression on his aquiline face was impenetrable. When he wanted to, Holmes could be close as a clam; his devotion to reason allowed him greater control over his emotions than most people had.

"Now," said the medium, "let us all join hands and begin."

Father Norton's hand was steady and cool, but Lady Cary's hand in mine felt icy. Impulsively, I squeezed it to reassure her, and she looked at me, apprehension in those beautiful blue eyes. Until that moment I had experienced no fear, but now I felt a thin little shiver of anticipation thread its way up my spine.

Madame Olenskaya bent forward and blew out the candles on the candelabrum in the center of the table, and the room was pitched into blackness. It was a dark, overcast night; not even a glint of moonlight filtered through the heavy curtains. Some coals still glowed in the fireplace, however, and as my eyes adjusted to the darkness I found I could see the dim outlines of shapes. Without the use of sight, however, my ears suddenly seemed unusually keen. I was aware of every sound within the house: the mournful ticking of the grandfather clock in the hall outside, the faint creakings and shudderings of an old house; I could even hear the breathing of the people sitting around the table. To my right, Father Norton inhaled slowly with a raspy, hoarse sound, and Lady Cary's breath came in soft little gasps. I was marvelling at this variety of sensory input when Madame Olenskaya spoke. Her voice was low and resonant, and while not loud, it filled the room.

"I call now upon the beings of the other world! Come, O ye spirits, reveal to us the secrets of your dark ways—we are listening!"

Her words died away, leaving only a faint ringing sound in the air which floated and dissipated like ripples on a pond. We sat in silence for a moment. Someone coughed. The metallic ticking of the grandfather clock in the hall seemed preternaturally loud.

Suddenly a pitiful groan emanated from the other side of the table. I had an impulse to leap from my chair to see who was in distress, but the sound of Madame Olenskaya's voice pinned me to my chair.

"Nobody move!" she said in a commanding voice. "Someone is in the room with us. Who are you? Can you speak to us?"

The groan gathered in volume. In the semi-darkness I could just make out the form of Elizabeth Cary, who was seated directly across from me. She swayed from side to side as the groans grew louder, and there was no doubt in my mind that she was the source of the sounds. Lady Cary's hand tightened around mine as Madame Olenskaya spoke again.

"Tell us—tell us why you have come. What knowledge do you bring from the next world?"

The groans stopped and I heard Elizabeth Cary making strange throaty sounds, as though she wanted to speak but couldn't quite get the words out.

"What? What is it?" asked Madame Olenskaya. "What have you come to say to us?"

"It—it is the hour . . ." She struggled to release the words.

"What? What hour is it?" Madame Olenskaya said in a husky whisper.

"The . . . hour . . . of . . . the . . . moon," the girl replied, and at that moment it struck me that *she was speaking in a voice other than her own!* It was a full octave lower, with a throaty quality which was normally absent from Elizabeth Cary's speech. There was also a hint of an accent—Spanish perhaps, or Portuguese.

"Please don't take me there—anywhere but there," the girl suddenly cried in a plaintive voice.

"Where are they taking you?" Madame Olenskaya asked gently.

"No," the girl went on, as if she hadn't heard the question.

And then she said something in a foreign language which I was fairly certain was Spanish.

"Elizabeth, are you all right?" I recognized the concerned voice of Charles Cary.

"She is no longer your sister," Madame Olenskaya replied. "She will not respond to you as Elizabeth."

"Not the barn," the girl whimpered. "Not there!"

Suddenly the air was rent by a piercing scream. I felt as though all the blood in my veins was instantly frozen. There was the sound of a chair hitting the floor, the sharp yellow flare of a match in the dark, and the gas lamp was lit. I looked up to see Charles Cary standing by the gaslight, a smouldering match in his hand. His overturned chair lay on the floor at his feet.

"That is quite enough!" he cried. He hurried over to his sister and put his arms around her. She sat limply in her chair, her head upon her breast, as though she had fallen into a faint.

I rose from my chair and went to Miss Cary's aid. Her pulse was weak but steady, and her pale forehead was wet and clammy.

"I think you should take her up to her room to rest," I said to Charles, who nodded and helped his sister to stand. The rest of the assembled company watched in silence as he helped her out of the room. Holmes remained seated until brother and sister had left, then he rose and examined the seat Miss Cary had been sitting in. He ran a long hand over the back of the chair, peering closely at the wooden arm rests, then he lifted the entire chair up a few inches from the floor. Evidently satisfied, he put it down again and lit a cigarette.

Father Norton turned to Madame Olenskaya. "What did she mean by the 'barn,' do you suppose?"

Madame Olenskaya shook her head. "I don't know. Perhaps Lady Cary can enlighten us." She looked at Lady Cary, who remained in her seat, trembling, her face white. "Do you know of this barn she referred to? Is it somewhere around here?"

Lady Cary looked around the room as if she were contemplating an escape route. When she spoke, her voice was unsteady. "The Spanish barn," she said softly.

"The Spanish barn?" said Lydia Norton with a look at her brother.

"Isn't that what they sometimes call the old tithe barn?" the vicar said. "It's something to do with the invasion of the Spanish Armada, I believe."

"What is the Spanish barn?" said Madame Olenskaya to Lady Cary.

Lady Cary looked at Holmes, but he stood in front of the cold fireplace calmly smoking, one arm resting on the mantel. Lady Cary sighed and shook her head.

"There is a legend concerning that structure. Like so many stories about Torre Abbey, it is bound up in the actual history of the place. In 1588, during the invasion of the Spanish Armada a galleon was captured off the coast of Devon. The crew were all taken prisoner and brought to the abbey, where they were housed in that building."

She paused and looked down at her hands. "It is not a proud moment in English history. There were four hundred sailors, and they were terribly overcrowded—many died of disease and starvation." She sighed deeply and continued. "The legend has it that among the crew was a young girl disguised as a sailor in order that she might follow her lover, whom she loved so much that she was willing to follow him into battle. The story goes on to say that she was among those who died. They say her spirit walks at night searching for her lover."

There was a pause and then Holmes spoke.

"Very touching," he remarked, and it was hard to tell whether there was an edge of irony in his voice or not. He looked at Lady Cary keenly. "Was your daughter aware of this legend?"

"The Cary family has lived in Torre Abbey for centuries, Mr. Holmes," she replied quietly. "Stories have been passed down among family members for as long as that."

Father Norton rose from his chair. "Well, there's one way to find out—we can simply ask her."

Madame Olenskaya smiled and leaned back in her chair. "I see. So then this event becomes nothing more than the overactive imagination of a romantic young girl?" She shook her head. "Believe that, if you want to; I cannot prevent you from thinking what you will. But surely I am not the only one who noticed that the voice we heard tonight was not the voice of Miss Elizabeth Cary. Does she speak Spanish?" she said to Lady Cary, who shook her head.

"No. A little French, but no Spanish."

"Ah," the medium replied, something like triumph in her voice.

She looked around the room at the others, who had no reply. Lydia Norton rose and stood next to her brother, as if drawing security from being near him. Her lean, aristocratic face was impassive but her jerky movements indicated that she was unnerved—as were we all, I think. Lady Cary wrung her hands and looked at me. I had nothing to say; Madame Olenskaya was right, of course. Unless Miss Cary was a gifted actress, it was all certainly very strange, to say the least. At length Holmes spoke.

"You know," he said, "I have always maintained that whenever you have eliminated the possible, whatever remains—however improbable—is the truth."

"And what do you think the truth is here, Mr. Holmes?" said Lydia Norton, taking her brother's arm.

Holmes shrugged. "It is too early to tell. There are many things yet to be ruled out. However, I have not yet eliminated the possibility that Torre Abbey is indeed haunted."

There was a little gasp of breath from the collected company. Their surprise at hearing these words from such a personage as Sherlock Holmes was no less than my own. Father Norton shook his head.

"Good Lord," he said. "Good Lord."

Only Madame Olenskaya seemed unmoved by Holmes's statement. A smile played at the corners of her mouth, an expression of undeniable satisfaction. She fingered the sandal-wood necklace around her neck. "There are many things under heaven and earth, Horatio," she said in a sly voice.

I was a little surprised to hear her quoting Shakespeare, but Holmes nodded. "Indeed there are, madame, indeed there are."

CHAPTER THIRTEEN

Elizabeth Cary's dramatic exit had broken the mood, and Father Norton and his sister went home shortly afterwards. After seeing Madame Olenskaya out, Marion Cary returned to the parlour.

"I hope your daughter will be all right, Lady Cary," Holmes remarked as she joined us by the fire.

"Elizabeth is a very fanciful child," Marion Cary replied dourly, and once again I was struck by the coldness in her attitude towards her daughter. It was so different from the way she treated her son; her azure eyes would light up when he entered the room, and her affection for him was evident in her every gesture. But with her daughter it was just the opposite; she treated her with an indifference bordering on disdain, as if she were dismissive of the girl's very presence in the house. I couldn't help but wonder if her mother's coldness was a factor in Elizabeth's nervous disorder.

"Well, if you will excuse me, I believe I will retire for the night. I have had quite enough excitement for one evening," Lady Cary said.

After she had gone I mentioned to Holmes her coldness toward her daughter.

"Yes, I've noticed it myself," he replied, emptying his pipe into the grate. "Curious, isn't it?"

"It isn't uncommon for a parent to favour one child over another," I said, "but this seems above and beyond favouritism to me."

"Yes, I quite agree," he answered, carefully stuffing the bowl of his pipe with shag tobacco. "No, it's something else, something buried in the family's past, perhaps. There are many things about the Cary family which have not yet come to light."

"Oh? What leads you to that conclusion?"

Holmes struck a match and lit his pipe before replying. "Unless I am very much mistaken, they are hiding all kinds of information from us, Watson."

I put my legs up on the sofa where I sat and lay back to contemplate his statement. I stretched out my limbs, which felt heavy and sluggish from the damp Devon air. Sitting here in front of a blazing fire, I was at last comfortable, and with a glass of cognac to warm me, I was losing the stiffness which had plagued my joints ever since we arrived at Torre Abbey.

"Family skeletons in the closets, do you think?" I said, leaning my head back on the armrest.

Holmes lifted his glass and peered at it as if it were a crystal ball in which he could read the future. "I don't know about skeletons, but I would say secrets, most certainly."

"Any of them pertinent to this case, do you think?"

Holmes smiled rather grimly. "Ah, well, that remains to be seen, Watson. But the past has a way of creeping up on the present just when you least expect it."

At that moment Charles Cary returned to the parlour. He looked drawn and weary, and sank into the chair nearest the fire with scarcely a word to us. He sat staring into the flames until finally I spoke.

"How is your sister feeling?"

He looked at me as though my words surprised him; then, sitting up, he ran a hand through his thick hair, which shone like burnished copper in the firelight.

"She is resting. The events of the past few days have simply been too much for her to handle. She does not have the strongest constitution and is somewhat given to nervousness, as you know." He sighed and stared moodily into the glowing flames of the fire. "I never should have given in to her desire for a séance; it was a foolish idea. It has only upset her."

"Your concern for your sister is touching, Lord Cary, since you yourself supply her drug habit," Holmes remarked drily.

Our young host reddened, the blood creeping up his neck to his fair-skinned face. He looked at Holmes with fury and I thought for a moment he might strike him, but then Cary turned away.

"You don't know how she's suffered—you can't possibly understand," he said quietly.

"Perhaps," replied Holmes. "Although suffering is unfortunately not restricted to the privileged classes. Maybe I understand more than you might think."

I supposed Holmes was referring to his own drug habit—or perhaps to some secret sorrow buried deep in his past. I knew little of his early life; outside of my acquaintance with his brother Mycroft, Holmes's family was a mystery to me. He rarely spoke of such things, and I was not one to pry.

"Our life here at Torre Abbey has not always been a pleasant one, Mr. Holmes, despite what you call 'privileges,' " Charles Cary said, a bitter edge to his voice. "Our father was not an easy man—far from it. I won't bore you with the sordid details of our family life, but poor Elizabeth, being of a delicate disposition . . . well, I did my best to shield her from my father's moods, but I fear I was not always successful."

I leaned forward. "What about a sanatorium? Surely you can afford that."

He looked at me imploringly. "I swear to you, I have urged her to commit herself to a sanatorium to conquer her addiction—without success. I've even thought about committing her myself, but I could not bring myself to do it." He stared down at his hands, which he wrung until the veins stood out. "I too have my limits, it seems. Perhaps it is the coward's way out to cater to her addiction, but I cannot bear to see her suffer."

Holmes rose from his chair, unfolding his lean body and stretching up to his full height before he spoke. "Lord Cary," he said in an icy tone which I recognized, "the longer you wait, the more difficult it will be to shake her from this deadly habit. And I trust Watson will agree with me—but one does not have to be a man of medicine to know that."

I nodded. "Surely you recognize that what Holmes says is true, Lord Cary."

Cary hung his head. "I know," he replied softly. "Your words strike me to the quick—really they do. I know I have been neglectful in my duties as a brother—and as a son—but I mean to make good on that now. Even if it means taking a semester off from medical school, I am prepared to do what must be done. I only hope it is not too late."

Holmes lifted his glass of cognac and swirled the golden liquid within so that it caught the glow of the firelight.

"I hope so too, Lord Cary."

I looked at my friend, his face grim in the dim light, and his words sent a shiver of dread up my spine.

"Did you remark the ornament on the necklace Madame Olenskaya wore, Watson?" he said.

"Yes, as a matter of fact, I did. It was a carved hand; the design looked familiar to me, but I can't think where I've seen it."

Holmes blew a puff of smoke into the air. "It is none other than the Hand of Fatima."

My Arabic lore was a little rusty, but I recognized the name. "You mean Fatima, daughter of Mohammed?"

"The same. In the right hands, it is considered to be a symbol of good fortune; however, in the wrong hands . . . well, let us just say it is one of those symbols which can work either way."

"I see. And Madame Olenskaya?"

Holmes smiled. "If that is really her name."

Charles Cary gave a short laugh. "Her real name is probably Gladys Birnbaum or something like that. To tell you the truth, I only hired her to help put my sister's fears at rest once and for all—and look what I accomplished," he added bitterly.

"I'm not surprised your sister is full of morbid fancies," I remarked. "I got quite caught up myself in a book of Devon legends yesterday while you were all at the funeral."

"Oh?" said Holmes. "You didn't mention anything about it to me."

"I found it in the library. Grayson says your father was quite fond of that particular book. I was quite caught up by the poem about the Demon Hunter."

Cary looked at me, but in the dimness of the room I couldn't tell what his expression was. "What drew you to that one?"

"I'm not sure, really. It was quite chilling, though, I thought."

"It's supposedly about one of my ancestors, Hugo Cary— the one whose portrait hangs in my father's study."

"Ah, yes—the Cavalier. I remarked upon it when we first arrived," said Holmes. "You said there were all sorts of stories surrounding this fellow."

Charles Cary warmed his glass of cognac between his slender hands. "The poem Dr. Watson read is the verse version of the tale. My father used to read it to me when I was a boy."

I told Holmes the story and he listened with interest, his long fingers pressed together. "I don't remember seeing that book in the library yesterday," he said when I had finished.

"Neither do I. Perhaps someone had taken it out and was reading it earlier."

"Perhaps."

I looked at Charles Cary. To my surprise, his face was crimson.

"Is there any truth to it, do you think?" I asked.

Charles Cary shrugged. "Who can say? They say that Hugo Cary went mad and was often seen riding about the moors on a black horse—and that when locals speak of seeing the Demon Hunter galloping over the moors, they are seeing the Cavalier—the ghost of Hugo Cary."

He paused and took a sip of cognac, and I couldn't help noticing the shiver which travelled through his thin frame.

THAT NIGHT I insisted on taking young William to sleep on the spare bed in my room. To my relief, Holmes agreed; I could see even his iron constitution was beginning to crack under the strain of too many sleepless nights.

"Mind you bolt your door from the inside, Watson," he cautioned me as we trudged upstairs. He gave the same reminder to the Cary family as we adjourned to our separate rooms. Though they grumbled when Holmes suggested moving the sleeping arrangements, eventually they acquiesced. Lady Cary gave up her elegant quarters and moved into a bedroom next to Holmes, and Elizabeth Cary took a room next to her brother so that he could keep an eye on her. That left only the servants to worry about; Annie gratefully agreed to move into a spare guest room on the other side of my room, but Grayson demurred, saying he preferred to remain where he was.

To my surprise, Holmes did not insist, and let the butler have his way. In fact, when Grayson suggested that whoever was behind this was not interested in him, Holmes nodded.

"I'm rather inclined to agree with you, Grayson," he remarked. "Still, you will be careful, won't you?"

"Indeed I will, sir. Thank you, sir," the butler replied smoothly as he turned down the gas lamps before padding quietly off down the hall.

"A singular character, Watson," Holmes commented when Grayson withdrew.

I had to agree with him, but I was exhausted myself, and went to my room. I found Annie there waiting for me, holding William by the hand.

"You'll be a good boy now, won't you?" she said, attempting to smooth the boy's unruly black curls. He nodded and shoved a thumb into his mouth, clinging tightly to her hand.

"Come along, William," I said, reaching for him, but he shrank from me and pressed up against Annie's plump body.

"Go along with Dr. Watson now, there's a good boy," she said, disentangling her hand from his. He made little whimpering noises and twirled a strand of hair around one finger.

"Perhaps I should help you put him to bed," she said. "He's been ever so lost since—well, since, you know."

"What did you tell him?" I whispered as we entered the room. Grayson had lit a fire in the grate, and the room looked inviting in the warm orange glow of the fire.

"I told him his mum had gone up to heaven to sleep with the angels."

"Did he understand you?"

She shrugged her plump shoulders. "Who can say, sir? It's hard to know as what he understands. Mind you, there are times I think he understands more than the rest of us, and other times when I'm just not sure."

William seemed pleased with my room—he let go of Annie's hand to investigate the intricately carved mahogany chest at the foot of my bed, running his fingers over the animal figurines, lions and tigers, that graced the top of the chest.

"That's ever so nice, isn't it, William?" Annie said as his hand rested on the head of one of the lions.

He looked up at her and made one of his little grunting noises, his lips moving as though trying to form words. Watching him struggle to speak, I felt a sudden rush of sympathy for this poor motherless wretch of a boy. It seemed cruel that Nature had robbed him of the usual means of communication with his fellow beings, so that he was stranded behind a wall of silence.

"I've got to go now, William," Annie said gently, backing slowly out the door. "Dr. Watson here will look after you. He's pretty good at communicating what he wants, sir," she added. "Aren't you, William? He likes it when you sing to him, sir. It seems to soothe him."

"What shall I sing?"

"Anything, sir. He just likes to be sung to. Well, if you have any trouble with him, sir, you can come get me."

"I'm sure we'll be fine, Annie, thank you."

"Very good, sir," she replied, and with a little curtsy closed the door behind her.

I looked over at William, who stood, hands in his pockets, staring at me with his great dark eyes.

"We're going to be fine, aren't we, William?" I said, but he just continued staring at me. "Here's your bed over here," I continued, pointing to the little single bed in the corner under the eaves. He must have understood, because he walked quietly over to the bed and sat on it, gazing at me expectantly.

Without his saying a word, I was aware that he was waiting for me to sing to him. I sat down on the edge of the bed. To my surprise, he immediately laid his head upon my shoulder, pressing his body against my side. Though I had no children of my own, there seemed something so natural—comforting, even—

about the warmth of his body next to mine. A pang of regret pierced my heart. At that moment fatherhood seemed like the most natural, most desirable thing in the world. Some deep, ancient instinct within me awakened, and without thinking I placed a hand upon the unruly black curls. I felt the weight of my duty: to protect this innocent child against whoever or whatever lurked outside the thick, vine-covered walls of the abbey.

"What shall I sing to you, William?" I said, stroking the boy's tousled hair.

He snuggled closer to me and murmured, a tiny soft sound which was indeed like the cooing of a baby bird. I looked out of the arched cathedral windows in my room, into the night sky, which lay like a starry blanket over the sleeping moors of Devon. The words of a song from my own childhood came to me, a song my mother used to sing to me. Softly, I began to sing.

"Hushaby, don't you cry
Go to sleep, my little baby
When you wake, you shall have all the pretty little horses
Dapples and greys, pintos and bays
All the pretty little horses . . ."

My voice floated through the dusky chambers of Torre Abbey, down dim hallways, mixing with the echoes of voices long gone, adding to the ancient whispers that still twisted around the thick pillars and columns late at night, flickering like bats through the stone arches. The boy's breathing became slow and regular, his eyelids heavier, until finally they closed. Still I sang, thinking as I did of lying in my own mother's arms, late on a fall evening such as this, ill with scarlet fever, the sound of her voice like a soothing balm, lifting the ache from my limbs, chasing the fever from my tired brow.

"When you wake, you shall have all the pretty little horses
Dapples and greys, pintos and bays
All the pretty little horses . . ."

Out on the lawn, a lone mourning dove called to his mate.
The sound, hollow and plaintive, floated across the courtyard,
but she did not answer.

CHAPER FOURTEEN

I WAS sunk deeply into sleep, in the middle of a dream in which I was walking through the abbey, turning down one corridor after another, unable to find my way. The more I turned the more lost I became, until it felt as if I was wandering deeper and deeper into the dark interior of the building, never to escape, like Theseus winding his way through the Labyrinth, except that I had no thread to guide me out. I wondered what Minotaur I would meet at the end of my journey, what horrible sight would greet me as I turned the next corner, but then I heard the sound of a dog barking. Relieved, I turned to retrace my steps, heading towards the source of the barking.

It continued steadily, and I felt if I could only focus on it I could escape this terrible twisting maze of corridors. To my disappointment, the sound stopped abruptly. Straining to hear it, I opened my eyes. I was surprised to find myself staring at the ceiling of my bedroom. Disoriented, it took me a few minutes to realize that it had all been a dream. Relief coursed through my body as I lay on my back, glad to find myself safe and sound in my bed.

The barking, however, started up again, and I realized that it was real enough, having worked its way as it did into the landscape of my dream. The sound came from within the building, and it was a hollow, lonely sound, not an aggressive angry bark.

I surmised that it was most probably Lady Cary's terrier Caliban, although I wondered what had disturbed the dog enough to set him off in the middle of the night.

I threw off the covers, pulled on my robe, and was halfway out the door when I heard a noise behind me. I turned to see young William standing beside his bed, his black hair shining bluish-silver in the moonlight. In my disoriented state I had quite forgotten about the boy, but now I saw that he appeared to be frightened, and was in need of comfort. I knew Holmes was probably already up and looking around the abbey, searching for whatever if was that had alarmed the dog. Still, I didn't want to leave my friend in the lurch; after all, I had my service revolver, while Holmes had no firearm in his room.

"It's all right, William," I said, going over to the bedside table to fetch my gun. "There's nothing to worry about."

Indeed, I hardly believed my own words until my fingers closed around the cool smooth wooden handle of the gun. I breathed a little more deeply as I slipped the gun into the pocket of my robe. I glanced back at William, who had lain down again on his bed, curled up in a tight little ball. I sighed; I didn't want to leave the boy alone, but I was afraid Holmes might need me. A knock on my door rescued me from my dilemma; I recognized the quick, impatient rap of my friend even before he spoke.

"Watson! Are you all right?"

I opened the door. Holmes stood in the hall, a lantern in his hand. Though he was fully dressed, the creases in his cheeks and lines around his eyes told me that he had until very recently been asleep. He wore his brown ulster, unbuttoned, over his shirt and vest.

"I'm quite all right, Holmes."

"Good," he replied with a glance at young William.

"Did you find out why the dog was barking?"

He shook his head. "He usually sleeps in Lady Cary's room, but somehow he got out and was roaming around downstairs."

"Is she all right?"

Holmes nodded. "She was quite undisturbed—aside from awakening from a deep sleep by her dog barking. I've checked on everyone else, and no one has seen anything; some of them even slept through the barking, it seems. I'm going out to have a look around the grounds," he continued, with another glance at the boy. "Will you look after everyone while I'm gone?"

"Certainly," I replied, "but why don't you take my revolver?"

Holmes considered it, and then nodded.

"Very well—Lord Cary has his if you should need it. I think, however, that you will find nothing in the house. I have instructed everyone to remain in their rooms with the doors locked, and I suggest you do the same."

"Very well, Holmes," I said, taking the gun from my pocket and handing it to him. I was disappointed that I was not accompanying my friend on his search, but I wanted to be useful, and would have to content myself with following his instructions.

"Thank you, Watson," he said. He slipped the gun into the pocket of his ulster and disappeared into the gloom. I watched the glow of his lantern become fainter and fainter, until at last it disappeared around the corner. I then returned to my room and bolted the door again.

William lay upon his bed, looking up at me with his large dark eyes. I sat next to him.

"Don't worry, William. It's only the dog barking."

But the barking had stopped, and the abbey lay in still silence. It was that dead of night when no bird sings, and even the creatures of the night—crickets, katydids, owls—seem to be asleep, all the world poised on the cusp between night and day, waiting for the first signs of dawn to break over the landscape.

William made his little cooing sound and I bent over him.

"What is it, William? What do you want? Do you want a glass of water?"

He shook his head and buried his thumb in his mouth.

I suddenly remembered a packet of candies I had bought at the Paddington Station in London just before we boarded the train to Devon; I had shoved a few in my mouth to ward off my hunger pangs at the time.

"How about a caramel?" I said. "Would you like a caramel?"

This produced a positive response. He removed the thumb and nodded, making a gurgling sound. I fished a candy from the bag and gave it to him. He sucked on it appreciatively, smiling at me.

"There, now," I said. "That's much better than a thumb, isn't it?"

There was another knock on my door, softer than the last. I went to the door.

"Holmes, is that you?"

"No, it's me."

I recognized the voice as belonging to Marion Cary. I opened the door, and once again the sight of her was startling. She stood, her hair loose about her shoulder, in a white nightgown under a deep-blue robe.

"May I come in?" she said. "I'm frightened."

It was then I noticed the little terrier at her feet. He looked up at me and wagged his tail; whatever had so concerned him earlier seemed to have vanished. Either that, or he had lost interest in it.

I opened the door to admit her, the little brown dog trotting obediently at her heels. When William saw the dog he gave a little yelp and leaped from the bed, charging towards the terrier. The dog lowered his ears and braced himself, but the boy stopped just short of impact and sat abruptly on the floor next to the dog. He reached for the animal's silky ears and stroked them gently, cooing and purring to himself.

Marion Cary stood by the door watching.

"Poor thing," she sighed, drawing her robe closer around her slim shoulders. "It just isn't fair, what he's been through."

"In my experience," I observed, "life is seldom fair." As soon as I said it, I realized the remark was something Holmes would have said.

Marion Cary sighed more deeply. "I suppose you're right, Dr. Watson."

I felt a little light-headed; the lateness of the hour, being awakened from a deep sleep, and above all the presence of Lady Cary in my room—all combined to make me feel more than a little off balance.

"Where is Lord Cary?" I said, attempting to cover my awkwardness.

"He's watching over Elizabeth. She's easily upset, as you know," she added. As usual, there was little warmth in her voice when she spoke of her daughter.

To my relief, before long there was another knock on the door. It was Holmes; his search had turned up nothing.

"Allow me to escort you back to your room, Lady Cary," he said, taking her gently by the elbow.

She looked at me as if she wanted to say something. But then she checked her impulse, and turned to follow Holmes out of the room. The little terrier trotted behind her, blithely unaware that he was the cause of all the uproar.

William climbed obediently back into bed and was soon asleep. I too returned to my bed, but slept restlessly.

I was awakened from my uneasy sleep by a scream followed by the sound of gunfire in the hallway outside. I leaped from my bed, not bothering even to look for my robe, and staggered out into the hallway. To my surprise, I saw Elizabeth Cary standing there, a gun in her hand, screaming hysterically. I rushed to her, grasping her shoulders.

"What? What happened?" I said, but she was hysterical. Carefully, I took the gun from her hand. The chamber was warm; there was no doubt it had just been fired. I heard the sound of footsteps, and turned to see Holmes coming from the direction of his room.

"What has happened, Watson?" he inquired. "Is that the gun I heard being fired?"

"Yes," I said, handing it to him.

"And what's that?" he said, pointing to a thin stream of smoke at the far end of the hall.

"He—he came to me in a ring of fire!" Elizabeth Cary cried.

"Who? Who came to you?" said Holmes, taking her by the shoulders.

"The Cavalier! He came to me surrounded by fire!"

"And you shot at him?" I said.

"Yes, yes—only the bullets went right through him!"

Just then Charles Cary arrived. Holmes turned to meet him.

"Lord Cary, is this your gun?"

"Yes, it is. I gave it to Elizabeth for protection."

Holmes shook his head. "Under the circumstances, it strikes me as a very foolish thing to do. She has just discharged it, and might have hurt someone."

"But the bullets went right through him!" she cried again, collapsing into her brother's arms.

We were soon joined by Lady Cary and Annie, who also had heard the shots being fired. Holmes insisted everyone go downstairs while he examined the hallway, and they complied. Elizabeth had calmed down somewhat, but kept repeating the phrase "ring of fire" as they took her away.

Holmes went over to where a thin wisp of smoke still trailed in the air. He knelt and examined the floor, sweeping up a powdery substance from the floorboards and smelling it. He then ran his fingers slowly over the wall opposite from where Elizabeth Cary had been standing.

"Look at this, Watson!" he cried triumphantly.

I stepped over to where he stood, and saw a small flattened chunk of what looked like wax upon the wall.

"What is it?" I said.

"Wax!" he exclaimed. "Someone put wax bullets in that gun, Watson—that's why she thought the bullets went right through him. She evidently missed him, but even had she hit him, it would do no harm. It's an old magician's trick," he mused. "I wonder . . . And look at this," he said, showing me some powder upon the floor. "This is your 'ring of fire'!—"

"What's this?" I asked, smelling it. It had a curiously familiar odor, like burnt mushrooms.

"Lycopodium powder," he replied. "A highly flammable powder used by magicians in their stage acts. It comes from a common form of club moss, is easily obtainable, and quite safe when used correctly."

"Yes," I said. "I am familiar with it—it is used sometimes in surgery as an absorbent."

"Indeed," he murmured, and then abruptly headed off toward Miss Cary's bedroom. "Would you be so kind as to ask her to join me here, if she is up to it, Watson?"

I did as he requested, and though she protested she was all right, her brother insisted on accompanying her upstairs. When we returned to her chamber, we found Holmes on his knees examining the bottom of the window ledge. With his thumb and forefinger he carefully plucked something from the edge of the open window. I could not make out what it was.

"You left your window open tonight, Miss Cary?" he said when she entered the room.

"Y-yes," she replied, looking at her brother, who stood behind her, frowning. "I like to sleep with an open window."

"I see," said Holmes. "Do you by any chance own a black wool dress?"

She shook her head. "No, I don't. I have a black dress, the one I wore to my father's funeral, but I am certain it is not wool."

"There may indeed be an otherworldly presence in the abbey," Holmes remarked sardonically, "but whoever visited Miss Cary's room tonight was real enough—that is, unless protoplasm can suddenly turn into black wool."

He held up a small piece of cloth. It was black, of a sturdy, thick weave, such as one might find on a man's cloak. He peered down into the courtyard. "Whoever it was, they were fairly athletic—even with the vines clinging to the outside wall, that is a decent distance to climb in the dead of night, and going back down is even more hazardous."

"So the intruder came in through the window?" said Charles Cary.

"Yes. You assured me earlier that you checked the locks yourself tonight, I believe?"

"Yes, I did."

"Miss Cary did as I instructed you all to do and bolted her bedroom door as well. The only point of entry is the window . . . and if you look closely, Watson, you will observe here a faint set of fingerprints on the outside of the glass."

"Yes, yes, I see," I said, peering at the smudges on the window panes. "What now?"

Holmes put the thread in his pocket and brushed off his hands. "Someone knew exactly what they were doing, in order to produce an effect like this."

"But who put the wax bullets in the gun?" I asked.

His eyes narrowed. "That is precisely what I intend to find out, Watson."

CHAPTER FIFTEEN

OUR QUESTIONING of the Cary family led us to no further clues; Elizabeth could tell us nothing more than when she fired at the Cavalier he disappeared in a puff of smoke, which Holmes said was undoubtedly the lycopodium powder. Charles insisted that the gun was loaded with real bullets when he gave it to her, and we could find no one else who admitted to handling the gun. At Holmes's urging, Charles took the gun back from his sister.

I was seated in the east parlour the next morning when Holmes entered the room brandishing a newspaper.

"I am convinced that whoever is behind this has employed the help of a professional magician," he announced, seating himself in front of the fire. "I took the liberty of procuring a recent issue of the local paper in Torquay this morning. It just so happens that a magician by the name of Merwyn the Magnificent was playing the old opera house in Torquay last week. Coincidence? I think not," he concluded with satisfaction.

"I think I've heard of him," I said. "He plays regularly at various theatres in the East End, I believe."

Holmes looked at me in mock amazement. "I say, Watson, you surprise me, really you do. I had no idea—"

"Very well, Holmes," I answered brusquely. "I didn't say I had ever gone to see him."

"Ah, well, I wouldn't think less of you if you had," he replied, his eyes twinkling. "In any event, I see that tomorrow night this Merwyn fellow has a performance scheduled in London." He stroked his chin thoughtfully. "It might be worth my while to pay him a visit."

"I need to go into town and check up on my practice," I said. "Why don't I go talk to him for you?"

"My dear Watson," Holmes replied, "you don't look at all well. I doubt that a trip to London would be advisable for you just now."

"Oh, well—if you don't trust me," I answered huffily, "why don't you just say so?"

"My dear fellow, it isn't a question of trusting you; I simply don't want you risking your health by tramping all over London."

"Nonetheless, I feel I should go in and make an appearance at the surgery—not that McKinney isn't doing a splendid job, I'm sure, but I just don't want him feeling I've left him in the lurch all this time."

Holmes sighed. "Very well, Watson; it seems your mind's made up about this. I would never think of standing in your way once you have settled on a course of action."

I looked at him in disbelief, but saw at once the mischievous twinkle in his eye.

"Really, Holmes," I muttered, but he laughed, not his usual dry sardonic chuckle, but a deep, full-bodied laugh.

"Come, come, Watson, I'm only tweaking you. You will let me have my fun, won't you?"

"I don't see how I can prevent it," I replied, feigning irritation, but the truth was I was pleased that Holmes would entrust me with such an errand. I only hoped that I would rise to the occasion; though I didn't say it, I was still weak, and my illness, though greatly diminished, was not yet altogether gone.

"There is another reason I would appreciate you doing this for me, Watson: I am loath to leave the Cary family alone just now."

"Oh? Do you think . . . ?"

Holmes shook his head. "I don't know what to think, Watson; I only know that I fear for their safety."

"What exactly do you want me to do with this Merwyn fellow?"

"Merely observe his reaction."

"His reaction?"

"Yes. When you suggest to him that you suspect him of involvement in a crime."

"Oh? What sort of reaction am I looking for?"

"You are a student of human behaviour, Watson. A flush to the face, stammering, vehement denial—anything that would indicate his guilt."

"I see. And then?"

Holmes leaned back in his chair and laced his long fingers together behind his head. "You offer him a bribe, Watson."

"A bribe?"

"Yes. That is, you pay him to reveal who he is doing business with."

"I see. And if he won't tell me?"

Holmes smiled. "Oh, he will—provided the price is right. And we shall see that the price is indeed not only right, but irresistible."

"I am very much flattered that you would entrust me with this responsibility," I said. "I hope I will not fail you."

"No fear of that, Watson—I wouldn't send you if I thought you were not up to it," he said with unaccustomed warmth in his voice. I confess I felt a twinge of apprehension at his words, but was all the more determined that I would not disappoint his trust in me.

I TOOK the early train to London the next day, and sat gazing out the window as the granite *tors* of Devon and Dorset flew by and were replaced by the soft grassy hillsides of Hampshire and Surrey. Lulled by the motion of the train, I let my head sink back onto the seat rest and dozed off. Dream images flitted through my head as I napped, the stately halls of Torre Abbey merging in my brain with thoughts of our flat in Baker Street. In my dreams I saw Lady Cary standing in a blue dress in front of the fireplace at Baker Street, the flames reflecting off her face as she lifted it to mine . . .

When I awoke, the train was just pulling into Paddington Station, the heavy exhale of air from the steam engine like the sigh of a great leviathan. I climbed stiffly from the train and took my place among my fellow Londoners, amidst the scramble of commuters coming and going, the endless daily rush which is modern city life. A thick pulse of white steam poured from the locomotive as I strode up the ramp leading to the street. The one-legged newspaper seller was in his usual place on the sidewalk just outside the station, and I bought a *Daily Telegraph* from him.

The hustle and bustle of London felt strange to me after the monastic quiet and solitude of life at Torre Abbey. I stood on the street corner for a moment and looked around: nowhere in the city was there more of a mixture of the upper and lower classes than in front of a rail station. Elegant gentlemen in top hats and stiff black frock-coats hurried past street vendors hawking their wares; rough-looking grooms in scuffed black boots leaned against the backs of their rigs smoking and trading jokes, their cloth caps pulled low over their eyes. Middle-class families hurried into the station, their picnic baskets packed for a day trip to Surrey or Kent. It was a brilliant October day, the air bright and clear, and even the many unsavoury smells of London seemed muted in the crisp air.

I hailed a cab to my medical offices, where I paid a call on Dr. McKinney to see how things were going. His report that everything had been quiet the past few days was reassuring; it seems the flu epidemic had worn itself out, gone as quickly as it had arrived. I then headed for Baker Street, to check in on Mrs. Hudson, sort through the mail, and put my feet up for a short time before my evening excursion began.

As I entered the front hallway of 221B I was greeted by the welcome aroma of roast beef, and no sooner had I closed the door behind me than Mrs. Hudson came bustling into the hallway, wiping her hands upon her apron. Holmes had sent her a telegram saying that I was on my way, and she was evidently well prepared for me.

"Now you just come right in and have a nice glass of something, Dr. Watson, while I get some dinner on for you," she said by way of greeting.

"It's nice to see you, too, Mrs. Hudson," I replied with a smile. In her own way, our landlady was as eccentric as her most famous tenant.

I took her advice and had a glass of claret in front of the fire. I dozed off for quite some time, because when I awoke the October sun was beginning to sink reluctantly behind the buildings, reflecting red and gold upon the window panes before sliding slowly behind the town houses across the street. Outside, the clop of horses' hooves along the cobblestones increased as people made their way home at the end of their workday.

At Holmes's request, Mrs. Hudson had gone over to the theatre earlier in the day to procure a program of the evening's events, and I studied it as I sipped my claret. The language of the flyer was rather amusing: "Merwyn the Marvelous Performs Astonishing Feats of Magic and Other Death-Defying Acts!" A picture of the magician swallowing a sword accompanied the assurance that spectators would be "amazed and astonished" by his "skill and courage," and promised the added attraction of Merwyn's "lovely assistant Miss Caroline Cocoran," the "Belle of Atlanta." A picture of Miss Cocoran showed her to be a fleshy blond wearing an outfit that looked as if it were from a Parisian dance hall: corset, garters, and tights, all under a filmy skirt which left little to the imagination. I settled back in my chair and permitted myself a smile—this was a far cry from my usual trips with Holmes to violin concerts at the Royal Albert Hall. I couldn't help looking forward to seeing Merwyn the Magnificent and his lovely assistant Miss Caroline Cocoran.

Mrs. Hudson's excellent roast beef complete with Yorkshire pudding put me in an even more receptive mood, and I went off to the theatre in a cheerful mood, ready for an entertaining evening. The night was cool but clear as I settled into the back of a hansom cab, the horses' hooves clipping smartly along the cobblestones. I felt a curious sense of contentment settle over me as I gazed out the window at the cozily lit windows all around me. On the streets people headed homeward, brown paper packages tucked under their arms—a joint of beef, perhaps, or a rack of lamb. After the oppressive atmosphere of Torre Abbey, there was something comforting in the thought of my fellow Londoners all around me, inside their houses fixing dinner or getting ready to go out for the evening. I hadn't realized until just then how claustrophobic I felt at Torre Abbey, hemmed in somehow—by what or whom I did not know, but now that I was back in London I felt a sense of liberation and escape, as though I were a prisoner newly released from a long jail term.

The mood outside the theatre was festive. Orange sellers and jugglers vied with purveyors of roasted chestnuts, sweetmeats and various other savouries for the attention of the crowd gathering in front of the theatre. I was greeted by their cries as I alighted from the cab and paid the driver.

"Oy—get your meat pies here—fresh and hot!"

"Oranges, ripe and sweet—heyo!"

"Pickled eel, pickled eel—best in London!"

The street swarmed with seekers of merriment: office clerks and their sweethearts, young families out for the evening, sailors with their fancy girls—and I found such liveliness refreshing after Torre Abbey, where the dead seemed to hold more sway than the living.

The large poster in front of the theatre showed a picture of Merwyn the Marvelous inside an elaborately decorated rectangular cabinet with half a dozen swords protruding from the box, their handles pointing in every direction. He had a broad smile on his face, and the lovely Caroline Cocoran stood just above him, a sword in her hand, ready to plunge it into the box. Underneath the picture, garish lettering proclaimed "See the Sword-Box and Other Death-Defying Acts!"

I smiled to myself as I climbed up the stairs to the ticket-booth. All the cheap tickets were taken, but there were still quite a few left in the orchestra section, and I purchased a seat in the third row centre. As I gave my ticket to the ticket-taker I was jostled by someone to my left, and, turning to look, I saw an elderly gentleman, wizened and bent over from age. His heavily creased face was like a ploughed field; the hand of time had clawed deep furrows into his skin, etching the passage of years into the canvas of his cheeks. He tipped his hat to me.

"Beg pardon, sir; my apologies to you. I'm old and my balance isn't what it once was. That's why I need this," he said, indicating his cane, which was of polished mahogany with an unusual and ornate handle, a bronze head of a falcon.

"That's quite all right," I replied, and entered the theatre. It had seen better days—the red velvet curtain which covered the stage was frayed at the edges, and the ceiling was blackened with soot from years of gaslighting. The performance was late in beginning, and I took the opportunity to study my program. Merwyn the Marvelous had just returned from a tour of Germany, it seemed, where he "stunned and delighted audiences everywhere with his magical expertise and showmanship."

Finally the ragtag band of musicians in the orchestra pit began to play a somewhat halting waltz, and I turned my attention to the upcoming performance. The curtain opened to reveal a stage bare except for a single pine coffin. The lighting on stage was dim, and suddenly there was a puff of smoke. The audience murmured as the lid of the coffin opened slowly and a little man got out. At first I wondered who he was, but then realized from his costume—formal evening wear, complete with a yellow-lined silk cape—that he was indeed Merwyn the Magnificent. The promotional posters had done a fine job making him seem a good deal larger, but now that he stood on the stage before us, I guessed that he was no more than five foot four in his stocking feet.

He looked out over the audience and smiled.

"Welcome," he said in a surprisingly deep and resonant voice, "to an evening of terror and magic!"

Merwyn the Magnificent did not disappoint. Assisted by the lovely Miss Caroline Cocoran, he performed the sword-box trick advertised on the poster, as well as various sleights of hand involving playing cards, little red balls, live doves, and even a live fish. Finally he came to what he referred to as "the most challenging, the most dangerous, the most death-defying challenge of all": to catch a bullet between his teeth while blindfolded—a bullet fired from the other side of the stage out of a gun held by Miss Caroline Cocoran. The feat, he said, had been taught to him by an Indian swami who had the ability to hold his breath underwater for half an hour or more.

By that time I was feeling somewhat sleepy. I had risen early, and Mrs. Hudson's excellent roast-beef dinner and the accompanying claret was beginning to have a soporific effect upon me. I sat watching the stage through half-closed eyes as Miss Cocoran took aim at the magician, who stood in a dramatic pose worthy of William Tell, his eyes covered by a red kerchief. I was aware of the heavy floral perfume of the lady next to me as Miss Cocoran raised the pistol, took aim and fired.

A gasp came from the audience as the shot rang out, echoing from the ceiling of the domed theatre. There was a moment of silence and then a louder gasp. I sat up in my seat and looked at the stage as Merwyn slumped to his knees, a red stain blossoming on the front of his shirt. Nervous titters came from the crowd; they assumed at first, as I did, that this was a ploy, an act of showmanship to heighten the effect of the trick. However, when his body pitched forward onto the stage, and was followed by a scream from Miss Cocoran, cries erupted from the audience. Miss Cocoran let the gun fall to the floor and rushed to the aid of the fallen magician. Her face stricken, she looked out at the crowd.

"Help! We need a doctor—please help!"

Without thinking twice, I leaped from my seat, and, bounding over the first two rows of horrified spectators, vaulted onto the stage. I am not certain how I accomplished this, but within moments I was at his side. A quick examination revealed that he had indeed been shot, the bullet piercing the left lung. I quickly removed the kerchief from his forehead and attempted to stanch the flow of blood from the wound. Caroline Cocoran looked on helplessly as I tried vainly to stop the pinkish flow of oxygen-rich blood from the lung. I could tell at once the wound was serious, probably fatal—the loss of blood was too swift, and I could see the life draining away from his face as he lay there, pale and still. Within minutes he had no pulse at all, and the blood which had bubbled so quickly from his body now only trickled from his lifeless form. I covered his face with my own handkerchief and attempted to calm Miss Cocoran, who was sobbing uncontrollably.

"It was supposed to be wax bullets!" she cried over and over, the tears streaking down her cheeks carving little rivulets through the heavy makeup she wore.

The appearance of several police constables did nothing to calm the spectators, who were on the verge of hysteria. The crowd appeared evenly split between those who were clearly horrified at the sudden tragedy and those who just wanted to get a better look, craning their necks to see over the huddle of people standing around the poor magician's body. Finally, with the arrival of more police, the crowd was ushered from the hall. Miss Cocoran was placed under arrest, but not even the sergeant who placed the handcuffs upon her looked as though he believed that was anything more than a formality.

"Wonder who changed those bullets?" he said as I followed the sad procession out of the theatre.

It was exactly the question I was asking myself.

CHAPTER SIXTEEN

I T WAS an odd assortment of people who shuffled into Scotland Yard late that night: three or four grimy-looking stagehands, a handful of startled-looking ushers and the ticket-taker, along with a teary-eyed Miss Cocoran and myself. We were greeted by an irritable Inspector Lestrade, who had evidently been roused from his bed. His sharp, ferret-like face was lined with sleep; his hair was rumpled and there were bags under his eyes.

"What's all this about, Watson?" he growled at me, drawing himself up to his full height, which was not much. He looked as though he had dressed hurriedly; his shirt collar poked out unevenly from his waistcoat, and his cuffs flapped about like small white wings, minus the restraining aid of cuff links. We stood in the foyer to his office, a waiting room undistinguished by its furnishings—wooden benches lining the wall, a few scattered chairs, and a desk at one end.

I explained as best I could what had happened, but did not mention the connection to Torre Abbey or the fact that I was at the theatre that night at the behest of Sherlock Holmes.

Lestrade sighed and shook his head as the desk sergeant entered and handed him a steaming cup of tea. "It's a bad business, Watson, when murderers take to killing magicians in front of a crowd of five hundred. What does it mean, I wonder?" He took a sip of tea and jerked back, waving his hand in front of his face. "Bloody hell!" he yelped. "Burned my tongue!" He turned to the desk sergeant, a ruddy-faced young man with a tiny blond moustache. "You could have warned me it was boiling hot, Flannery," he said sharply.

Sergeant Flannery rolled his eyes. "I thought tea was supposed to be bloody hot," he muttered under his breath.

"What was that?" Lestrade said.

"Nothing, sir," the sergeant replied with a glance at me. I admit I agreed with him—when Lestrade was worked up, as he certainly was now, discretion was indeed the better part of valour.

"So now what have we got, Watson?" he said, rubbing his forehead wearily. "We've got one dead magician and a couple of stagehands with no motive whatsoever for killing him. Puts them out of work, in fact—closes the show right up, a thing like that, I should think." He looked over the motley collection of backstage fellows, who stood silently staring back at him, their eyes wide with disbelief. I didn't blame them—it must have been quite a shock for them to find themselves suddenly at the police station when less than an hour ago they were going about their business backstage at the theatre.

Lestrade took a wary sip of tea. "Take them downstairs and get them some tea and a bite to eat, will you, Flannery?" he said. "It's going to be a long night."

"Right you are, sir," Flannery replied. "This way, lads," he said to the crew, who followed him obediently down the hall.

"Wait just a moment—Miss Cocoran, is it?" Lestrade said as Caroline Cocoran turned to go with them. Covered in a long cloak, she had been standing behind one of the stagehands, as if she did not want to be noticed. With her blond curls and heavily rouged cheeks, however, she couldn't help standing out from the dishevelled company of stagehands who shuffled meekly after Sergeant Flannery. She stood in front of Lestrade, trembling a little as she pulled the cloak tighter around her shoulders.

"Let's go into my office," Lestrade said, and Miss Cocoran and I followed him into the small room. A thick oak desk littered with papers sat underneath a pair of tall French windows overlooking a courtyard at the back of the building.

On top of a tall filing cabinet was an improvised tea service: a cracked blue-willow teapot sat among several mismatched mugs. Lestrade poured some tea from the pot and handed it to Miss Cocoran.

"Sugar?" he said as she took the chipped white porcelain mug of tea from him.

"Yes, please," she replied. She looked at me with tragic eyes. "Do you know who killed poor Merwyn?"

I shook my head. "I regret to say that I do not, Miss Cocoran."

"I understand you were the one who fired the fatal shot," Lestrade said to Miss Cocoran, handing her the sugar bowl.

Her hand shook as she spooned three lumps of sugar into her tea. "It was a trick we'd done a hundred times," she said softly. "I thought the bullets were wax, so help me God—I swears I did."

Lestrade poured me a cup of tea, then settled himself in the scarred old captain's chair behind his desk. "Do you have any idea at all who might have switched the bullets?" he said, putting his feet up on the desk. As he did I saw that his socks were unmatched—one dark-blue, one brown. He didn't seem to notice, however, and waved Miss Cocoran to a chair. "Please have a seat—make yourself comfortable." He seemed less irritable now; the combination of tea and the presence of an attractive woman appeared to have cheered him up.

Miss Cocoran sat down gingerly, as if she were afraid she might break the chair. "I don't know as who might have wanted to kill poor Merwyn," she said sadly. "I mean, he could be a right bastard sometimes when he didn't get his own way, but mostly he was a lamb, really he was." She looked at Inspector Lestrade with large, tear-streaked blue eyes.

"Hmm," Lestrade replied, studying her. "Were the two of you . . . ?" He paused and coughed delicately.

Her cheeks reddened through the thick pancake makeup she wore. "Why—what does that matter?" she said softly, her voice unsteady.

Lestrade shrugged. "It might not matter—but then again it might. Perhaps someone who also cared for you wanted Mr. Merwyn out of the way—or perhaps you yourself wanted him out of the way so you would be free for another man."

Miss Cocoran's lower lip trembled as tears gathered at the corners of her eyes. "No, it wasn't like that. I cared for him— truly I did. I don't know what I'll do now that he's gone. Or how I'll live," she added, a tragic edge to her voice which didn't sound entirely ingenuous—after all, she was an actress. She wiped a tear from her eye. "He was my bread and butter, you know."

Lestrade studied her, his dark eyes narrowed, his sharp little face looking even more like a ferret's than usual. "Yes," he said slowly. "Yes, I can see that."

Miss Cocoran leaned forward in her chair. "May I . . . ?" she said quietly.

"What?" said Lestrade.

"I have to . . . do you have a loo here I can use?" she said with a nervous glance at me.

"Oh, by all means," Lestrade replied, rising from his chair. "Just ask Flannery—he'll show you."

"Thank you," she replied. A faint aroma of musky scent lingered after her as she slipped through the heavy door of Lestrade's office.

"Well, Watson, what do you think? Is the lady a murderer?" Lestrade asked, draining the last of his tea and setting the cup down among the mound of papers which covered his desk.

I leaned back in my chair as if I were considering the question. I wasn't sure if Holmes wanted our business in Devon to be made known to Scotland Yard, but I felt it was important to clear Miss Cocoran from any suspicion of murder, however faint.

"I believe the magician was killed by forces as yet unknown to us," I said slowly, choosing my words carefully.

Lestrade stared at me, his small eyes wide with puzzlement. "Good God, Watson, what on earth are you talking about?" he said, his voice thick with disdain.

I took a deep breath. It was now or never—I must either explain what I meant or be silent upon the point.

I chose the former, praying that Holmes would not be upset with me for sharing the details of his investigation with Scotland Yard. I explained to Lestrade the circumstances of how I came to be at the theatre that night, including the whole history of the mysterious hauntings at Torre Abbey, and when I had finished he leaned back in his chair.

"Well, I'll be blasted," he said finally, and burst out laughing. "Has it finally come to this, then—Mr. Holmes investigating ghosts at country houses?" he said through his laughter. "I wouldn't have thought it, truly I wouldn't—Sherlock Holmes, of all people!"

I was naturally irked at his reception of the information I had volunteered, and it showed in my voice.

"I can assure you, Inspector Lestrade, that Holmes is not chasing will-o'-the-wisps out in Devon—there is no doubt in my mind that something very evil is at work at Torre Abbey, and I am equally certain that whoever is behind these 'hauntings' is also responsible for the death of this unfortunate magician!"

There was a knock on the door and Sergeant Flannery poked his head into the room.

"Yes, Flannery, what is it?" said Lestrade.

"Begging pardon, sir," the sergeant replied, "but one of the lads backstage says he saw something, and I thought you might want to know."

Lestrade sat up in his chair. "Oh? Where is he?"

"Just outside, sir."

"Well, what are you waiting for? Show him in!"

The sergeant withdrew and ushered into the room one of the stagehands, a young lad of fifteen or so. He was dressed in a shabby brown jacket two sizes too small for him, over a pair of patched and faded grey trousers. He clutched his cloth cap in his hands, and when he saw Lestrade his pale face went a little paler.

"Sergeant Flannery says you have some information for us, Master—?"

"S-Stevens, sir," the boy stuttered, his nerves getting the better of him.

Lestrade evidently noticed the boy's discomfort, for he continued in a more kindly voice. "Well, then, Master Stevens, what have you to tell us?"

Master Stevens glanced at me and then at the pot of tea on top of the filing cabinet.

"I'll bet you would like some tea," I said. "Lestrade, I suppose you have some biscuits around here somewhere?"

"What? Oh, yes, of course—by all means. Try the bottom drawer of the filing cabinet."

I opened the drawer and found an opened box of chocolate biscuits nestled in among the files and papers. I fished it out and poured Master Stevens a cup of tea.

"Ta very much," he said, greedily slurping down the tea while piling as many biscuits into his mouth as he could manage. "Mmm," he said as he stuffed in yet another, "I like chocolate."

"Good," said Lestrade, drumming his fingers upon his desk.

"Now that you are suitably refreshed, I believe you have something to tell us?"

"Right," the boy replied, his mouth still full. "What I seen was this: about quarter of an hour before the show was s'pposed to start, I sees this old gentl'man wandering around backstage. And I says to myself, 'Now, who could that be?' Seein' as I ain't never seen him before, I takes it upon myself to find out who he is, like—I mean, he's well-enough dressed an' all that, but still—"

"So you spoke to him?" Lestrade interrupted.

The boy shook his head and stuffed another biscuit into his mouth. "No, I was comin' to that. Like I said, I was about to ask 'im who he was, but just at that moment Mr. Dawson calls me to do somethin'—he's the boss, is Mr. Dawson—and then a few minutes later when I come back, the old fellow is gone."

Lestrade leaned forward and laced his fingers together on top of his desk. "You say he was well dressed?"

The boy nodded, his mouth full. "Mmm—like a proper gentl'man, he was. Carried a cane, real fancy like."

I suddenly remembered the old gentleman who had bumped into me as I entered the theatre, and how his cane had struck me as unusual. "Did you get a good look at the handle of the cane?" I said to Master Stevens.

"It was some kind of bird, I think—had a nasty look in its eye, if you ask me."

I turned to Lestrade. "I'd be willing to bet that's the same man I saw upon entering the theatre."

"Oh?" he replied. "What man?"

I told him about the incident, which had not struck me as much of anything at the time; it was only the ornate handle of the cane which caught my eye.

"Hmm," he said when I had finished. "Are you telling me that our main suspect is an elderly gentleman with a cane?"

I shifted in my chair. "I suppose it looks that way."

Lestrade rose from his chair, went to the window and looked out at the faint glow of gaslight in the sky. London was never entirely dark; there was always the reflection of gaslights in the sky, even in the middle of the night.

Lestrade ran a hand through his disheveled hair. "Why kill a bloody magician?"

CHAPTER SEVENTEEN

T HE ANSWER to that is quite simple, Watson," Sherlock Holmes said, stirring sugar into his tea. "The real question is not *why*—but *who*."

"Why, then?" I said, unable to conceal a certain irritability from my voice. I had spent the entire night before at Scotland Yard, taking the first train to Devon in the morning, without so much as an hour of sleep, and now I was feeling a bit put out by Holmes's superior attitude. After relating to him the events of the previous night in their entirety over breakfast, I was now feeling light-headed from lack of sleep.

We were seated in the spacious dining room. The mid-morning sun was pouring in through the creamy lace curtains, filling the room with an ethereal glow that, tired as I was, I found mesmerizing.

"Merwyn was killed so that he would not talk, Watson," Holmes said, taking a piece of toast from the tray. I noticed that out here in Devon, even Holmes ate with a hearty appetite. The country air appeared to have done him some good—his cheeks glowed with an unaccustomed ruddiness, and, though still lean, he had lost the gaunt look which had so often caused me to worry about his health.

"Oh?" I replied. "Do you mean that whoever killed Merwyn knew that I was coming to talk with him?"

"Most certainly. There can be no doubt of it now—I am only glad that you yourself were not injured," Holmes replied, all traces of flippancy gone from his voice. "I would never forgive myself had I sent you into danger, Watson. I quite honestly did not expect so desperate a step from our opponent—really I didn't." He stood and gazed out the window at the bright day, at Nature apparently so unaware of the darkness which had descended upon the Cary family.

He turned back from the window and sighed. "But now I see more of what—or whom—we are dealing with. By performing so desperate and violent an act, our opponent has tipped his hand, so to speak. We now know something I suspected but can now confirm: we are undoubtedly being watched."

I shivered in spite of the warmth of the room.

"Someone is aware of our every move," Holmes continued, "and so we must take the utmost caution to act in secrecy and avoid discussing our plans with the Cary family as much as possible."

"Do you mean you suspect . . . ?" I said, but Holmes shook his head.

"I don't know as yet who it is," he replied solemnly, "and until I do we cannot afford to trust anyone." He turned back to the window, his sharp profile etched against the soft morning light.

Our conversation was put to an end by the arrival of Charles Cary, who came striding into the room with his usual energy. One look at my friend's glum face and it was clear to our host that all was not well.

"Good heavens, Dr. Watson, what's happened?" he said. "Did things not go well in London?"

"That would be an understatement," Holmes replied.

I shook my head. "My trip to London was a failure, I'm afraid."

Holmes proceeded to tell Lord Cary of the unfortunate Merwyn's demise, leaving out, I noticed, any mention of the mysterious elderly gentleman with the curious cane handle.

"Good Lord," Cary said when Holmes had finished. "Thank goodness Dr. Watson wasn't injured."

"Yes, indeed," Holmes replied, and I could not tell if he suspected Lord Cary of any part in poor Merwyn's death. I could hardly imagine Charles Cary would have called us down to Devon to help, only then to conspire against us, but I was beginning to think that everything at Torre Abbey was topsy-turvy.

"You look tired, Dr. Watson," Cary observed.

I admitted that I was feeling a bit dizzy from fatigue.

"Why don't you go upstairs and rest, Watson?" Holmes said. "You've done quite enough for the time being."

I took his advice and trudged upstairs to my room. Throwing myself upon the bed, I fell instantly into a deep slumber, as though I had been drugged.

By the time I awoke, it was mid-afternoon, and I lay in bed trying to rouse myself from the languor of sleep which had wrapped itself around my limbs. There was something about Torre Abbey, in the very air itself, which seemed to pull one deeper into sleep than normal. The barrier between consciousness and sleep felt thinner; dreams were more vivid, and it was harder to awaken each day from the torpour of sleep.

There was a knock on my door.

"Yes?" I called, rubbing my eyes.

It was Holmes. "What do you say to a trip to visit the Nortons?"

"Very well—I'll just put on my coat," I said, sitting up in bed. I felt woozy and disoriented, but the nap had done me some good.

Holmes was waiting for me by the front door, and we set out across the fields toward the village of Cockington, which was only about a mile to the west of Torre Abbey. As we climbed over the crest of a hill, I could see the thatched cottages of Cockington, all nestled together like eggs in a basket. The rounded Norman doorways of Cockington Church attested to its ancient lineage, and as we approached the church, surrounded by majestic elm trees, I saw the rectory, a long low building set next to the church itself. The chapel contained a polygonal turret on the north side, with medieval-looking slit windows, which added to the considerable charm of the place.

Holmes knocked on the thick oak door and we waited while the sound reverberated through the building. After a moment, we heard the sharp click of footsteps upon stone, and then Lydia Norton's voice called to us from somewhere within the building.

"Come in—I'll be right there."

The entrance door was so low that even I had to bend down to get through it. We entered the vestibule, which smelt of apples and nutmeg. The room was dominated by a large crucifix on the far wall. Underneath it was a sturdy oak table, upon which sat a bowl of apples. At that moment Lydia Norton appeared to greet us, wearing an apron and wiping flour from her hands.

"Ah—Mr. Holmes, Dr. Watson, come in. My brother was called away suddenly, but he shouldn't be long. Pardon my appearance," she added, whisking the apron from around her waist and tossing it onto a chair. "One of our parishioners has been taken ill and I thought an apple tart was in order for the family."

"How very public-spirited of you, Miss Norton," Holmes replied.

"It is expected of a parish priest's sister, Mr. Holmes," she answered with a smile. "Tending the sick does not come especially naturally to me, but when it comes to cooking for them I have no objections to augmenting my brother's duties. If you'll just follow me, I'll get you settled while I go finish up in the kitchen," she said, leading us through a narrow twisting corridor. Stepping through a low doorway, we entered a simple but comfortable sitting room. Two long, narrow stained-glass windows looked out over a small courtyard. The furniture was comfortable but worn; a rich Oriental carpet covering the floor was the only outward sign of opulence.

"Make yourselves at home while I see about some tea," she said, indicating two leather armchairs by the fire. I sank into one of the chairs gratefully; the chill in the air in Devon was unremitting, and I could still feel the effects of my illness.

"Please don't go to any trouble," Holmes replied, but she shook her head.

"It's no trouble at all, I can assure you; I was going to have some myself. I'll just pop the pies in the oven and then we'll have some tea."

She disappeared and returned some minutes later with a tea tray. "We have no servants," she explained, setting the tray on the sideboard. "My brother thinks his parishioners might object to any show of opulence on our part, so we make do without. It's not so bad—he helps out in the kitchen when he can, and even does a spot of dusting from time to time."

"I see," said Holmes.

"My brother is a great one for setting an example, Mr. Holmes. He believes in the good old-fashioned Christian ethic of hard work, and he tries to practice what he preaches."

Holmes leaned back in his chair and interlaced his long fingers. "And you, Miss Norton? What do you believe?"

The question appeared to catch her off guard.

"Well, Mr. Holmes, I don't know if I can answer that directly. I'm not exactly sure what you mean."

Holmes smiled. "What about the Cary family? Are they good Catholics, do you think?"

Lydia Norton fixed her quick, intelligent eyes on Holmes.

They were large, hazel in colour, and bright as a spaniel's. "The Cary family history is not without its blemishes, you know."

Holmes raised an eyebrow. "Oh?"

She nodded. "Oh, yes," she replied, unable to disguise the satisfaction in her voice. Here, I thought, was a woman who liked nothing better than a good piece of gossip, especially about a family so much more illustrious than her own. Everyone in Torquay lived in the shadow of the Cary family in one way or another, and it must have been an especially bitter pill to her to be the spinster sister of a parish priest without even a maid, while Marion Cary lived in luxury just down the road.

"How much do you know about the Cary family?" she said slowly.

Holmes shrugged. "Far less than you, I've no doubt. You've lived here for . . . ?"

"Twenty-six years," she shot back, as though the words weighed so heavily upon her that she could hardly wait to be rid of them. "Twenty-six years," she repeated softly, shaking her head as though she couldn't believe it herself. Her face softened, and for instance I had a glimpse of the young woman she must have been, the lines of her handsome face softened and rounded with youth. It was the kind of face which, if it didn't turn heads, would grow on you, and I imagined that when she was young some might have called her beautiful.

She sighed, and in that sigh I felt all the disappointments of a life spent as the sister of a parish priest—a handsome woman, intelligent and lively, destined never to have a family of her own, a husband to warm her bed at night, but to live instead as a spinster, in the shadow of the rich and glamorous Cary family. And then to know, on top of it, that her brother was in love with Marion Cary . . . there was no doubt in my mind that he was, of course, just as I could feel myself falling under her spell.

Lydia Norton rose and poured Holmes and myself more tea. "So, Mr. Holmes, what do you want to know?"

"Anything you feel would be of interest," he replied evenly.

She smiled, showing a row of small, even white teeth, sharp and pointed as a terrier's.

"Well, now, that could take a while . . ."

"What do you know of Marion Cary's life before she married Victor Cary?"

Lydia Norton shook her head. "What everyone else in town knows, I suppose—that she lost the real love of her life, and that Victor Cary was a consolation prize."

"Really?" said Holmes, but our conversation was interrupted by the appearance of Father Norton. Instead of his clerical garb, he was dressed to go out, wearing a blue pea jacket and oilskin cap.

"Why, hello," he said when he saw us. "To what do we owe the pleasure of this visit?"

"I hope we have not inconvenienced you or your sister," Holmes replied, but the vicar shook his head.

"Not at all. You rescued Lydia from her baking—not one of her favourite tasks, eh, Lydia?" he answered jovially, to which his sister responded with a tight smile.

"I was just telling Mr. Holmes and Dr. Watson something of the history of the Cary family."

"Ah, yes," her brother replied. "The illustrious Cary family. The villagers around here love to gossip about them—the closest thing we have here in South Devon to a royal family, I suppose. I say, Mr. Holmes, I don't suppose you'd like to go letterboxing with me?" said Father Norton as he pulled on a pair of rubber boots.

"I can think of nothing more delightful," Holmes replied, to my surprise. Though my friend was astonishingly athletic when he chose to be, he seldom took exercise for its own sake, preferring instead the life of the mind. Indeed, it had occurred to me that only his highly strung nature and his periods of complete disregard for food kept him from turning into the whale-like creature his corpulent brother Mycroft had become.

"You know of the sport, then?" Norton said.

"Yes, indeed—in fact, I was just telling Watson about it the other day," Holmes answered. "What do you think, Watson? Shall we accompany Father Norton on his ramble?"

"I don't see why not," I replied.

"Excellent! If you'll just bear with me for a moment, I'll find you something suitable to wear," Father Norton said, fishing through a bundle of coats in the hall closet. "You may thank me for these later," he continued, extracting two rubber raincoats. "It can get quite nasty out there, and it's good to be well prepared."

"I, for one, enjoy a good hike, though I'm surprised Holmes here agreed to it so readily," I said as the priest handed us each a rubber jacket.

"There's a lot about me still to surprise you, Watson," Holmes said as he donned the rain gear.

CHAPTER EIGHTEEN

⁓

I T WASN'T too far to the moors, and soon we were tramping along behind Father Norton, sweat gathering inside our heavy rubber raincoats. To our left were gently rolling green farm fields; to our right, the vast, forbiddingly beautiful waste-land of the Devon moors. It was populated only by hard-scrabble shrubs and the occasional stunted tree; otherwise, it was a lonely, arid plain of stubborn weeds and gorse. Dotted with bogs and swamps, the soil was uncultivatable and uninviting, save to those few travellers who, like ourselves, sought out the subtle splendours of its barren beauty.

We followed the priest in silence for some time, with only the sound of the wind across the heath as company as we trudged along single file, each of us lost in our own thoughts. The wind on the Devon moors is unlike anywhere else; it lies still for a time, then, when you least expect it, rushes suddenly at you like a freight train. Weather in the West Country, Father Norton told us, is as unpredictable as in the Lake District; sun and rain come and go without so much as a by your leave, fol-lowing after one another with hardly any time in between. It is possible to step from a perfectly sunny day into a pocket of rain and come out the other side half a mile later back into the sun.

As we approached the crest of a hillock, Father Norton

turned towards us. His usual sardonic expression was gone, and the look on his face was that of a happy child.

"You perhaps think it odd, Mr. Holmes, but I find I am never more at peace than when I am tramping about the moors in my rubber boots, looking for the next clue to find a letter-box."

"On the contrary, Father Norton, I don't find it odd at all," Holmes replied. "After all, a man of the cloth may find the presence of the Deity all around in Nature."

Father Norton stopped walking. He studied the ground, turning a stone over with his toe. At first I thought he had found a clue, but then I saw he had something on his mind.

"I may not strike you as someone eminently fitted out for the priesthood, I suppose," he said in a low voice.

"Not necessarily," Holmes answered.

"I suppose all sorts of men answer the call of the Church," I offered.

Norton let a brief laugh escape his lips—a quick, bitter sound. I was surprised; his jaunty manner had not led me to suspect there was any hidden sorrow beneath it.

"Yes, I suppose they do," he replied, and continued walking. "In my case, however, it was rather a matter of the call answering me."

"Oh?" said Holmes. "How so?"

The priest let a out a sigh. We stood in front of an outcropping of rocks and boulders such as one finds scattered across the hillsides of Devon. He set his walking stick next to a large grey boulder jutting out of the ground like a sleeping leviathan.

"I see no point in trying to hide from you something which is bound to come out sooner or later," he said, fingering the handle of his walking stick, which was a brass lion's head. He ran his fingertips along the animal's wavy metal mane and looked down at his shoes.

"It may not have escaped you that I harbour certain . . . feelings . . . for Marion Cary," he continued. "I know Dr. Watson here, observant fellow that he is, has seen me in her company enough to notice that even though I wear this dog collar"—he pointed to the white priest's band around his neck—"I am still a man, and subject to what any healthy man may feel towards a beautiful woman. I just want you to know, Mr. Holmes, that although you may consider me a suspect in this case, I would never—*could* never—do anything that would cause Marion Cary a moment's unease."

Holmes leaned back against the rock and regarded the priest through half-closed eyes. "I am glad to hear it. However, I am not at all convinced that Lady Cary is the target of these strange occurrences."

"Who, then?" I said, but Holmes shook his head.

"There are several points upon which I am clear, but there are many curious aspects of this case, and I have found that nothing is so detrimental to the investigative process than reaching erroneous conclusions early on." He turned to Father Norton. "But I am most interested in what you were saying. You and Lady Cary have a—history, then?"

The priest sighed again. "I don't know if you could call it that. Years ago I had hope that my feelings might some day be reciprocated, but that was before . . ."

He trailed off and looked in the direction of the eastern sky, where clouds were beginning to darken the rolling landscape. Patches of sun escaped through the cloud cover, shafts of yellow spilling down onto the hills here and there. The effect, I thought, was curiously biblical, like the hand of God descending from heaven to dispense beams of sunlight onto a darkening land.

"You were going to say that was before she met Victor Cary?" I said.

Norton looked at me, confusion registering momentarily in his swarthily handsome face. "Victor?" A sound escaped him which was in between a laugh and a snort of disgust. "Good Lord, no! Victor was . . . well, he was there to collect the spoils in the end."

Holmes said nothing, but his keen grey eyes were fixed upon the priest's face.

I could not resist, however. "Your sister spoke of someone else in Lady Cary's life—it was not you, then?" I said, my heart beating faster in my chest as I thought of our twilight visit to the cemetery and the lady in white.

Norton looked back at Holmes. "I thought you knew. I never—I mean, with your ability to ferret out details of people's lives, I just never imagined you would miss something like that. I mean, forgive me, but everyone in town knew, for God's sake."

"Knew what?" I said, bursting with curiosity.

"Now I *am* in a quandary, gentlemen," Norton said slowly. "I feel it would be inappropriate for me to reveal something which is really entirely between the lady and her conscience."

"Your reticence does you credit," Holmes replied. "However, rest assured that I am not entirely ignorant of the presence of this personage in the lady's past. I will of course do everything in my power to treat whatever you may tell me with the utmost delicacy and discretion. Nonetheless," he added, peering intently at the priest, "I will use any information you give me to aid my efforts to rid the Cary family of whoever—or whatever—is tormenting them."

Norton pushed a lock of black hair from his forehead. The wind had picked up, sweeping briskly across the broad flat plain, cutting through my raincoat and sending a chill through my body.

"Very well, Mr. Holmes. I believe you and Dr. Watson to be men of honour, and I hope you take me for the same." He paused and took a deep breath.

"There was a man before Victor Cary, a man who I believe truly captured Marion Cary's heart. His name was Christopher Leganger, and he was a dashing fellow—even I could see that." He paused and wiped a bit of mud from his cheek. "Christopher means 'Beloved of God' . . . odd irony, isn't it? And here I am, the one who entered the priesthood. Still, I suppose I'm the lucky one in a way, though it may not feel like it."

"What do you mean?" I said.

"I'm the only one of Marion Cary's suitors who is still alive."

"Yes," said Holmes. "This Leganger fellow—we saw his grave. How did he die?"

"He was killed in a hunting accident," the priest replied. "Fell off his horse. Odd, really—he was the best horseman I've ever seen, myself included. I don't want to sound immodest, but I once knew my way around a jumping course . . . still, Leganger was fearless, and could tame any horse. In the end the Grim Reaper comes to all of us, I suppose, and it's not a bad way to go.

"After he was gone, I thought I might have a chance with Marion, but . . . well, I suppose I can't blame her for choosing Victor Cary. He could give her everything I couldn't: money, security, even a title." He looked down at his feet. "I could never believe that she loved, him, though—or maybe I just didn't want to believe it."

He sighed and poked at the ground with his walking stick. "Well, a man can stand being disappointed in love by the same woman once, but somehow twice was too much for me, and that's when I entered the brotherhood of the Church. I know what you're thinking," he said, smiling ruefully. "Even at the time it felt a bit like a melodramatic gesture to me, but the Church seemed like the perfect place to hide from my feelings.

"I found out that there are some things you can't really hide from, of course, but by then I had grown accustomed to the regularity of religious life, and there was something comforting in the rituals of the Church. There's something to be said for routine, for having one's choices narrowed down. I didn't have to think about the subject which tormented me most."

"So that's what you meant when you said that the Church didn't call you, but you called it," I said.

"Something like that," he replied with a wan smile. "Do you think it very wicked of me to enter the Church without being a man of fervent faith? I've tried to be a good priest, and I have taken the vow of chastity seriously—something which was not easy for me at first. I got used to it, though," he said. "It makes for a certain peacefulness of spirit, believe it or not. And I'm not a hypocrite; I have faith, in my own way."

"And for some years you have been Marion Cary's priest and confessor?" said Holmes.

Father Norton looked at him, his black eyes solemn. "You know that to reveal anything Marion said to me would be a violation of my oath and a violation of the sanctity of the confessional."

"Yes, indeed," Holmes replied. "I wasn't suggesting such a thing. This . . . hunting mishap in which Leganger died. You say it was an accident?"

Father Norton looked at Holmes, alarm in his eyes. "Why do you ask that?"

Holmes shrugged. "It just seems odd, as you say, that such an excellent horseman would fall from his horse."

"Even the best riders fall sometimes, Mr. Holmes. Luck as well as skill plays a part in every endeavour in life—even your own profession is not without the element of luck."

Holmes smiled. "Touché . . . and, as you say, even the best riders fall sometimes."

Father Norton looked up at the sky. "I don't mean to rush you, gentlemen, but I believe a storm is brewing."

"Really?" I said. Even though clouds gathered in the west, the dying sun was still shining through them upon the gently rolling landscape with its sparse dotting of gnarled and stunted trees. The wind had picked up, though, I noticed.

"When you have lived in the West Country as long as I have, you begin to know these things," Norton answered, looking at his map. "If I have read my clues correctly, we are almost there."

We followed him past a copse of slanted trees, bent over from fighting against the wind which whipped so fiercely across the flattened landscape. At the bottom of a shallow gully he gave a little cry and bent down to pick up a metal object from the ground. I recognized it immediately from my days in India: it was an old ammunition tin, bent and battered, but still solid enough.

"We use all sorts of strange containers as letterboxes," Father Norton remarked as he opened the tin. "Ammunition tins are common, actually, because they're sturdy and durable. That's odd," he said. "There's a message inside."

"What's so odd about that?" I inquired.

"Well, I've never seen one before—usually the letterboxers just leave their stamp."

"May I see it?" said Holmes, his eyes gleaming with curiosity.

"I don't see why not—since it doesn't say who the intended reader is," Norton replied, handing it to Holmes.

The note was written upon a simple piece of good quality bond paper torn in half. In large bold strokes someone had written simply: "Monday—4."

"Most curious," said Holmes, examining it carefully.

"But what can it mean?" said Father Norton.

"Perhaps it was left here on a Monday which fell on the fourth of the month," I suggested.

Holmes shook his head. "It's possible, but I rather think not. In that case you would have expected the message to include the month. And neither the fourth of this month nor the last fell upon a Monday."

"What do you think it is, then?" said Father Norton.

"I have my theories," Holmes replied, "but one thing I am certain of: we must replace it so that it can be read by its intended target, otherwise it will do us no good at all."

"What good might it possibly do us?" said Father Norton, bewilderment stamped across his sensual face.

"Possibly none at all," Holmes replied, carefully folding the paper and replacing it in the tin receptacle. "Now then, Father Norton, I don't suppose I can persuade you not to stamp the registry just this once?"

"Why on earth not?" the priest replied. "We came all the way out here—"

"Yes, I know," Holmes interrupted. "It does seem a pity, but what if I tell you that a life may depend upon it?"

"Mr. Holmes, I know they say you have strange methods, but I fail to understand how leaving my stamp in this letterbox could possibly cause harm to anyone?"

"Because that would be evidence we were here. If whoever left this message knows that we saw it, it greatly diminishes my capacity to help the Cary family."

The priest shook his head. "Very well, Mr. Holmes. I don't understand, but I'll do what you say."

"What makes you think the message was left by—" I began, but Holmes shook his head in reply.

"I'll explain later," he said, looking up at the sky, where the sheet of dark clouds was blowing in more swiftly now from the west. "In the meantime, it appears Father Norton is right: we'd better curtail our hike and make our way back as quickly as possible if we want to avoid getting thoroughly drenched."

"We're closer to Torre Abbey now than to Cockington," the priest said. "I suggest we head there."

We turned back and made our way across the moors as rapidly as we could while the clouds, swollen with rain, gathered above us. Before long the rain began to fall, a fine spray at first, followed by big heavy droplets which fell from the sky like bullets, pelting our shoulders so hard it hurt. We pulled our coats tighter around us and ran for it.

"That's the thing about the West Country," Father Norton shouted as we dashed across the muddy ground. "You never have much warning in case of rain! But sometimes these showers end as abruptly as they start," he added, leaping over a puddle.

Unfortunately, this was not one of those showers. A fierce wind whipped up, sending our coats flapping around our ankles, and the fury of the storm only increased as we ran. We covered a good mile or so in the rain, and by the time we were in sight of the abbey we were soaked. The clock tower was a welcome sight, standing stolid and gloomy in the downpour, and we hurried inside, stamping our feet on the stone floor.

We were met by Lady Cary, who soon saw to it that we warmed ourselves before a blazing fire in the west parlour, plying us with brandy as we peeled off our wet outergarments. The raincoats had done a tolerable job of keeping us dry. We hadn't been settled long in the parlour when Charles Cary strode into the room.

"I hear you had quite the afternoon," he remarked upon seeing our wet clothing spread out upon the grate, steam rising from our sodden garments as the fire warmed them.

"Yes, indeed—it was quite exhilarating," Holmes replied.

Cary joined us in a glass of cognac, and soon we were all sitting slumped in armchairs, staring into the fire.

"Torquay seems to be quite the place to be—it's a pity it isn't really the season just now," my friend remarked.

"Right you are, Mr. Holmes—thanks in part to the Cary

family," the priest replied, staring at the honey-coloured liquid in his glass.

"Oh?" I said.

"Yes," said Father Norton. "Victor Cary was instrumental in developing Torquay, in part by selling off abbey land to the town."

"I see," Holmes replied. "Well, progress can't be halted, I suppose, though it is a pity he had to sell off family land," he added with a glance at Charles Cary, who sighed and picked restlessly at his hair.

"The rain seems to have stopped," he said, suddenly rising from his chair. "I don't suppose you and Dr. Watson would like to take a look at the stables now, would you?"

"On the contrary; I can't think of anything I'd rather do," my friend replied. "That is, if Father Norton will excuse us."

"Oh, certainly," the priest replied with a wave of his hand. "I know how Charles likes his horses, and with good reason. It's a fine lot he's got out there—that black stallion is as good a horse as you'll see in Devon or anywhere else, I'll wager."

"Thank you for the compliment," Charles Cary said, but his voice was tight and his lean body shimmered with tension.

Father Norton smiled and poured himself some more cognac. "I suppose I should know. After all, I was a jockey for a while."

Holmes looked at him with interest. "Really? You do continue to surprise, Father Norton—really you do."

The priest laughed. "Well, if you're looking for anything more exotic about me, I'm afraid I'll disappoint you there. I'm really just a simple parish priest."

Holmes smiled. "Oh, I shouldn't underestimate yourself, Father. In my experience, there's more to just about everyone if you look hard enough."

Father Norton looked at Holmes as if he were not sure how to interpret this remark, but he was too shrewd to show any discomfort he might feel at being under the great detective's scrutiny. Instead, he too rose from his chair.

"I'd best be getting on, I suppose—Lydia's bound to be wondering where I am," he said, pulling on his raincoat, which had more or less dried by now.

"Give my regards to your sister," Charles Cary said as the four of us headed towards the front hallway.

"I will be sure to tell her you said so," the priest replied, buttoning his coat. "And thank you for a most convivial afternoon. I've always believed in enjoying life's little pleasures, and I'm glad that my vows do not include abstinence from a good French cognac."

"Yes, indeed," Holmes murmured as we followed Charles Cary out through the vaulted entryway of the abbey. The rain had abated, and a thin, pale rainbow was beginning to form in the rays of the setting sun as we trudged across the sodden lawn.

THE STABLES were on the other side of the Spanish barn, and as we approached that structure I couldn't help feeling a sense of dread. The stables were cheerful enough, however, with the sweet smell of hay filling the air as we approached. Lord Cary owned four horses: a big black stallion by the name of Richmond, a fat little white pony which had been Elizabeth's as a child, a beautiful palomino, and an elegant little strawberry-chestnut mare. I noticed there was one empty stall at the end of the row.

"This will be your horse for the hunt, Dr. Watson," Cary said as we stopped in front of the chestnut mare's stall. Her arched neck, shapely little head and small, sharply pointed ears indicated the presence of Arab blood. She snorted gently as we approached, leaning her head out of her stall, her delicate nostrils flaring.

"This is Ariel," Cary said as she nuzzled his hand with her soft, finely sculpted nose.

I held out my hand and felt the velvet softness of her muzzle as she sniffed my palm, hoping no doubt to find an apple or a sugar cube.

"I hope she doesn't live up to her name," I said, thinking of the mercurial, troublesome character in *The Tempest*.

Cary laughed. "Not in the least. She is the most compliant, good-natured of animals—aren't you, Ariel?" he said, stroking her thick red mane. In response she nickered—a low, barely audible rumbling from deep within her chest—and nuzzled his shoulder.

"All right," he said, extracting a carrot from his jacket pocket. "Here you go—there's no fooling you."

She took the proffered carrot, holding the thick end between her lips as she chewed on the other half.

"Ariel can eat a whole carrot without dropping any of it— can't you?" Lord Cary said with a pat on her neck. "She's a very clever girl, very clever."

"Is it a family tradition to name your animals after characters from Shakespeare's plays?" Holmes inquired.

Cary smiled. "Not at all. She was born here, and my mother named her when she was just a young filly. Perhaps she was reading *The Tempest* at the time; I don't really know. But as with all horses of good blood, as you probably know, the name of the horse should include something from the names of both the sire and the dam. Her mother was Airy Morning, and her father was an Arab named El Dorado."

"I see," I said, stroking the mare's muscular neck. "Your mother rides, then?"

Cary looked away. "She used to."

"Oh? She gave it up, then?" said Holmes.

"Yes."

"Did she have an accident or something?" I said.

"No," Cary replied, and I could sense the subject was a delicate one. I glanced at Holmes, but Cary was already walking towards the next stall.

"What about you, Mr. Holmes—do you think you can handle Richmond?" said Cary, standing in front of the huge black horse. The animal stood looking at us, his enormous head draped over the door of his stall, ears forward.

"I don't see why not," Holmes replied. "He looks to be a capable enough animal."

"Actually, he had a brother, Mystic Rider, who belonged to my father, but after his . . . well, we sold him to a neighbouring estate."

"That explains the empty stall," I remarked.

"Yes." Cary patted the big horse. "Richmond is a stallion, and they can be a bit harder to handle."

Holmes shrugged. "I've always believed it's more a question of your will over theirs, Lord Cary, if you don't mind my saying so. The smartest horse is no match for a really strong-willed rider."

"Yes, I suppose you're right," said Cary slowly, "so long as they know you're not afraid of them."

"Holmes isn't afraid of many things," I hastened to interject.

"Very well, Dr. Watson," Lord Cary replied, smiling. "Then it's settled: you shall have Ariel and Mr. Holmes will take on Richmond. Mind you let him run out ahead of the pack, Mr. Holmes—Richmond likes to be in the lead at all times."

Holmes nodded. "Very well. With those long legs I don't foresee that being a problem."

Just beyond the stables was a fish pond, where a few mottled orange carp swam lazily about just below the murky green surface of the water. I stood watching them while Cary fed and watered the horses.

I thought I heard a bird nearby, and turned to see young William and Annie standing behind me. She held his hand, and

in his other hand he carried a small bouquet of wild flowers—
Queen Anne's lace, fall daisies, goldenrod.

"He picked them for you, sir," said the chambermaid as
William handed me the flowers, a shy smile on his face. William
was under Annie's close supervision during the day; Holmes had
arranged that the girl would keep an eye on him, not letting him
out of her sight, though he did not tell her why he was especially
concerned about the boy's safety. I was glad to see she took her
duties most seriously. I had grown fond of the boy since we had
become roommates; he had a sweet, innocent nature, and far
from finding his lack of language a barrier, I found him better
company than many adults I knew. Holmes had made several
attempts to get the boy to communicate further what he had
seen the night his mother died, but without success; he had
revealed what he knew, it seemed, and could only repeat the
same mimed actions we were already familiar with.

"Why, thank you, William," I said as he handed me the flowers. "That's very thoughtful of you. They're lovely—where did
you find them?"

"They grow in the fields and along the streams all around
here, don't they, William?" said Annie, and the boy nodded
vigorously.

"I think there may be some fish in this pond, if we look
carefully and are very quiet," I said.

"Oo, fish, William—he loves watching fish, don't you?" said
Annie. "Why don't we sit next to Dr. Watson and look for them?"

Again he nodded his consent, working his mouth as hard as
he could, but all that came out was a kind of strangled yelping
sound, rather like the bark of a small dog.

"Come on," said I, "come sit right here and help me look."

They were just about to sit down on the grass next to me
when suddenly I heard a commotion back in the direction of
Torre Abbey. I turned to see Lady Cary running from the building, crying hysterically.

"It's the mistress!" Annie exclaimed. "What's wrong, do you think?"

"I don't know," I replied, "but I'm going to find out!"

I immediately jumped to my feet and ran as fast as I could to her aid, Annie and William following me not far behind. I was not the first to arrive—Holmes and Charles Cary were already there by the time I had covered the several hundred yards of ground. Lady Cary had collapsed in her son's arms, crying uncontrollably.

"He's dead!" she wailed.

"Who? Who's dead?" said Holmes.

She raised her tear-streaked face. "Caliban! Someone's killed Caliban!"

"Killed him?" said her son. "Who on earth would do that?"

"I don't know," she responded, "but I found him just now, poor little thing! He's dead and I'm afraid he's been poisoned!"

Annie shook her head sadly. "Why would anyone kill a poor little dog?"

I looked at Holmes and thought he suspected, as I did, the answer was related to Caliban's sudden fit of barking the other night. I took a deep breath; it was clear that not even the animals at Torre Abbey were safe from the vengeance of a desperate and ruthless killer.

CHAPTER NINETEEN

ADY CARY was inconsolable over the death of her beloved terrier, and I gave her some valerium drops to calm her down. Everyone in the household now was quite unnerved; even placid, stoic Annie trembled at the sight of the poor animal's little corpse. The dog was lying just outside the butler's pantry, not far from his food bowl, and Lady Cary's conclusion of poison seemed reasonable to me.

Holmes instructed everyone to leave the kitchen immediately so that he could work undisturbed. Charles Cary escorted his mother and sister to their rooms and saw to it that Annie and William were out of the way. The boy evidenced curiosity, but was not allowed to see the poor dog, nor was Elizabeth, whose already delicate state of mind was becoming increasingly fragile.

Grayson alone seemed unmoved by the turn of events, expressing sympathy over the death of the dog, but his implacable manner remained intact throughout.

Holmes bent over the dog, sniffed at it, examined the floor all around it, then turned his attention to the partially eaten bowl of food.

"I think in this case Lady Cary is not far off," he remarked, removing a sample of the food and placing it in a small saucer.

"I say, Lord Cary," he said to our host as he entered the kitchen, having seen to it that the other members of the household were settled.

"Yes, Mr. Holmes?"

"I noticed when I was in your quarters that you have a small laboratory set up."

"Yes, that's true."

"Is everything in good working order?"

"Yes; as you know, I'm a medical student. I use it occasionally in my studies."

"May I use it?" Holmes inquired. "I have one or two tests I should like to perform."

"Certainly. Everything is at your disposal."

"Come, Watson, we have work to do," he said, starting to leave the kitchen. "Oh, one more thing, Lord Cary, if you don't mind my asking?"

"Yes?"

"I suppose in your laboratory you have either sulphuric or hydrochloric acid?"

"Yes, I have a container of hydrochloric acid. It is clearly marked."

"Good. And might you by any chance also have a sample of pure metallic zinc?"

"As a matter of fact, I do. I just updated my supplies so that when I am not at school I might be able to—"

But Holmes was already gone, walking swiftly from the kitchen, head down, lost in thought, intent on his next move. I followed behind, curious as to what he had in mind.

Lord Cary's laboratory was not bad—not as complete as the one Holmes had set up in our rooms at Baker Street, perhaps, but sufficient, apparently, for his purposes. I watched as he lighted a Bunsen burner and watched as he adjusted the bluish flame to the proper height.

"What do you intend to do, Holmes?"

"Watson, have you heard of the Marsh test?"

"Yes, I believe I have, but I couldn't tell you what it is exactly."

"A very simple and effective way to determine the presence of arsenic," he said as he poured out hydrochloric acid into a beaker containing a small amount of zinc. "There are other tests as well; the Reinsch test, for example, is more precise, and able to detect much smaller concentrations, but I suspect this will be quite sufficient for our purposes." He then added the sample of the dog food to the solution and placed it over the flame. Once the acid had evaporated, he pointed to a white substance left at the bottom of the beaker.

"Arsenic oxide, Watson! Just as I thought—the poor animal was given arsenic in his food. Lady Cary was right—someone deliberately poisoned her dog!"

UNFORTUNATELY, THE constabulary of Torquay were singularly unimpressed with the poisoning of a dog. Such crimes were apparently not uncommon in and around the town, so we were told; with the quickly expanding population of the region, people who had come to live in a quiet, remote seaside village now found themselves increasingly surrounded by newcomers. Given such conditions, a certain amount of resentment and hostility was inevitable. Though there was very little violent crime around Torquay, apparently pets were often considered fair game in the settling of local feuds. The fat sergeant told us that he had received several reports of suspected poisonings over the past few months. I suspected, however, that his obvious indifference to the fate of the Cary family owed more to the bad blood created by Victor Cary during his lifetime.

"Well, Watson, it seems we are on our own once again," Holmes commented as we returned to the abbey in the Carys's brougham.

"What next?" I replied. "Perhaps we should not go on tomorrow's hunt."

"Oh, no, by all means we should attend the hunt. First of all, I am most concerned about the safety of Charles Cary and want to keep an eye on him; and I am further convinced that the killer may very well reveal his or her hand tomorrow at the hunt."

"Really? How so?"

Holmes shook his head. "I cannot say for sure; I wish that I could. All I can say is that we must be on our guard, Watson."

THAT NIGHT I had trouble sleeping; even a cognac after dinner couldn't calm my overwrought mind. I lay in my bed tossing and turning, listening to the creaking and groaning of the ancient building around me. In the middle of the night I heard a soft rain begin to fall, splashing on the eaves, pattering gently upon the window panes, and I finally fell into a fitful slumber.

I dreamt I was riding across an open field at twilight on the little strawberry mare. It was growing dark and I was anxious to get somewhere. The field seemed to stretch on and on, though, and there was no sign of a building anywhere. I called out at one point, but there was no reply, so I kept riding. I had the strange sense I was being followed and looked over my shoulder, and to my horror I saw a rider on a black horse wearing long flowing robes: the Demon Hunter! Panicked, I urged my horse into a gallop, but still my pursuer was gaining on me. Faster, faster we rode along the moors, until we reached the cliffs overhanging the sea, the waves crashing upon the rocks beneath. I dismounted and looked down into the abyss, at the swirling water which lapped at the jagged edges of the boulders beneath. Behind me, that sound of hoofbeats grew louder. I closed my eyes and jumped, and felt myself falling, falling . . .

CHAPTER TWENTY

THE MORNING of the hunt the day dawned bright and clear, the air as crisp as the tiny green fall apples which lay scattered on the ground underneath the spreading branches of the Carys's apple trees. I awoke early, excitement creeping up my spine as I pulled on the breeches and boots Cary had lent me the night before. The breeches fit well enough, but the boots were a bit tight around my calves. Nevertheless, I succeeded in pulling them on and crept downstairs to avoid waking the rest of the household. The rattling of pots and pans coming from the kitchen told me that I was not the only early riser that morning; I could make out the voices of Grayson and Annie over the clatter of cutlery.

I arrived in the dining room to find Holmes already seated at the breakfast table, a steaming pot of tea in front of him. The early morning sun shone shyly through the French windows upon the immaculate white linen tablecloth.

"Ah, Watson, join me in a cup of tea, won't you?" Holmes said, pouring me a cup from the blue-flowered china teapot. "Nothing like a good Assam blend to fortify us for the day ahead," he said, placing the cup in front of me as I took my place at the table across from him. He looked more comfortable in his riding boots than I was in mine. Lord Cary's jacket was a little short in the sleeves, but other than that, the riding habit fitted him admirably.

"Well, Holmes, you look quite to the manor born," I said, taking a sip of tea, which was hot and strong, with the stringent taste of Assam.

"I am sorry about your boots, Watson; I hope it doesn't spoil the day for you."

"Oh, is it that noticeable?"

Holmes smiled. "Perhaps they will be more comfortable once you are on horseback."

Just then Grayson entered with a fresh pot of tea, and as he set the pot upon the table, Holmes addressed him.

"You are a man of many talents, it would seem, Grayson."

"I don't know about that, sir," the butler replied as he removed the empty teapot.

"Oh, come, don't be so modest. You spent time in the theatre in India, did you not?"

"A little," Grayson replied without looking up from his task. "Will that be all, sir?" He was clearly not anxious to talk about his time in India.

"Yes, thank you," Holmes said, and the butler withdrew to the kitchen.

"How on earth did you know that?" I said when he had gone.

"I didn't, Watson. For once, I was just guessing—though I'll admit it was an educated guess. The fact that he plays the flute so well, the pierced ears, a certain way he carries himself and uses his voice—all of this indicated he's had training as an actor."

"And what might that lead you to conclude?"

"Possibly nothing, Watson—or possibly a great deal."

Soon the rest of the household was stirring, and before long Charles Cary appeared, looking every inch the lord of the manor in his smart white jodhpurs, shiny black boots and red hunting jacket.

"Ready for the big day?" he said as he seated himself at the breakfast table.

"Yes," I replied, although I was more afraid than I would have willingly admitted; still, I was determined to make a good show of it and acquit myself with honour on the field.

The hunt was to gather at the bottom of the apple orchard, and, once mounted, Holmes and I followed Cary on his horse down the path to the orchard. Riding behind him, I noticed Charles's horse was walking strangely, and seemed to be favouring one leg. I trotted up next to him and pointed it out.

"I thought something seemed odd," he said, dismounting.

"I believe it's the left hind leg," I observed, and he bent to examine it.

"Can't see any sign of injury . . . wait just a moment—hullo! Here's the problem—a loose shoe!" He lifted the horse's hoof up so I could see, and sure enough, the shoe hung loose upon it.

"I say, that's irritating," he grumbled. "I had the blacksmith in just last week. I'll have to have a word with that fellow about this!"

"What's the matter?" Holmes asked, drawing up alongside of us on Richmond. The big horse tossed his head and pawed the ground, as if eager to be on his way. He could smell the excitement of the upcoming hunt, and was no doubt impatient for a good gallop across the moors.

"Lord Charles has a loose shoe," I remarked.

"Really? May I see?" said Holmes.

"Nothing much to see, just sloppy work, I'm afraid," Charles replied, "but be my guest."

Holmes dismounted and examined the offending shoe. When he had finished, Charles Cary took up the reins and led his horse back to the barn.

"Go ahead without me—I'll catch up," he called to us. "I just need to tighten this up and then I'll be right along."

As we trotted out towards where the rest of the riders were beginning to gather, Holmes slowed his horse to a walk and turned to me.

"That was not sloppy workmanship, Watson—someone deliberately loosened that shoe."

"Really? Are you certain?"

"Oh, yes. The scrape marks on the loose bolts indicate a different kind of tool was used to loosen them—and most probably not by a professional blacksmith."

"But who would . . . ? I mean, why would someone . . ."

"I can think of several reasons, Watson. Whoever it was may not have wanted Charles Cary to ride in the hunt today. Either that, or . . ." He paused and looked out over the gently sloping hills of Torre Abbey.

"They wanted his horse to have an accident."

"Precisely."

I shuddered. "Are you going to tell him?"

Holmes paused to consider the question. "Later, Watson, not now. But I will tell him. I think he has a right to know that someone may be out to do him harm."

The atmosphere at the hunt was one of suppressed excitement as the horses and riders began to arrive. The sight was a festive one: the Master of the Hunt in his bright-red jacket and top hat, the horses all immaculately brushed and groomed, some with braided manes and tails, their polished hooves glistening with oil. The horses felt the excitement, too: many of them pranced and fretted at their bits, anxious to be off, their breath coming in cloudy little bursts in the crisp air.

Holmes's black stallion was one of the more excitable animals, but Holmes kept him firmly in hand, his fingers wrapped tightly around the double reins of the pelham bit. My little chestnut mare stood quietly, though, as if she did this every day of the week and couldn't be bothered to get worked up about it. Even the simple snaffle bit she wore seemed hardly necessary; I sat upon Ariel with a loose rein and she gazed about her placidly as if wondering what all the fuss was about.

There were about twenty-odd horses and riders; the usual assortment of chestnuts and bays, with one or two spotted Appaloosas, a couple of greys, and of course Charles Cary's beautiful palomino. Though a couple of the bays were quite dark, Richmond was the only truly black horse. The other horses seemed afraid of Richmond, and gave him a wide berth as Holmes walked the big horse around the broad circular drive.

The braying of dogs announced the appearance of the Huntsman, the hounds swarming around the feet of his bay gelding, their moist noses to the ground, occasionally lifting their heads to bray with the peculiar hoarse voices of foxhounds. He was followed by the Whippers-in, also wearing scarlet jackets.

The horses ignored the dogs, but the tension in the air increased with their appearance. The horses seemed to know it was nearly time to depart; they fussed and fretted even more, prancing in place, tossing their heads and pulling at the reins. Ariel, however, remained calm as ever, regarding the dogs with the same disinterest and serene detachment as she viewed the other horses, as though she had only disdain for their foolish expenditure of wasted energy.

Finally, with one shrill blast of the Huntsman's horn, we were off. The horses in front lurched forward, and the whole pack lunged after them at a brisk trot. I was pleased to see that Ariel trotted as steadily as she did everything else; she pricked her head up and followed her stable-mate, Richmond, as we trotted down a dirt lane leading away from Torre Abbey. Ariel was no match for Richmond's long legs, however, and I soon found a place at the rear of the pack, while Holmes's horse rode grandly off to the front. As we turned onto a broad meadow, Lord Cary cantered up from behind me on his handsome palomino.

"How do you like Ariel, Dr. Watson?" he said, drawing up beside me.

"I've never seen a steadier mount," I replied. "Is she always this calm?"

"When she trusts her rider," he answered. "She must think you know what you're doing."

"I hope she's right," I answered as Cary went off to the front of the hunt.

A white dew still lay heavily on the grass as we cantered across the first field; lit by the pale October sun, the meadow grass sparkled like crystal. I breathed in deeply, filling my lungs with fresh, clean Devon air. The ascending sun glinted off the back of the riders in front of me, the rhythmic beat of hooves pounding the ground, softened from rain the night before. The rocking motion of the horse under me as we cantered slowly across the field put me into a kind of trance state, and I felt lucky to be alive, to be in this field at this moment, with these people, joining them in an ancient and time-honoured sport.

For a little while I forgot about the grim errand which had brought us here; all thoughts of mysterious spirits and hauntings vanished from my head as I rode across the field. Up ahead, the dogs had entered the woods, and I could hear them baying as they sniffed rocks and trees in search of the elusive fox.

I followed the others into the woods, ducking under tree branches as Ariel crashed through the undergrowth in pursuit of the other horses. The cries of the Whippers-in could be heard up ahead as they urged the dogs on.

"Get on it!"

"On-y, on-y, on-y!"

Ahead I saw a low stone wall, presumably a property marker. The other riders were jumping their horses over it with apparent ease, so I gave Ariel a squeeze and urged her over it. She cleared the jump easily and I gave her a pat for a job well done.

At the other side of the wall Lord Cary was seated upon his palomino, watching me. "She jumps like a dream, doesn't she?" he said, smiling.

"Yes, indeed," I replied, feeling quite pleased with my mount and myself.

"Yards of daylight between her and that jump," Cary went on, "not even a challenge. There's a larger one up ahead which should make for some good fun," he said, turning his horse to rejoin the group. He spurred the big palomino onward and called out over his shoulder to me. "See you in a bit."

"Right," I replied, and followed after him, albeit somewhat more cautiously. My mare seemed to know these woods, but I did not, and I wished to avoid a branch across the face if at all possible.

The woods rose to a low hillock, then the trees thinned out a bit along a shallow ravine, which was plastered with fallen leaves and other woodland debris. We walked our horses through the ravine, as the leaves were still wet from the night before and could be treacherous footing. The woody smell of dead leaves rose from the ground and mingled with the aroma of horse sweat as I approached the ravine, which looked to be a dried-up river bed. It occurred to me that all of Torquay was so close to the sea level that it was not far down to the ground water level anywhere.

Up ahead I could see the fence Cary had mentioned to me. It was a cross-slatted wooden fence in a zigzag pattern, a good four feet high, and the sight of it was intimidating. But the other riders were already taking it in ones and twos, and I urged Ariel forward at a brisk canter.

Her take-off was strong and well-timed and we sailed over, but as we hit the ground something caused her to shy and lunge to one side. Still forward in a three-point jumping position, I was unprepared for this sudden change of direction—and before I knew it I found myself seated unceremoniously on the ground, the wind knocked out of me. Other than being surprised and winded, though, I was sound enough; nothing appeared to be broken. I picked myself up, hoping no one had seen me, and went to collect my mount, who stood a few yards away calmly munching on a clump of grass growing under a scrub oak tree. I was grateful at least that she was waiting for me; having divested themselves of their rider, many horses would rush off to join the rest of the pack without a thought to their stranded rider.

"What frightened you?" I said, walking up to her slowly so as not to scare her off. She raised her head, her mouth full of grass, and regarded me with the calm serenity which seemed to be her only expression. She chewed contentedly, lime-green grass juice seeping out of the sides of her mouth, as I checked the girth. I reached for the reins but as I did I heard a noise behind me, the sound of footsteps in the underbrush. I turned to see what it was. The rest of the hunt was not far in front of me, and though I could hear the thick baying of the hounds, I could not see any of my comrades.

When I turned toward the noise, it stopped. Ariel evidently heard it too, for she pricked her ears forward and stood still as a statue. Then she let out an enormous whinny, so loud that it hurt my ears. I assumed she was calling to Richmond, her stable-mate, who had gone on ahead. I took one more look around me but the trees were as still and silent as the great boulders which dotted the hillside.

I took up the reins and remounted, feeling a bit stiff but mostly just grateful that no one had been there to witness my ignominious fall. I gave Ariel her head, and she trotted through the woods, scattering dry leaves in every direction. Horses are social animals, and I could tell she was eager to join her companions. I put my head down almost level with her neck to avoid any pesky branches and let her have her head. We skirted the dry river bed for a while and then, coming upon a twisted, barren oak tree, I let her stand still for a few moments to catch her breath. The tree stood by itself at the top of a little hill, and with its bare, blackened branches, it looked as though it was the victim of a lightning strike. A solitary crow sat upon one of the higher branches, its harsh hoarse caw piercing the air, a mournful sound.

I shivered a little and sent Ariel on. Before long I saw the other riders up ahead of us, galloping across a broad plain. Without any urging from me, Ariel took off at a fast clip, almost leaving me behind. The hunting horn sounded as we raced along the moor—the fox had been spotted! The cry of the dogs mixed with the sound of pounding hooves, and my melancholy was soon replaced by exhilaration. Galloping a horse across a field is sure to send the heart racing and the blood pounding even in the most phlegmatic of men—and I was no exception. To my surprise, at a flat-out run, Ariel was a match for any of the larger horses in the hunt, and she soon caught up with the others, racing past the pack until she was almost at the front.

Up ahead I saw another stone wall surrounding the meadow. It looked like a formidable jump, but I was feeling my oats now, and headed for it.

"Mind you jump that wide—there's a ditch on the other side!" Lord Cary called out as I prepared for take-off. Ariel sailed over it, though, as if she had wings, clearing the ditch with ease, and we galloped on ahead. Having trailed behind the others until now, I was exhilarated to be out in front. I hadn't travelled far when I heard a cry from behind me, and then came the call:

"Rider down!"

Disappointed, I reined Ariel in and turned her around. As a doctor, I felt a responsibility to come to the aid of the fallen rider. My disappointment turned to cold fear when I saw the riderless horse trotting toward me: it was Richmond!

I spurred Ariel back to the jump, where, to my horror, I saw

Holmes lying motionless on the ground. In an instant I dismounted and knelt beside him to feel for a pulse. To my great relief, he lifted his head and spoke.

"I'm all right, Watson," he said, though he did not look it. His face was pale, and in addition to having the wind knocked out of him, he was holding his shoulder as he struggled to sit up.

"Easy, Holmes," I said as he attempted to stand. "Why don't you let me check for broken bones?"

He shook his head and struggled to his feet.

"There's nothing broken, Watson, but it is as I suspected." He pointed to an object lying in the grass just beyond the ditch, and I saw at once what had caused the fall: a broken stirrup lay on the ground.

"Look," I said, holding up the stirrup. The leather had torn clean through—and as the leather was shiny and new, it was unlikely that it had broken on its own.

Holmes examined the stirrup leather, holding it up so that I could see. "You see where it has been cut clean through?"

I did indeed—the leather had clearly been sliced with a sharp instrument; except for the little bit which had been left uncut—and which had torn through on the jump—there was no doubt that this was a case of deliberate sabotage.

"It's been very precisely cut," I remarked, "and with great skill. It's almost as though . . ."

"What, Watson?"

"Well, it's almost as though it were done by a scalpel," I said reluctantly.

To my surprise, Holmes nodded. "I was thinking the same thing."

Both of us knew that Charles Cary owned a scalpel, though neither of us said as much. Just then Cary trotted up to us on his palomino, Holmes's horse in tow. He held Richmond's reins in one hand, and with the other he pulled his horse to a stop.

"Are you all right, Mr. Holmes?"

"Yes, quite," Holmes replied, though he still clutched his shoulder and I could tell from his face that he was in pain.

"Will you be all right to carry on, or do you want to go back?"

"Oh, I'll carry on."

"Holmes," I said, "why don't you go back?"

"Because I don't know what else may happen, Watson," he replied, taking Richmond's reins from Lord Cary. I helped him mount the big stallion, but I did not feel good about his decision. However, I knew better than to argue; once Holmes's mind was made up, that was that. He attached his stirrup to the saddle with what was left of the leather and mounted.

To my relief, the hunt did not last too much longer. The three of us trotted to catch up with the rest of the hunt, but the dogs had stopped in front of a hay-strewn corner of the field where meadow met woods. Underneath a crumbling stone wall was what appeared to be the entrance to a burrow.

"Well, it seems the fox has gone into his den," the Huntsman said as we all gathered around the yelping hounds. Some ran in frantic circles around the burrow, sniffing at the ground, driven wild by the scent of the fox, which was so enticingly present everywhere—but the little animal was safe in his underground hideaway now, and I breathed a silent prayer of thanks as we turned our horses around and headed for home. I had no desire to see a fox ripped apart by hounds, and was glad that he had escaped.

Mud-spattered and matted with dried sweat, our horses were tired now, drained as we were of the adrenaline of the chase. It was over, and every horse and rider plainly felt it; even Holmes's black stallion walked quietly, his proud head drooped forward like the head of an old cart-horse.

Dusk was gathering over the fields as we limped homeward.

Every bone in my body was beginning to ache, and I thought fondly of a bath and a glass of brandy in front of the fire when we returned to the abbey. Holmes and I were in the rear, a fathom or so behind the others, and as we rounded the crest of a hillock I suddenly realized I no longer had my gloves. I had removed them when I stopped to assist Holmes, and I must have left them on the ground by the stone wall.

"I've left my gloves behind," I said. "I'd better go back and get them."

"Shall I accompany you?" said Holmes.

"No—go ahead and I'll catch up," I replied. The truth was I was concerned about my friend, and wanted him to get back to the abbey as soon as possible.

Holmes must have sensed what I was feeling, because he didn't argue. "I'll ride on ahead and tell them to slow down a bit," he said.

"Oh, don't worry—I'm sure Ariel knows the way home," I replied as he rode off at a trot.

I turned Ariel around and headed back across the wide field. She gave me some resistance, unwilling to turn away from the direction of home when all her companions were up ahead; not only had I separated her from the pack but now I was heading in the wrong direction! Horses have a very keen sense of direction, and always know exactly where their barn is, even if they are travelling through unfamiliar countryside.

"Don't worry, old girl," I said softly as she pulled against the reins, "we'll be on our way in a moment."

I found the gloves just where I had left them. I dismounted, put them on, and swung myself back up in to the saddle. No sooner had I done this than Ariel gave a start, tossing her head to the side as if frightened by something.

"What is it, old girl?" I said, looking around. A thick mist was gathering over the field as the cool evening air settled over the land. Visibility was limited, and I could barely see the edge of the woods, which lay to the west. Straining my eyes, though, I could see a form standing among the trees where the woods and meadow met: a tall black horse and rider. Thinking that Holmes had doubled back and gone into the woods for some reason, I turned Ariel in the direction of the horse and rider. She went a few steps, but then suddenly stopped and would go no farther. I squeezed her hard, but she fought me, pulling at the bit and shaking her head, and I finally gave her the first kick I had given her all day. Shocked, she took a few more steps towards the woods, but then suddenly stopped and reared. It was clear that Ariel did not want to go any closer to that woods. I would not admit it to myself, but I had no great desire to go there either; perhaps Ariel was simply picking up on my reluctance. I did not have a good feeling about the spot where the horse and rider stood; I could not say why, but something about it made my flesh creep. I could not make out the rider's face or figure very well, but I had the distinct impression he was looking at me.

"Hello!" I called out. "Who are you?"

Both horse and rider stood motionless for a moment, and then suddenly took off into the woods at a furious canter. I attempted to prod Ariel into following them, but once again she fought and reared; this time I very nearly came off, and had to grab on to her neck to steady myself. Finally I gave up and allowed her to follow after the rest of the hunt, which she did at a brisk trot. I looked behind me as we went on, but the mysterious stranger had disappeared into the woods.

I let Ariel have her head and we cantered across the field, accompanied only by the sound of her breathing and the muffled thud of her hooves upon the soft soil. I could see only dimly now, and hoped that Ariel would not step in a gopher hole or some other obstacle, but she proved as sure-footed in the twilight as she was during daytime. After a while I thought I could hear the others ahead of us, and as we came to the top of the crest of a hillock I could see them through the fog, the horses' breath coming in thick white clouds of steam.

"Well, Watson, what kept you so long?" Holmes said as I trotted up beside him.

"I—I saw something," I said.

"Oh? What?" Holmes inquired.

"A black horse and rider," I replied.

Holmes stopped his horse. "Are you certain of that?"

"Fairly certain. It was somewhat dark, and at first I thought it might be you, since the horse was jet-black and Richmond was the only black horse in the hunt today. But when I called out they turned and went back into the woods. I tried to follow, but Ariel would have none of it. I finally gave up and rejoined the hunt."

" 'And I saw, and behold, a black horse, and its rider had a balance in his hand.' "

I looked at Holmes. I recognized the quote as being from Revelations, but it sent a chill up my spine nonetheless. Holmes shook his head slowly.

"The scales of justice, perhaps, Watson . . . I think that whatever is going on here, revenge is not far away from the centre of things."

"What makes you think that?"

Holmes shrugged. "A process of elimination. There are a limited number of drives which motivate human behaviour, and once you have eliminated the others . . . well, time will yet tell. Come along," he said, turning Richmond in the direction of the abbey. "We must return or the others will wonder what happened to us."

We walked along for a few minutes without speaking. I heard the gentle cooing of quail in the underbrush as we walked alongside the hedgerows leading up to the abbey. As we started up the long drive to the abbey, Holmes turned to me.

"Well, we have at least one corroborating piece of evidence now, Watson."

"Oh?" I said. "What's that?"

A chill crawled its way up my spine as I heard his reply.

"Why, the Demon Hunter, Watson—now you have seen him, too."

CHAPTER TWENTY-ONE

L ATER THAT night, after the rest of the family had gone to bed, we sat with Charles Cary in front of the fire, sharing a glass of claret before retiring.

"Well, I think I'll turn in," our host said with a yawn, setting down his glass and stretching before rising from his chair.

"One moment, Lord Cary," said Holmes. "I think there is something you should know."

Holmes proceeded to tell Cary his theory about the loosened shoe—that it was done deliberately. He also told him about the broken stirrup leather. As he spoke, Cary's blue eyes grew wider.

"Are you sure, Mr. Holmes? I mean, could you be mistaken?"

The detective shrugged. "I think not. I believe it was meant as a warning."

Cary sat down again, a look of bewilderment on his face. "But who would do such a thing—and why?"

Holmes explained his various theories and then added, "Of course, there may be another reason I'm overlooking . . . anything is possible."

Cary stared into the fire for several moments without moving. Then, collecting himself, he took a breath and rose from his chair. "Well, that is a sobering thought, gentlemen—sobering indeed."

"I'll tell you one thing, Lord Cary," Holmes responded.

"Oh? What's that?"

"Ghosts don't go around loosening horseshoes and cutting stirrup leathers—at least none that I know of."

Cary shook his head slowly. "No, I don't suppose they do."

I looked out the window at the black skeletons of the branches rattling on the window panes, blown about by the wind.

At the hour of the moon the Demon Hunter is abroad
On his black stallion o'er the fields he does ride . . .
The lovers now lie buried in the deep dark glen
But the Hunter on his great black steed will ride, and ride
—and ride again.

I was seated in the dining room over a late breakfast the next morning when Holmes came striding into the room.

"Good morning, Watson," he said, seating himself.

"You're up early, Holmes. Where have you been?"

"I've been to town," he replied, plucking a napkin from the table and unfolding it onto his lap. I noticed he still favoured his right shoulder.

"Oh? What did you do there?"

"I was looking for a man who doesn't exist."

"And did you find him?" I asked, familiar with my friend's cryptic ways.

"I did. Or at least I found people who had seen him, which was close enough for my purposes," he said, helping himself to a thick slab of bacon with eggs.

"I see. And who is this nonexistent personage?"

"Do you remember the strange little man you saw at the theatre in London?"

"Yes."

"And one of the stagehands also reported seeing someone who was very likely the same person?"

"Yes, I remember telling you about it."

"Well, Watson, it seems that odd character has been a recent guest at the Lambeth Hotel in Torquay."

"Really? You don't say!"

"Yes, even in a place like Torquay such a colourful personage is bound to make an impression. The hotel clerk particularly remembered the curious cane handle you described so well."

"The falcon head, or whatever it was—"

"Just so," he replied, pouring a cup of steaming coffee from the pot.

"And what do you think his involvement in this affair is?"

"That remains to be seen, Watson, though I have my theories."

But any further discussion of his theories was interrupted by the entrance of Marion Cary into the dining room. She had only just greeted us and sat down when her son Charles strode into the room.

"Has anyone seen William?"

"Not today," Marion Cary replied. "But then," she added, turning to me, "days can go by without my setting eyes upon him. And the abbey is so big that if you want to hide from others, it's fairly easy."

"Yes, I can see that," Holmes remarked.

Charles Cary paced impatiently from one side of the room to the other, the heels of his boots clicking upon the hardwood floor. "Well, he hasn't cleaned out the stable yet today, and no one seems to know where he is."

Holmes rose from his chair. "Annie has been instructed to keep close watch on him during the day. I think we should search the abbey."

Cary looked at Holmes, evidently surprised by his response. "Good Lord, Mr. Holmes, you don't think . . . ?"

"I make it a practice never to predict without the proper facts, Lord Cary."

Just then Annie came rushing into the room, panting. "I can't find William—I just turned around and he was gone!"

Elizabeth insisted upon helping us, claiming that she knew of all the boy's favourite hiding places. After searching all through the house, however, we came up empty-handed. As we stood huddled in the foyer comparing notes, Holmes suggested gravely that we might try searching the grounds next. Grayson entered the room with a tea tray, and we stood in the foyer hastily gulping down steaming cups of tea to fortify ourselves for the raw weather outside. A blustery offshore wind had begun to blow in from the sea, whipping the bare tree branches about with an increasing insistency.

We went outside, and as we all were about to set off in different directions, a cry came from Elizabeth Cary, who was standing a few yards away from the rest of us.

"What is it, Elizabeth?" said Charles Cary, hurrying over to where his sister stood staring at the ground.

"There—there!" she replied, pointing to the body of a blackbird upon the ground. The dead bird lay on its side, the wind ruffling its shiny black feathers, its lifeless orange eyes staring up at us from death. There was no visible mark upon the bird's body; it appeared to have fallen out of the sky onto the ground where it lay.

Whatever the cause of death, the girl was transfixed by the sight, trembling and pointing to it as we joined her one by one.

"It's only a bird, Elizabeth," Cary said, putting his arms around her.

She buried her head in his shoulder. "Please—take it away!" she wailed piteously.

"Very well; don't worry," he murmured, stroking her shiny dark curls, black as the feathers on the dead bird.

Holmes and I watched as he led the disturbed girl away, back into the abbey.

"What on earth was that all about?" I said when they had gone. "Why get so upset over a dead bird?"

Holmes looked down at the dead bird, its body still except for the fluttering of its feathers ruffled by the wind.

"Why, indeed, Watson; why indeed?"

We continued the search, spreading out in all directions; Holmes headed towards the orchard, Cary and I southwest in the direction of the stables. Leaving Cary, I skirted the edge of the Spanish barn and headed toward the little pond just beyond the stables, set in among a grove of poplar trees. I entered the grove and walked towards the pond, clutching my coat around me as the wind gathered in strength and tried to tear it from my body. As I neared the pond, I saw what I thought at first was a dark log protruding from the water's edge. I took a couple more steps, and my heart was suddenly caught in mid-beat.

I had found William.

The boy lay at the water's edge, half submerged, the lower part of his body in the pond, the upper half lying facedown on the muddy bank. I knelt and felt for a pulse, but I knew at once from the icy-cold feel of his skin that he was dead.

There was no injury immediately apparent upon his body, no sign of blood on his clothing, no rips or tears that I could see which might indicate stab wounds. I guessed the cause of death to be drowning, though, not being a pathologist, I was not equipped to determine it. His pale face was parched of all colour, white as birch, and his skin was already beginning to look swollen and bloated. My heart felt heavy and tears welled up in my eyes; I had grown fond of the boy these past few days, and it was almost more than I could bear to see his poor, lifeless body.

I pulled him a little farther onto the shore so that he did not slip back into the pond, then ran to get the others. I soon found Holmes in the orchard, then the two of us went to get Cary, whom we found standing just outside the Spanish barn.

"Whatever will we tell Elizabeth?" he murmured minutes later as we stood over the body watching as Holmes examined the ground around the pond. "She will be heartbroken, poor thing."

Holmes straightened up and wiped the mud from his trousers. "There are no tracks coming from the house other than ours and the boy's," he observed tersely. "Someone may have come from another direction—but you see here where the soil has been smoothed over? They took care to cover their tracks."

Cary rubbed his forehead. "This is bad, Mr. Holmes. I don't know what I'm going to tell my family."

Holmes wiped the mud from his hands, his face set and grim. "Anything is possible, Lord Cary, but I think it was very likely the boy met his death through the infliction of violence."

"In other words, he was murdered."

"I'm afraid so."

He went on to explain to Cary William's impromptu performance for us several days ago, and the conclusion it had led us to: that the boy had been present when his mother died.

Cary listened thoughtfully. "But that doesn't necessarily mean—"

"No, it doesn't," Holmes replied in a tight voice, cutting him off. I could tell William's death had hit him hard, too. His movements were stiff and more precise than ever, and there was a barely suppressed rage in his voice.

After Holmes had finished examining the scene, we carried William's body gently to the house. Holmes asked Lord Cary if he wanted to leave the scene intact for the police, but Cary shook his head.

"I'd rather not involve the police just now, if you don't mind. The whole town doesn't need to know about this, and besides, there's no certainty this was murder. As Dr. Watson pointed out, William's brain disorder—"

But Holmes cut him off. "And there's no conclusive evidence your cook was the victim of foul play, either. But if you want my opinion, Lord Cary, I must tell you that I believe neither of these deaths can be blamed on accidental causes."

"Very well, Mr. Holmes, but if it's all the same with you, I'd still rather not involve the police."

Holmes shrugged. "As you wish."

Later, as we sat in the parlour waiting for Grayson to round up the rest of the household, Holmes stood in front of the window looking out at the wind which chased and whipped the tree branches to and fro. "By God, this has gone too far, Watson!" His jaw was set and his grey eyes burned with anger. I could not remember ever seeing him so furious. "Now he has drowned a child!"

I shook my head. "I'm not a pathologist, but I know that a diagnosis of death by drowning is really a matter of elimination, once other causes have been ruled out. It's a tricky call."

"Damn!" Holmes muttered, his jaw clenched. "He has covered his tracks once again, giving us precious little to go on. This murderer is very clever—and very evil. What kind of person is this, who could kill a poor helpless half-wit child?"

"William isn't—wasn't—a half-wit," I corrected gently. "He just had a condition—"

"Yes, yes!" he barked impatiently. "He was still a *child*, defenseless and harmless." The rage in his voice gave way to fatigue. "He was harmless to everyone—to everyone, that is, except his killer. And that, Watson, is the closest thing we have to a clue in solving his murder."

CHAPTER TWENTY-TWO

"HERE IS devilry afoot here, Watson," Holmes observed grimly as we gazed out at the greyish-green water of Tor Bay. It was later that day, just before nightfall, and Holmes had gone for a walk along the seashore to clear his head. I accompanied him on his lonely hike, lowering my head against the strong offshore wind blowing in from the bay.

"Are you quite convinced, then, that neither of the deaths at Torre Abbey were accidental?"

Holmes looked out at the sea stretching before us, its surface dark and moody as a willful child. "No more than I believe that real bullets ended up in Merwyn's gun by accident. No, Watson, I am convinced that our antagonist will stop at nothing to gain his or her ends." He drew a hand over his brow, and in the dull light of day his face looked worn and haggard. "The trouble is, Watson, I don't yet know what those ends are." He sighed and shook his head. "There is evil at work here, Watson. Someone is playing a very dangerous game, and playing it in earnest, leaving bodies wherever they go. And now they are desperate enough to strike in broad daylight. These are deeper waters than I ever suspected—deeper and more treacherous."

I looked out across the gently swelling waves, a blank surface of water as far as the eye could see. The sea was so opaque in the grey light that it looked almost as if you could walk upon it. I knew this was an optical illusion, however: like so many things at Torre Abbey, appearances were deceiving, and the placid surface of the sea hid the dangers swirling just beneath it.

As I feared, following the death of William, Holmes began driving himself even harder than usual. In spite of my remonstrations, he blamed himself for the boy's death, and, determined to break the case as soon as possible, began ignoring his own health. I came down the next morning to find him sitting in front of a cold fire, staring moodily into the grate, his pipe and a bag of shag tobacco next to him, wearing the same clothes as the day before. It was obvious he had not been to bed all night.

"I don't see how ruining your health will help solve this case, Holmes," I said, perching upon the arm of the settee.

He looked up at me, great dark circles under his grey eyes. "Time is running out, Watson. My health is of no concern to me at the moment."

"That may be," I countered, "but if you drive yourself into the ground you will be of no use to anyone."

He dismissed this with a weary wave of his hand. "I have trained my constitution, Watson; I have done without sleep before."

That much was true. His willpower was remarkable; I had seen him endure privation that would have stopped a lesser man. "Still," I grumbled, "you might have some breakfast."

He appeared not to hear the last remark, for he sat sunk in his own thoughts until I left to go into the dining room, where Grayson had prepared a lavish breakfast. At the sight of eggs and sausages I turned heel and went back into the study, where Holmes was sitting where I had left him, about to light his pipe.

"I will not leave you alone until you eat something," I said firmly. "Punishing yourself for William's death does no good to anyone."

He looked at me, his haggard face registering surprise. "My dear fellow, what on earth makes you think I am punishing myself?"

"This refusal to take care of yourself—I don't know what you call it, but I call it punishment," I replied coldly. "And I don't see how it can possibly help you to solve this case."

He rubbed his forehead and sighed wearily. "Very well, Watson, I shall do as you ask—or rather, as you command," he added with a little smile. "I see you have quite made up your mind in the matter."

"Quite," I replied, trying not to show my surprise at the ease of my victory as he followed me into the dining room.

Holmes really was famished, as was I, and we both tucked into the plentiful platters of food which emerged from the kitchen. Annie was very upset over poor William's death, as her red eyes attested, and she sniffled a little as she served us. It seemed as though everyone had been fond of the boy, and all of us were still in shock from his death.

I⊤ wɪʟʟ all come to a head soon, Watson," Holmes said later that day as I sat in the library cleaning my revolver. The thick salt air had done it no good; the action was sluggish, and I noticed the bullet chamber had a tendency to clog and stick. If we were soon to come face to face with our foe, I wanted to be prepared.

Holmes lifted the heavy brocade curtain and let a stream of sunlight into the room. I watched the dust particles swirling about, caught in the yellow beam, tiny travellers trapped in a whirlwind of sunlight.

"Clues present themselves in the strangest manner," Holmes mused. "For instance, did you happen to remark the number of pork chops served at dinner last night, by any chance?"

"No, I can't say that I did. How many were there?"

He let go of the curtain and turned to me. "There were eight, Watson."

"And what is the significance of that?" I asked, confused. I had no idea where he was headed with this.

"I distinctly heard Grayson tell Lady Cary that eleven chops were purchased," he continued, "and yet there were eight served to us."

"So presumably the servants each had one."

"That would be . . ."

"Grayson and Annie."

"Yes—which leaves ten chops. What happened to the other chop, Watson?"

"Perhaps one of the staff ate two."

Holmes shook his head. "An old man and a girl? They were extremely generous chops, Watson—you yourself remarked upon it."

"What are you suggesting?"

"Merely that there is one pork chop still unaccounted for."

Holmes sat in a chair opposite me. His long fingers twitched and every muscle in his lean body seemed poised for action. He watched me for some moments, fidgeting and sighing, until finally he could remain seated no longer and began to pace back and forth in front of the stacks of books which lined the walls.

"It is just as well the weather is fair," he remarked, almost to himself. "We will need the advantage of moonlight."

"How do you know it will be tonight?" I inquired.

He stopped pacing and ran a hand through his black hair, which looked shaggy and in need of a combing. I knew this meant Holmes was preoccupied; usually meticulous in his personal grooming, this inattention to such details could only mean he was focusing every bit of his impressive intellect upon the problem at hand.

"If you will just bear with me a little longer, Watson, all will become clear," he replied apologetically.

I sighed and returned to my task, but I couldn't help smiling a little. Holmes liked to play his cards close to his chest, keeping details even from me until the last minute. I've no doubt he had his reasons at times, but sometimes I thought his innate sense of theatricality was to blame. There was more than a little bit of the magician in Holmes himself—given a wand and a red-lined cape, I could just see him enjoying the breathless gasps of a stunned audience as he revealed the tricks of his trade.

As if reading my mind, Holmes spoke. "No doubt you think me unduly parsimonious with my information, Watson, but I assure you it is for your own protection."

"Oh?" I said, amused and irritated at the same time. "This information is so dangerous, then, that I would be in peril if you told me?"

"My dear fellow, I promise that soon—very soon—all will be revealed. Until then, if you can only bear up with patience, I would be most grateful." He looked at me earnestly, his grey eyes pleading.

"Holmes, when have I ever failed you?" I said, my voice suddenly thick.

He turned away without speaking for a moment, and when he did, I thought I detected a catch in his voice as well. "Never, Watson, and you have my gratitude for that." There was another pause, and he cleared his throat. "But now, if you will excuse me, I must see to a few things," he said, and left the room without looking back. I watched his spare from recede, saw the determined set of his shoulders, the kinetic energy in his stride, and smiled. In a world which was beginning to change at a dizzying rate, Holmes would always be Holmes, and there was comfort in that.

I WAS not prepared for his pronouncement over tea later that day.

"Well, Watson, I think it's time we left Devon and went back to London."

I was flabbergasted. "What are you talking about, Holmes?"

He laid a hand on my arm. "Calm yourself, Watson. I am merely suggesting a ruse to lure out our opponent. We must find a way to make the predator the prey."

"And you think the way to do that would be to *leave?*"

Holmes smiled. "Or rather, to pretend to leave. Consider, Watson: what does this person behind all these threatening events want?"

"Well . . ."

"Precisely. You are not certain. These events, terrible as they are, have mainly been threats aimed at the Cary family. If he or she—"

"Oh, Holmes, surely a woman is not capable of such—"

Holmes shrugged. "You know my views on women, Watson."

I frowned. "I do indeed, and I do not agree with them."

He laughed softly. "Poor Watson, always the romantic."

"That may be, but—"

He dismissed me with a wave of his hand. "We are wasting time on trifles. The point is, Watson, that if our antagonist wanted the Cary family dead, he would have carried out that scheme long ago. He clearly has both the resources and required ruthlessness to do so. We must therefore ask ourselves, what *does* he want? And the answer, I believe, is that he wants them gone."

"Gone?"

"Yes, gone from Torre Abbey, that is."

"I see. So you think whoever is behind this is trying to scare them out of the abbey?"

"Precisely. And our intervention has only slowed down the process. Therefore, if we leave—or pretend to leave—he will finally play out his hand, therefore laying all his cards upon the table, to use a perhaps trite but useful analogy."

I nodded slowly. "I see. So we'll pretend to go back to London—"

"Yes; we'll invent some excuse or other, pressing business at Baker Street or some such thing, and then we will go so far as to get on the train—but when the train leaves we will not be upon it."

"Hmm. I only hope we will not be placing the Cary family in further danger."

Holmes rubbed his forehead. "Who can say? I only know that I am tired of playing cat and mouse, and that it is time to confront our opponent."

Holmes insisted that no one be in on our scheme; that even if the members of the family could be trusted, it was best we not reveal ourselves to them for their own safety.

"You remember, perhaps, Watson, that I allowed you to believe I died at Reichenbach Falls, partly for your own safety, and partly because I did not believe you could convincingly act the part—"

I cut him off. "Yes, I remember, Holmes; there's no need to remind me." Though my relief upon his unexpected "resurrection" had been great, his actions of those years still rankled; I was still hurt that he had let his brother Mycroft into his confidence instead of me. But I agreed to go along with him and pretend we were really leaving, even though it was difficult. I was not the natural actor Holmes was, and furthermore, I feared the family's reaction when we told them the news.

As I expected, the Cary family did not receive the news of our imminent departure well. Charles Cary was angry, and Marion Cary just stared at us with those blue eyes, and I felt shame creeping up my neck to my face. Holmes had invented an excuse involving a telegram and "urgent business pertaining to the government"; I tried my best to lie low and not answer questions as we prepared to leave. It was all I could do to avoid blurting out the truth as we climbed into the brougham, with Grayson waiting to drive us into town that evening. We were to catch the last train to London, and though we had promised to return as soon as we could, I knew our departure was wreaking havoc upon the mental state of the family. Of course, as Holmes pointed out, we might just be witnessing some very good acting performances, though he still would not tell me which member of the family he suspected.

We boarded the train as Holmes had arranged, and watched through the window as Grayson drove away from the station; we even went so far as to buy one-way tickets to London to further the ruse. But shortly after the final boarding call we slipped out of the last car and secluded ourselves behind a copse of trees until the train left. After it had chugged away into the night, belching blue smoke from its smokestack, Holmes stepped out from behind the tree.

"Good, Watson," he said, looking around. "I don't think anyone saw us." The platform was indeed empty, and the station house was closed and deserted. "We must now make our way back to the abbey on foot."

We had packed light, and I slung my overnight bag over my shoulder and followed Holmes.

It was not far from town to Torre Abbey, and as I walked down the country lane alongside Holmes I could hear the crickets chirping and the woodland creatures scuttling about in the bushes all around us. The call of a hoot owl came from a grove of birch trees, their white bark shining silver in the moonlight. We soon reached the edge of the Cary property, and the abbey loomed in front of us, dark and heavy-set against the clear October night sky.

To my surprise, Holmes did not go directly to the abbey, but headed in the direction of the stables.

"We must be prepared to meet fire with fire, and in this case that means being ready with mounts of our own," he said as he fetched a saddle and bridle from the tack-room. He saddled and bridled Richmond, and I did the same with the little chestnut mare, Ariel. My heart pounded as I tied up the girth under her; I did not know what Holmes expected to happen, but resolved to prepare myself for whatever might be required. To that end, I had placed my revolver in my coat pocket before leaving the abbey, and now I was glad to have it.

We led the horses around to the side of the abbey and tethered them to a small tree, then Holmes led me up the stairs to the Abbot's Tower, where a shaft of moonlight shone in through the window.

We sat huddled in the darkness for some time, listening to the soft chortle of doves outside the window give way to the slow cascade of night noises. The sounds were so different from the ones I was used to in London that I found myself listening to them with intense interest. The movement and murmurings of the night creatures came together in a symphonic blend of cooing, clicking, rustling and cawing, a nocturnal concerto which was as mysterious as it was foreign to me. I peered out of the window at the sliver of pallid moon which hung in the starless sky.

I looked at Holmes, crouched besides me in the semi-darkness. Pale moonlight fell upon his aquiline face, his profile sharp as the crag of a wind-swept hill. A cloud passed over the moon, leaving us in its shadow. I could hear in Holmes's steady breathing the tension of every coiled muscle in his body. Hours passed, and we sat, speaking in whispers, until I began to wonder if my friend was wrong, and that whatever we were waiting for would not happen after all. But I was wrong, and Holmes, as usual, was right.

The first sign that something was happening was the sudden silence of the nocturnal creatures. All at once, there was a pause in their clatter and chatter; the air itself seemed to pause and hold the stillness within the breath of a breeze. I glanced at Holmes as I felt his body stiffen beside me. My fingers closed around the cold metal handle of my revolver. In spite of the chill in the air, my palm was clammy with sweat. My index finger sought the reassuring feel of the trigger; I checked to see if the safety was on and removed my hand from my pocket. My forehead, too, had begun to sweat, and I wiped a few drops from my temples.

At that moment I felt Holmes's hand upon my shoulder.

"What is it?" I whispered as a thin thread of fear wormed its way through my stomach.

"It is time!" he hissed, and crept soundlessly to the window.

I followed behind him, and looked down onto the lawn in front of the abbey, where, to my astonishment, I saw the shadowy figure of a man on horseback. A sudden parting of clouds from the moon revealed details of his elaborate seventeenth-century attire: it was the Cavalier! He looked up toward the Abbot's Tower, and I was afraid he had seen us, but he continued to sit silently upon his horse, a huge gelding, black as pitch. I couldn't make out the features of the man's face, but I had the same queasy feeling I had experienced when I saw the horseman at the edge of the woods during the hunt.

However, I had no time to contemplate my response.

"Come, Watson, we have no time to lose!" Holmes cried, and sprang toward the stairs. I followed after him, stumbling down the dimly lit steps as I fumbled for the handrail. Within moments we were pushing open the heavy wooden door, emerging into the courtyard, only yards away from the man on horseback. Our sudden appearance frightened the animal, who shied and began to rear, but the rider immediately controlled his mount, shifting his weight forward and reining the animal in so that it could not easily rear. He then wheeled the horse around and took off at a dead run.

"Quickly, Watson!" Holmes cried, dashing to where Richmond and Ariel stood waiting. Though Holmes had not explained his plan to me in detail earlier, I now knew why we needed them.

Vaulting into the saddle, Holmes urged Richmond forward; the big horse needed little urging, so charged was the air with excitement. The little mare was equally excited, and my feet were barely into the stirrups when she took off after Richmond at a gallop.

The mystery horseman headed in the direction of the apple orchard, past the ruins of the old church, whose crumbling stones shone a dull grey in the pale moonlight. Holmes and I followed after him, our horses' hooves kicking up clods of soft dirt as they raced across the lawn. Veering around the edge of the ruins, I saw a large fallen stone right in our path just as I rounded the corner, and was forced to jump it. Throwing my weight forward at the last moment, I nearly lost my balance, but Ariel gathered herself without stumbling and sailed over the rock. I landed heavily upon her neck on the recovery, almost losing the reins.

"Sorry, old girl," I muttered, regaining my seat as we thundered after the others. The orchard was just ahead, and I had to duck as we entered the thicket of low branches, heavy with late-fall apples still clinging to the trees. Ariel slowed to a brisk trot, head erect, ears pricked forward, her breath coming in excited little puffs. I could barely make out Holmes ahead of us, threading his way through the trees in pursuit of our quarry. Branches scraped across my face, scratching my cheeks; finally I buried my head in Ariel's mane and let her carry me through the dizzying maze of branches, which seemed to reach out to snag us at every turn. As we bounced along over the uneven ground, trotting jaggedly over exposed tree roots, I blessed the herding instinct of the horse; I knew Ariel would follow Richmond without my urging, and that all I had to do was hang on as best I could.

Finally we cleared the orchard, and took off once again at full speed across the farm fields surrounding the abbey. When she saw open land stretched out in front of her, Ariel put her head down, flattened her back and ran at a dead gallop, her sturdy legs churning up the soil beneath us. The little mare soon caught up to Richmond, following so close behind that I could feel my face being pelted by bits of dirt thrown up by his hooves. The land lay spread out in front of us, illuminated by moonlight. Even with the moonlight, I was afraid the horses would stumble on unseen obstacles, but they raced across the fields as if their hooves had eyes in them.

Ahead of us loomed the jagged cliffs just outside the town of Torquay, where meadows gave way to the rugged rocky landscape overlooking the harbour. To the left was the road leading into town; to the right woods, and straight ahead the sheer cliffs overlooking Tor Bay. I expected our mystery horseman to turn at any minute in the direction of town, but to my surprise he continued straight towards the cliffs. We followed doggedly after him; the only sound in my ears was the pounding of horses' hooves upon the ground combined with the heavy breathing of my chestnut mare. I was beginning to worry about her, and hoped we would soon slow our pace. She was no racehorse, and I did not want her to injure herself in the chase. She showed no signs of slowing down, however, and galloped along after the others.

Suddenly, a shot rang out and I felt a thread of fire tear through my left shoulder. At first I didn't know what had happened, but then I realized I had been shot. I grasped my shoulder with my right hand, somehow managing to hang on to the reins with my left. My shoulder was wet, and I knew it was blood; I could feel the ripped place in my jacket sleeve where the bullet had torn through it. At the same time, I did not think the bullet had hit bone. I felt dizzy and disoriented, though, as we galloped over the field, but it would take more strength than I had now in my hands to stop Ariel; the chase was hot in her blood, and she raced after the other two horses as if her life depended upon it. I resolved, therefore, to hang on as long as I could.

My left arm was beginning to go numb, so I grasped a piece of Ariel's mane with my good hand and bent down low over her back, so that if I fell I could roll, lessening the impact. My gun was still in my pocket, but there was no question of using it now; I had only one good hand, and my aim would be poor even if we were not riding at such a clip and it were not dark. It was pure chance, I thought, that our quarry's bullet had found its way to my shoulder, and I cursed his good luck as I held on to my galloping horse, trying not to faint.

The edge of the cliffs loomed closer and closer, and my heart began to race as I contemplated our quarry's next move. Did he plan to charge off the edge of the cliff into the sea, some forty yards below? I couldn't see how anyone could survive such a fall, and was about to call ahead to Holmes when suddenly the man on the big black horse pulled abruptly on the reins, attempting a sharp turn to the left, towards the road leading into Torquay. His horse tried to adjust and make the turn, but was going too fast, and, thrown off balance, stumbled and fell heavily onto his side.

I watched as the man fell along with his mount, landing under the entire weight of the enormous animal as rider and horse hit the ground with a loud thud. The horse seemed momentarily stunned, but soon clambered onto its feet; however, the man remained motionless on the ground where he had fallen. Holmes reined in his horse and leaped from the saddle, going over to where the fallen rider lay unmoving upon the ground. I followed suit, looping my reins together quickly so that my horse would not stumble over them.

We bent over the still figure. He lay on his back, his face drained of all colour in the pale light of the moon, eyes wide open, his head twisted at an odd angle from his body. I had seen those staring eyes before, both as a physician and as a soldier, and knew immediately that I was looking at the face of death.

"Broken neck, Watson?" Holmes said softly as I felt for the pulse that was gone forever from the inert body which only minutes ago was so full of life.

I stood up and wiped the dirt and sweat from my hand. "I think so—it certainly looks like it."

It was only then that I took a closer look at the face, a face I had never seen but whose features were somehow familiar even in death. I knew Holmes was right the instant he said it.

"So, Watson, at last we meet Victor Cary."

I believe it was then that I fainted.

CHAPTER TWENTY-THREE

I AWOKE to see Holmes bending over me, a look of concern on his face.

"Watson, you're hurt. Why didn't you say something?"

I sat up slowly. "I meant to, but somehow . . . is it really Victor Cary, Holmes?" I said, staring at our dead antagonist.

"Do you recognize him as the man you saw at the theatre in London?" said Holmes, tearing off his own sleeve to make a tourniquet for my arm. It was, as I had surmised, not a deep wound, but it continued to bleed.

"Well, he's a much younger man," I remarked. "Was that really him I saw?"

"I believe it was. With the aid of his confederate, who was something of a virtuoso at theatrical makeup, he was able to move about freely in the alias of an old man," he replied, tying the tourniquet.

"Well," I said slowly, "I supposed it could be the same man. I can't really say."

We did not stay long over the body of Victor Cary. I expressed misgivings about leaving him lying there upon the ground, but Holmes observed that the Torquay police would conduct an investigation into his death, and it was perhaps best not to move the evidence. We turned our horses around and headed back towards the abbey.

"It's about time they were brought in," he remarked as we trotted back across the fields. Cary's horse followed us; stripped of its rider, the big black wanted nothing more than to join its companions.

"Are you sure you are all right, Watson?"

"Yes, quite," I replied. "So how did you know he would come tonight?"

"Do you remember the message in the letterbox Father Norton found?" he answered.

"Yes . . . it was Monday—4. I see—Monday 4 A.M.!"

"Yes. Communicating with his confederate was tricky, and rather than take the chance he might be seen, Victor Cary fell upon using the back-up plan of letterboxes."

"I see," I said as the stone walls of the abbey loomed in front of us. I was dying to ask him who Victor Cary's confederate was, but I was to find out soon enough.

When we rode up to the gatehouse, Grayson was waiting for us with a lantern in his hand. If Holmes was surprised to see him there, he showed no sign of it. "Your master's dead, Grayson," he said solemnly.

"I thought as much when I saw the two of you returning alone," the old butler replied. "So your trip to London was a ruse after all."

"Loyalty is a commendable virtue, is it not, Grayson?" Holmes said. "However, in this case you were willing to do things in the name of loyalty which no virtuous man would contemplate. Isn't that so?"

I looked at Holmes, surprised. "Holmes, do you mean that Grayson . . . ?" I stared at the old butler, his furrowed face grim and haggard in the dim light. A cloud had passed in front of the moon, and the single lantern provided the only illumination.

The old man stared Holmes straight in the eye. "What I did I did for a man who was much wronged," he replied, his voice dry as the brown leaves swirling at our feet. "I had a debt to him that could never be repaid."

"Ah, yes," Holmes murmured. "It isn't often a man saves your life, is it?"

Grayson drew himself up to the full extent of his height. "When he gave me my life, I pledged it to serve him always. I could do no less," he replied proudly.

"Even when it meant taking the lives of innocent women and children?" Holmes said sternly.

"Innocent!" Grayson scoffed. "Sally was hardly innocent. She seduced my master, and then, when she was with child, he took her in and cared for them both."

"But then he killed them," Holmes replied. "And still you stood by him."

"I could do no less—I was bound by my oath!"

I looked at Holmes. "Sally—and William? Victor Cary killed them both?"

He nodded, his face grim.

"I killed the boy," Grayson said, no remorse in his voice. "It was regrettable, but necessary." I looked at him in disbelief. "You weren't there in Calcutta!" he cried suddenly. "That mob would have torn me apart had it not been for him."

"Ah, yes—your days as a snake charmer were over, I expect," Holmes remarked. "What happened—did the snake bite a bystander?"

Grayson's eyes narrowed. "What are you, a wizard?"

Holmes smiled grimly. "No, merely a man who observes. You see, Mr. Grayson, most people *see* but they do not *observe*."

"Oh—the flute!" I said. "So Grayson was a snake charmer, then?"

"Yes," Holmes replied. "But now, we must go inside and tell the family what has happened." As we walked across the grounds towards the main building, a murky dawn was just beginning to push its way through the clouds, the sky lightening ever so slightly in the east. Grayson walked meekly in front of us, and though I tightened my hand around the revolver in my pocket, I didn't think I would need it.

"So William was the bastard son of Victor Cary," I remarked. "That explains why he was so willing to take Sally in—it was *his* child she was carrying!"

"You yourself remarked upon the resemblance between William and Elizabeth."

"Yes, but . . . he had his own son killed?" I said, hardly able to believe it.

"Yes, because he realized, as we did, that William had been present the night his mother died, and might give him away."

"Foolish woman!" Grayson muttered. "He never intended to harm her in any way. If she hadn't been nosing around that night she never would have seen him." He frowned and shook his head. "No one knew she had a weak heart."

"No, indeed," Holmes replied. "But the sight of a man she thought was dead could make anyone's heart skip a beat."

We were now standing under the Abbot's Tower. At that moment a light went on in one of the rooms above us, and presently we heard footsteps upon the stairs. Moments later, the front door opened and Charles Cary appeared, his face ringed with sleep.

"What's going on here?" he demanded.

"I'll be glad to explain everything," Holmes replied, "but why don't we go inside? It's quite chilly out here, and Watson has been injured. I rather think we could all use a cup of something hot to drink," he added, noticing I had begun to cough a bit. My lungs were still weak from my illness, and the damp air was making me cough.

"Yes, certainly," Cary said, looking confused. "Grayson, would you . . . ?"

"I think we'd best see to it ourselves," Holmes intervened.

"I don't see why—" Cary protested, but Holmes laid a hand upon his shoulder.

"Please, Lord Cary, if you will only come inside, I'll explain everything. In fact," he added, "perhaps you should awaken the rest of your family. They also need to hear what I'm about to tell you."

And so shortly afterwards we were all seated around the fire in the west parlour. Annie, too, had joined us, and sat wrapped in a blanket on one end of the sofa, her white nightcap pulled down over her ears to keep out the chill. Lady Cary sat in the chair closest to the fire, her golden hair loose about her shoulders. She wore a pale-blue dressing gown; her daughter occupied the chair opposite her, her knees pulled up to her chest, a woollen scarf around her neck.

Grayson sat a little apart from the rest of the group, perched upon a straight-backed chair, his spine as stiff and hard as the wooden chair. I had some concern that Grayson might still attempt to harm a member of the family, but Holmes assured me quietly that with his master dead, the old man was not likely to provide any further threat. Still, I kept a watchful eye on him as Holmes addressed the rest of the group.

"Well, Mr. Holmes?" said Charles Cary when everyone was assembled, steaming cups of tea clutched in their hands. "What have you to tell us?"

"Some of what I have to say will be a shock to some of you," Holmes began slowly. "And some of you have secrets of your own which I will be forced to reveal."

At these words Marion Cary looked away, averting her eyes from the gaze of her son.

"Whatever it is you have to tell us, Mr. Holmes," he said, "I've no doubt these 'secrets' will seem harmless by the light of day."

I looked out the window, where the day was indeed dawning, pale shafts of sunlight spreading across the ground, still wet with dew, the blades of grass glistening like tiny jewels as the early morning light fell upon them. My shoulder was beginning to throb, but my mind was more at peace than it had been for days.

"These secrets have done enough harm already," Holmes replied seriously. "After Victor Cary discovered one of these secrets, he became bent upon destroying his family."

Charles Cary took a step forward. "But why would Father . . ."

"There is something you must know, Lord Cary," Holmes interrupted. "I'm afraid that Victor Cary was not your father."

There was a pause, and then Charles Cary snorted softly.

"Oh, really?" he responded coldly. "Since you seem to know so much about our family, would you kindly tell me who *is* my father?"

"Perhaps I should leave that to your mother," Holmes replied with a glance at Marion Cary, who sat stiff as stone in her chair, her eyes straight ahead.

There was a pause, during which I could hear the soft coo of the mourning doves in the eaves outside.

Charles Cary stared at his mother. "What's he talking about?" There was a note of uncertainty in his voice I had never heard before.

She sighed heavily, a sound so deep within her chest that it seemed to come from the very centre of her being.

"You have perhaps heard that there was another man in my life before Victor Cary," she said, avoiding looking directly at her son.

"Yes, but he died," Charles replied, his voice tight. "And you married Father."

There was another uncomfortable pause, and I could hear the loud ticking of the grandfather clock in the hallway. I looked around the room at the rest of its occupants. Grayson sat immobile upon his chair, stiff and expressionless as a sphinx;

Annie had curled herself into a ball at her end of the sofa, tightly bundled in her blanket, staring with wide eyes at her employers. At her end of the couch, Elizabeth Cary sat wrapped in her woollen scarf, her head cocked to one side, staring at her mother.

Marion Cary sighed again. "I have not been entirely forthcoming with you, Charles, I'm afraid."

"In what way?"

"It is true that Christopher Leganger died, as you say, but I loved him very much, and . . ." She paused to collect herself, but it was more than Charles could bear.

"And . . . ? And *what?*"

"I was already carrying you when I married Victor Cary." She parcelled the words out tersely; it was less like a confession than a challenge.

The effect upon her son was as if he had been shot. He slumped back in his chair and clutched his chest. He struggled to speak; his mouth moved but no words came out at first. Then he managed a strangled "*What?*" He looked at Holmes, his eyes blazing. "Is this—some kind of joke?"

"I'm afraid not, Lord Cary," the detective replied. "I imagine that your mother kept it a secret all these years in part so that your father would not attempt to disinherit you."

"I did it for you, Charles, can't you see that?" Marion Cary cried, her voice full of anguish, but her son just stared at her as though she were a madwoman.

"And what about me?" Elizabeth Cary suddenly spoke up from her end of the couch. "Who is *my* father?"

"Oh, Victor Cary was your father, all right," her mother replied coldly. "That should be plain enough."

"So that's why you hated me all these years—because I wasn't *his* child!" Elizabeth responded bitterly.

Marion Cary stared at her daughter as if confused by this accusation, but Elizabeth continued angrily, spitting the words out in a torrent of fury. "Oh, yes, don't think I don't know you hate me—I'm not stupid, no matter what you think!"

Marion Cary looked at her son for support, but he stared blankly at her. I couldn't help feeling sorry for her—in the short space of a few minutes she had alienated the affection of both her children.

"How can you say that?" she said. "Charles, tell her she's wrong!"

Charles Cary shook his head. "I don't know what to believe any more. How could you keep this from me all these years?"

Holmes broke in, his voice like a splash of cool water over the heated emotions of the family. "In order to keep it from her husband, she had to keep it from everybody—except, of course, her confessor."

Lady Cary stared wildly at Holmes. "Father Norton told you?"

Holmes shook his head. "Oh, no, madam; he is the very soul of integrity. No, you yourself told me."

"I . . . ?" Colour crept up her cheeks, her pale skin flushing crimson.

"At first I wondered why your attitude towards your son was so very different from that towards your daughter. I also could not help noticing how different your children were physically, your daughter taking so much after her father, while Charles . . . well, these things happen in families, of course, but then that day Watson and I saw you visit the grave of your dead lover, my suspicions grew stronger. A woman may love a man very much, but when she has had a child by that man . . . well, the bond often grows that much stronger."

I stared at Holmes with some surprise; I wouldn't have thought he was so versed in matters of the heart. Nonetheless, there was truth in what he said.

"Then I saw the broken lock on your desk drawer," he continued. "Your lie to cover up the real reason was quite transparent; I eventually came up with the theory that your husband had broken the lock—and discovered your secret."

Marion Cary hung her head. "Yes," she answered in a defeated voice, "that is where I kept the letters I exchanged with Christopher telling him I was with child."

"And it was shortly after you discovered the lock had been tampered with that your husband supposedly drowned."

Marion Cary lifted her head again. "Supposedly . . . ? What are you saying, Mr. Holmes?"

He turned to Elizabeth Cary. "Miss Cary, I regret to inform you that your father is dead."

The girl's lips trembled, and she looked up at Holmes, her large dark eyes wide. "But . . . but I knew that."

Holmes shook his head. "No. These past months you all thought he was dead, but he lived. He wanted you to believe he was dead, but he was very much alive."

Elizabeth Cary shifted her gaze to me. "But . . . I don't understand. How . . . ?"

"He took a fall from his horse earlier this morning and broke his neck," Holmes interjected.

The girl blinked and looked at her brother. "So then . . . he didn't drown?"

Holmes shook his head. "No. He faked his own death, and then arranged the series of hauntings and other bizarre events which have occurred recently."

"But why would he do such a thing?" Charles Cary demanded.

"In order to make Torre Abbey a place no one would want to live in."

Elizabeth Cary stared up at Holmes. "Then the apparitions . . ."

Holmes shrugged. "Cleverly staged events, done with the help of a professional magician, who is also unfortunately dead. Victor Cary planned to drive his wife out of her mind—or at least out of Torre Abbey. And somewhere along the line he planned to kill you, Lord Cary," he said, turning to Charles, "in such a way as to make it look like an accident."

Cary sat upright in his chair. "The loose horseshoe!"

Holmes nodded. "He also planned to do away with me, by cutting my stirrup leather."

"He didn't want to hurt me, did he?" Elizabeth asked softly.

"No," Holmes replied. "In fact, once your mother and brother were out of the way, I believe he planned to make a miraculous appearance, claiming amnesia, and reclaim Torre Abbey for you and himself. Am I right, Grayson?" Holmes said, looking at the butler.

All eyes turned to the old man, who sat still as stone in the corner. "More or less," he replied, his chin lifted proudly in defiance.

Charles Cary leaped to his feet. "Grayson? What is the meaning of this? Is this true? Did you . . . conspire against us?"

The old butler stared straight ahead, his face expressionless. "When he gave me my life I pledged it to serve him," he said tonelessly, as if reciting by rote. "He never meant for the boy to get hurt, miss," he said to Elizabeth.

Elizabeth Cary's eyes grew even wider. "William?" she cried. "You killed William?"

The old man continued staring straight ahead. Elizabeth jumped from where she sat and threw herself at him, but Holmes intervened, catching her firmly by the shoulders before she could attack the butler.

"I'm afraid there's another bit of disturbing information I must relay," Holmes said. "William was Lord Cary's bastard son."

"Good Lord," Charles Cary murmured, shaking his head. "So he arranged the murder of his own *son?*"

"His bastard son," Holmes corrected him. "William could never inherit Torre Abbey or the Cary name. But he was unfortunately present when his mother died, so Victor Cary was afraid he would spill the beans sooner or later."

"But he couldn't even talk," Marion Cary protested. "Why kill a poor innocent—" but she stopped mid-sentence. "I knew Victor Cary; I of all people should know what he was capable of," she added bitterly.

"Poor little bird," Elizabeth whispered, tears forming at the corners of her eyes. "Poor little bird."

"Yes, Sally's death was an unfortunate accident," Holmes continued, "but William's was cold-blooded murder, and only served to draw the noose tighter around Victor Cary's neck."

He went on to explain how he had discovered one of the methods Victor Cary used to communicate with Grayson when out letterboxing with Father Norton; how he had tracked Victor—in disguise as the old man I had seen at the theatre—to the Hotel Lambeth in Torquay; his discovery of the cigar ash in the Spanish barn; and finally, he described our midnight pursuit across the moors.

When he finished, no one spoke for a few moments. Then Annie, whom we had quite forgotten about, broke the silence.

"God help us," she murmured, expressing the thoughts of everyone in the room, I thought.

CHAPTER TWENTY-FOUR

ONE THING I don't understand, Mr. Holmes," Charles Cary remarked as we waited for the police to arrive. "If you were riding Richmond," he said, "where did my fath—Victor Cary—get a black horse?"

"Perhaps you know the animal, Lord Cary," said Holmes. "He's just outside."

We went out to where the horses stood tethered in front of the abbey.

"Good Lord—I'll be damned if it isn't Mystic Rider!" Cary exclaimed when he saw the animal. He ran a hand over the great horse's flanks. The horse seemed to know him, for it nuzzled his shoulder.

"Mystic Rider?" I was puzzled.

"Yes, he's Richmond's brother—"

"Oh, yes—the horse you sold to your neighbour, the one that used to belong to your father," I said.

"It's a fitting name for a 'ghost horse,' " Holmes remarked. "I should imagine your neighbour will be glad to see his horse again. He probably thought this was the work of horse thieves."

Cary's face darkened. "It was the work of someone much worse than that."

Detective Jonathan Samuels, the police detective from Torquay, arrived shortly afterwards, flanked by the fat sergeant and two equally well-fed constables, whose round faces registered surprise when they were introduced to Mr. Sherlock Holmes. After Holmes had explained the salient details, Detective Samuels shook his head. He was a short, blunt-faced fellow, with a tangle of salt-and-pepper hair and a rumpled overcoat. The constables continued to stare at Holmes while their superior officer spoke.

"That's quite a story, Mr. Holmes, and I'll have to hand it to you for sorting everything out—though I wish you'd come to us sooner, sir, as we could have offered you some protection," he added, addressing Lord Cary.

"Your colleagues seemed uninterested, to say the least, in our family's problems," he replied sourly.

The detective looked stunned. "I've been on vacation, sir, and just returned yesterday. I had no idea—"

"Never mind," said Holmes. "He never would have shown his hand if the place had been crawling with police."

The detective looked at him with admiration in his blunt face. "Oh, no offense, Mr. Holmes—round here you're something of a legend, you know, and I wouldn't dream of—"

"I'm quite sure you wouldn't, Detective," Holmes intervened. "However, we do have someone for you to place under arrest, so if you wouldn't mind . . ."

"Oh, no, not at all, sir—not at all," the detective sputtered, his face growing red.

Grayson offered no resistance when Samuels placed him under arrest; now that his master was dead, he didn't seem to care what happened to him.

"Before you take him away, Detective, there's something I'd like to clear up," Holmes said as the constables placed the handcuffs on the butler. We were standing in the front hall of the abbey.

"What's that, sir?"

Holmes went over to where Grayson was standing and

said something to him in a voice too low for us to hear. Grayson nodded his head, and said something back to Holmes. Holmes frowned and nodded, and then he came back over to us.

"Very well, Detective—thank you." With that he turned and went back towards the parlour, where the Cary family were gathered.

Detective Samuels looked at me. "What'd he say?"

I shook my head. "I'm sorry, but I don't know."

He sighed. "Pity." Then his face brightened. "Well, I expect I can look forward to reading your account of it someday, Dr. Watson."

"Yes, I suppose so."

"Mind you get my name right—it's Samuels, with an *s*."

"Right you are—Samuels."

"Right. Well, if that's all, we'll be getting along, I expect," he said, obviously reluctant to leave. "I've heard about this place, you know," he added, taking a last look around the abbey, "but I'd never been inside before. It's grand, isn't it?"

"Yes," I replied, "it is that."

"What was it you asked Grayson?" I said to Holmes as we stood watching the policemen load the butler into their coach.

Holmes frowned. "It's as I suspected, though I see no need to tell Lady Cary about it."

"Tell her what?"

"I suspected Victor Cary's involvement in Christopher Leganger's death when Father Norton told us what a good rider Leganger was. Grayson just confirmed my suspicion."

"So Victor Cary murdered him, too?"

Holmes nodded. "I'm afraid so, though it might be difficult to prove in a court of law. According to Grayson, he deliberately spooked Leganger's horse as it was going over a jump."

"Good Lord," I said as we watched the police coach drive away.

Not long afterwards we all sat over a long-delayed breakfast, which the ever-stalwart Annie had prepared with the help of Elizabeth Cary. The atmosphere in the room was strained as Annie shuffled in and out of the room with plates of eggs and sausages, but finally Charles Cary broke the silence.

He turned to his mother. "So you knew Father had discovered your secret before his 'death.' "

She hung her lovely head and studied her hands. "One day I came upon him in my room. He claimed to be there because the chambermaid had seen a mouse under my bed, but I thought at the time it was odd he didn't leave a job like that to Grayson." She sighed and flicked a stray hair back from her face. "I keep a box containing all my letters from Christopher locked in my desk, and, well, that was the lock Mr. Holmes saw had been tampered with."

Holmes nodded, his eyes narrow. "And did you know William was Elizabeth's half-brother?"

Marion Cary heaved a great sigh and looked out at the barren trees in the orchard, their branches stripped of fruit and leaves. "I suspected, certainly. Sally had a fellow in town, or so she said— and while I was happy enough to welcome her child into our house, I was surprised at my husband's willingness to overlook such an indiscretion on the part of a servant. He was not the most forgiving of men, as I suppose you know by now," she added sadly.

Charles Cary went over to his mother and wrapped his arms around her shoulders, burying his head in her hair. "Why didn't you tell me?" he murmured.

She looked up at him, her azure eyes full of pain. "I wanted to . . . I tried, but things were already difficult enough between you and your father, and I was afraid that if you knew, you'd—"

"Hate him even more?" Charles replied bitterly. "At least I'd have known I had a father I could be proud of."

"Imagine Victor Cary's rage when he found out that he had married a 'tainted' woman," Holmes mused, "and that the fact had been kept from him."

Marion Cary sighed again. "I know I'm to blame for so much of what has happened." She turned to her daughter, who sat still and silent across from her. "Can you forgive me, Elizabeth?"

The girl regarded her mother coldly. "I don't know . . . someday, perhaps. Right now it's hard to imagine how I'll feel about you . . . or about anything else."

Charles Cary went around to his sister and took her hand. "Elizabeth, I know it's difficult, but things will be better soon, I promise. I'm going to take the semester off and take care of you until you're all better, and then I'll go back to medical school."

"Oh, Charles . . ." said Marion Cary, but Charles put his hand to his lips.

"It's all settled, Mother—I've missed too many classes as it is. Elizabeth needs looking after, and I'm the one to do it."

Marion Cary put her head down. "I suppose you're right. After all that's happened, it's probably for the best." She turned to her daughter. "Perhaps in time you'll come to trust me, but . . . well, I can't say I blame you for feeling the way you do."

"It wasn't her fault, after all, who her father was," Charles added.

"No," Lady Cary agreed. "It was my fault."

HOLMES AND I stayed one last night at Torre Abbey, more to comfort the Cary family than because either of us wanted to stay. I for one was anxious to get back to my practice; after the events of the past few days, it seemed to me that even another flu epidemic would be a relief. We took the first train to London the following morning.

As we were preparing to leave for the train station, Father Norton rode up on his horse. I was in front of the abbey, loading our bags into the Carys's carriage.

"I heard what happened," he said, jumping down from the saddle. "It's all over town—everyone's talking."

"Oh?" I replied, lifting a bag into the back of Lord Cary's brougham. "Detective Samuels is evidently not the most discreet of policemen."

"No," Norton answered, giving me a hand with the luggage, "but gossip has always spread through Torquay like wildfire. Everyone always knows everyone else's business. Is Lady Cary about?" he said as we finished loading the last of the luggage.

"I believe she's inside."

"Thank you," he replied, and went into the abbey. Some moments later Holmes emerged from the building shaking his head.

"What is it about women, Watson, that makes perfectly sane men act like utter fools?"

I laughed. "I don't know, Holmes, but you should be grateful that whatever it is, you've been spared."

After we said our goodbyes, Charles Cary drove us to the train station. "I don't know how to thank you for all you've done," he said, holding his hat in his hands to avoid its being blown off his head by the strong gusting wind that whipped around the corner of the station building.

"Just take care of your family, Lord Cary," Holmes replied.

"And as for Elizabeth," I began, but Cary shook his head.

"Don't worry, Dr. Watson—I have already spoken with her, and together we'll solve her problem, I promise you." He looked down the tracks which extended into the distance as far as the eye could see. "I almost wish I were going with you. I feel as though I've had enough of Devon for a while. But I have responsibilities here," he sighed, "and I expect medical school will wait."

"It will," I assured him, "and when you get there, believe me, you'll have days when you want to leave."

He smiled. "Yes. Well, thank you again," he repeated, shaking hands with us. Then, placing his hat securely upon his head, he turned and went down the steps to his waiting carriage. We watched him go, and Holmes sighed.

"I hope he is up to the challenges ahead, Watson."

I sighed, too, but for a different reason. I knew that in all likelihood I would never see Marion Cary again. "I'm sure he will be fine, Holmes."

I looked down the track and could see the train, far away in the distance, chugging towards us. I inhaled my last breath of West Country air for what I now hoped was a good while. As beautiful as the Devon coast was, I was not sorry to bid it good-bye. I had had enough of ghosts who roamed drafty hallways at night, of ancient curses and family secrets. I longed for our sitting room at Baker Street, and wanted nothing more than to settle into my chair in front of the fire and while away the fall evening with a book and a glass of claret while Holmes scraped away at his violin or performed experiments at his chemistry table.

On the train, I sat staring out the window at the countryside rushing by, scenery which had once looked picturesque to me but which now seemed a mask to hide all human evil behind its façade of bucolic loveliness. Round stacks of hay lay upon freshly mowed fields, bulky and stolid as the fat grey sheep which grazed upon the farms all around us. I looked at Holmes, who was leaning back in his seat, his hat pulled low over his eyes. I thought he was asleep, and was surprised to hear him speak.

"Well, Watson," came the familiar voice from under the hat. "What do you think of the behaviour of the Cary family?"

I shook my head. "Pretty shabby, if you ask me. What I don't understand, though, is how you figured Grayson was part of it."

Holmes removed his hat from his face and propped it on top of his head at a rather crooked angle, so that it gave him a rakish, rascally look. "Grayson was the key all along, Watson, but it was essential that he not be aware that I was on to him. That is why I couldn't risk telling you. Forgive me, dear fellow, but I can't say that you number acting ability among your many talents," he added gently. "If Grayson had even suspected I was watching him, he would have alerted his master and that would have been that."

"So that extra pork chop was for Victor Cary?"

"Yes. He was no doubt hiding in the Spanish barn, waiting for his chance to strike, and Grayson brought him his dinner.

"The first clue I had to Grayson's involvement was when he called Charles 'Master Cary' instead of 'Lord Cary.' It was a subtle sign, but telling enough. It indicated to me that possibly he had not accepted Victor Cary's death, but it also suggested another possibility."

"That Victor Cary was not dead," I suggested.

"Precisely. And there can, of course, be only one Lord Cary at a time. Besides, all signs pointed to someone who, if not an actual member of the family, was at least very close to them— someone who knew them well. Do you recall when I asked Grayson who in the household smoked cigars?"

"Yes—and Lord Cary was surprised you hadn't asked him about it, instead."

"I did it to observe Grayson's reaction. I was just fishing at that point, but if Grayson knew where the cigar ash came from, then he was very likely to be implicated in the plot."

"And?"

"His reaction was very interesting. He did not ask me why I was asking the question, which means he knew—or guessed— why I was asking it. He responded, and then was hoping I would pursue the matter no further in front of his employer."

"I see. So that day at the Spanish barn, while I was in the grips of imagining the fate of those poor sailors, you were calmly collecting facts, as usual," I replied somewhat ruefully.

Holmes permitted himself one of his rare smiles. "Don't be so hard on yourself, Watson. After all, if it had not been for your somewhat over-active imagination, I likely would not have arrived at some of the conclusions I did—or at least not as quickly."

I brightened. "Really?"

"Most certainly." He sighed. " 'Oh what a tangled web we weave when first we practise to deceive' . . . it's interesting, by the way, that the Carys named their animals after characters out of *The Tempest*. Victor Cary *was* rather like Prospero, trying to control his own little island, even using magic to attain his goals."

"Like Prospero, he couldn't keep his little kingdom intact," I observed. "He failed to control his creatures, and there were always elements beyond his powers."

"Indeed," Holmes answered. "His magic wasn't strong enough in the end to overcome the forces of justice." He sighed and closed his eyes. "Would that it were always thus, Watson— the forces of justice prevailing at last. It strikes me as a terrible thing, Watson, that a man would care so much for his bloodline that he would be willing to kill for the sake of it."

I looked out at the golden farm fields flying by, at snug thatched cottages nestled against each other like the fat sheep huddling in the corners of the gently rolling hillsides.

"There are some things I don't understand, though," I said. "How is it that Elizabeth Cary was suddenly able to speak Spanish?"

Holmes looked at me and smiled enigmatically. " 'There are more things in heaven and earth, Horatio . . .' You yourself experienced something, did you not, Watson?"

I shook my head. "Something, Holmes, though whether of heaven or earth, who can say?"

"Who, indeed, Watson, who indeed?"

"You'd think there was enough suffering in the world without the need for man to add to it with his foolishness," I sighed. "Justice prevailed in the end, it's true, but at what cost?"

"Yes, indeed, Watson, you would think so—but you would be sadly mistaken. However," he said, sliding his hat down over his eyes once again, "I shall at least be able to report a successful outcome to Inspector Lestrade of Scotland Yard of what must have been for him a most vexing case. And, beyond that, there are at least some comforts in this evil world."

"Oh? Such as what?"

He lifted his hat ever so slightly and peered at me through one eye. "I for one am looking forward to Mrs. Hudson's excellent rack of lamb, a glass of burgundy by my own fire, and then perhaps a bit of Bach at the Royal Albert Hall, time permitting. What do you say—are you game? How is your shoulder?"

"It's much better," I replied earnestly. "I can't think of anything I'd like better."

"Capital! And now, if you'll excuse me, I'm going to catch a well-deserved nap."

With that he replaced the hat and I was left alone with my own thoughts. I thought about the Devon coast, and Torre Abbey, so full of enchantments but also treachery, and of Marion Cary's face and figure, also enchanting, but, like the mask of Nature's beauty, not to be trusted. I looked at Holmes, asleep so peacefully across from me, hands folded in his lap, his long legs stretched out in front of him—the picture of contentment.

I looked out the window once again. A sluggish mist was descending over the farm fields of Devon as they disappeared rapidly behind us, falling away into the background, replaced by a smoky fog in the thickening air. I sighed, leaned back in my seat and closed my eyes. I could not shake from my mind the feeling that there *were* more things in Torre Abbey, perhaps of neither heaven *nor* earth . . . I contemplated our return to the gaslit cobblestone streets of London, and its more familiar follies and pleasures, buried beneath back alleyways or exposed to the casual onlooker with the sudden flare of a street lamp. It was perhaps no better a place than the one we were leaving, but come what may, it was, after all, home.